The long

lushness. The verandah wrapped

structure that was perched high above the jungle. It was in a place where rising water levels and forest life could not reach. Along the eastern wall of the longhouse, glass winked quietly as sunlight grazed the building. On the dock, a boy stared at them, his mouth slightly open and a hand wedged in the pocket of his too-big shorts.

Savannah was exhausted. They'd walked miles through the interior, finally meeting up with a branch of the same river she'd lost track of earlier. From there, it had been a mile walk to the longhouse along the tributary that led even farther from the main river.

She nodded at the boy, who dodged her eyes and fixated on Drew, who was pulling the stretcher with what was left of Malcolm.

"No," she murmured. She turned toward the stretcher, thinking to block the child's view.

"Leave it," their rescuer ordered in his rough and sexy voice.

Praise for Ryshia Kennie

"..Ryshia's writing keeps you hooked from beginning to end, constantly adding in unexpected twists and slowly revealing parts of the story. Ryshia creates characters that you can connect to and grow to love and puts them into a story like no other.

...there are so many possible scenarios that could have led to Malcolm's death, the truth was quite a surprise and not something I had expected. The sexual tension ... was just crazy."

~ *inspirationsbysimone*

"...An original story line, believable characters and a great writing style, what more could you ask for? This book is a must read."

~ *Katie*

Fatal Intent

by

Ryshia Kennie

Fatal Intent

Contact Information: info@thewildrosepress.com

Cover Art by *Lisa Dawn MacDonald*

The Wild Rose Press, Inc.
PO Box 708
Adams Basin, NY 14410-0708
Visit us at www.thewildrosepress.com

Publishing History
First Edition, 2022
Trade Paperback ISBN 978-1-5092-4021-0
Digital ISBN 978-1-5092-4022-7

Published in the United States of America

Dedication

This book is dedicated to you, the reader. Enjoy!

Chapter One

She saw him floating headless through a mist of tears.

Even the river's roar was not enough to mask her scream, as overhead the Borneo midday sun skidded a brilliant reflection across the river's surface.

Savannah Cole clapped her hand over her mouth and squinted against the bright sun, as if that would shift reality or change the fact that all that stood between Malcolm and anonymity was the San Diego Chargers logo on his torn, water-soaked T-shirt. Instead, tears washed her vision.

Malcolm's smiling face—his smiling, missing face. She choked and her foot slipped, bringing her dangerously close to the riverbank, and the body.

Brush crackled and something screeched. The sound was harsh and loud even in a place where there was never silence. It would have sent chills through the uninitiated, but it was only an insect, an oversize bug. An insect that might not be classified or identified. There were so many and that was what brought her here. But now her guide was dead, headless. That thought alone was preposterous, even when the evidence lay in front of her. She wanted to weep. She wanted to run. But it was up to her to get her team out of here. She needed another focus before panic clouded everything. And then she caught sight of Ian spewing into the tall grass that grew wild and untamed on the edge of the clearing.

"Ian!"

It was only the two of them—for now. She and Ian. Ian, who was all about screams and hysteria in a crisis. But there'd never been a need to worry about that—there was no crisis, there should have never been a crisis.

Her fingers trembled and she clenched them into her palms, nails pinching the skin.

Her thoughts jittered everywhere.

There was no answer as Ian began to cry in large gulping sobs.

"Ian!" she shouted, trying to use tough love, hoping that would bring him back from the edge. There was no time for sympathy and neither of them could afford hysteria. They had to survive.

Small choking sounds came from the brush.

"C'mon, Ian," she muttered, swallowing her own bile as it crept up the back of her throat.

Dead.

Only yesterday morning she had laughed with Malcolm. It had been over some inane joke one of the other Iban had told him. Something that related back to his heritage and the Iban's history as headhunters.

"Headhunters," she whispered. "Don't be ridiculous."

There were no headhunters, not anymore. Just tribal people who took great pride in a history that once had included headhunting. Once, she reminded herself, no more. Her gaze flitted back to the corpse, the corpse that was minus a head.

I'll be back before dark. Keep to the river. I'll find you.

The last words Malcolm had spoken, at least to them.

Keep to the river.

Savannah and her team had kept to the river as instructed. They'd followed that trajectory until it began to get dark. But he hadn't returned. Now, here he was, one day later, headless. She almost gagged at the thought except she needed to remain strong.

She remembered her father's words: "There's money to be had in the jungle and as a result, it breeds violence and greed. Money does strange things to men. Don't trust anyone."

Savannah knew that her father, a member of the university board that funded her expedition, had been referring to the resources being stripped from the tropical rain forest. Stripped legally and illegally, with no thought to anything but money. What had Malcolm stumbled on? For she was sure that's why he died—why else? And where were his killers now?

"It could be an accident," she whispered and, despite what she believed, she prayed it was.

The body shifted and broke free of the bank.

"No!"

She raced to the river. Everything seemed to move in slow motion. Then, she was wrestling from the water what had once been a man. She clutched the waterlogged T-shirt, reluctant to touch the water-pulverized skin for fear of what she might take away. For fear that the skin would slough off, leaving raw meat, leaving…

She closed her mind, clutched the material, prayed it would hold, and pulled. The San Diego Chargers logo on the T-shirt, which he'd bartered from Sid only the other day, ripped down the middle. She sucked in air and touched flesh. His arm felt normal, just cold. Then, maybe her foot slipped or maybe it was all too much. Whatever it was, one minute she was standing and the next she was flat on her butt. The body was now partway out of the water but still lifting in the current. It looked as if, at any moment, it would break free and head downriver.

She looked across the rushing water to the undisturbed forest. She refused to look at what lay at her feet.

Malcolm.

Even though he lived in the city, in Kuching, he was so proud of his tribe—the tribe of former headhunters. He had claimed that a hundred-year-old skull still hung in his tribe's longhouse. The last man hunted. Or was it? Somewhere in the depths of this forest was Malcolm's head. Or maybe—she covered her mouth with her hand, the thought too horrible to contemplate. She thought it anyway…that it was at the bottom of this river.

She remembered something else, another quote of her father's: "Things can get deadly out there. Expedition of '72 we lost a member of the group. It was horrible. He was missing parts of his body. He was…" He had dragged the last bit out, leaving her in a strange mockery of suspense.

"His head. We assumed a monitor got him."

She dropped her head in her hands.

A woman has never led an expedition.

Not possible, not at her age.

The voices of the board of entomologists, her father's cohorts, came to her as if they were here. Her father had stood up for her. Her father, the same man who had once said that fieldwork was not for a woman and definitely not for his daughter. Her father had always been distant with her and passionate about his work. It was a fact she resented most of her life.

There was no time for memories. She took a deep calming breath.

"We have no choice. We're going to have to take the body."

She rose.

"We'll drag him to civilization?"

Ian's tone was dubious as he followed her. "Why?"

"We can't leave him here. That's so wrong." She shook her head and pushed wet hair off her face. "It's not even that. We don't know what happened to him. If we leave him here, no one ever will."

She glanced at Ian. Tears welled in his eyes. "Don't, please."

"His body would be gone in hours," he whispered. "I won't let him be eaten by lizards or ants, or…" Ian broke off as he began breathing in hitches and bent over, clutching his belly.

And the mention of ants only reminded Savannah of what she was leaving behind, and she chastised herself for even thinking that. To put it in layman's terms, bugs were her passion, and this expedition was the cumulation of months of planning. But they were ending an expedition with only a dead specimen, a beetle like none of them had seen before and a hunch that this was special. No live specimen, no live colony, just one unclassified insect and the hope that this would make her career. She rubbed the back of her neck and pushed the guilty thought to the background.

Malcolm was dead and she was thinking of her career. She turned her attention to Ian.

"We'll stick as close to the river as we can." She glanced to the forest. "Of course, we'll wait for the others. Oh, never mind waiting." She pulled a walkie-talkie from her vest pocket.

The small radio crackled as she pressed the on button. “Sid, do you copy?” More crackling.

“Savannah?”

“Sid, there’s been an accident.”

“What? Are you all right?”

“We’re fine, Sid,” she said, and it was true. The two of them, she and Ian, were fine—physically anyway. “Just get back here. Now. Please.” She ended the call. She’d update the rest of her team when they arrived. Only then would she tell them what little she knew. She swallowed, pushing the threat of tears back forcing herself to be tough, in charge.

“Let’s get him out of the river.”

She glanced at Ian, who looked like he was going to throw up again. “Ian?”

He nodded and shuddered. “I’m okay. Move over a bit. I’ve got his belt.” But his hands were still shaking. “It’s just…” He dragged the back of his hand across his face. “Such a crappy way to die.”

Savannah glanced at him. “Crappy?”

“Sorry. Maybe I understated.”

“A tad,” she said. She grimaced at the mundane conversation amid the grisly circumstance. But there were no rules of decorum. Not any that she knew of, not for any kind of venture into the Borneo rain forest that ended liked this. Malcolm was dead and the rule book was lost, or maybe it had never been written.

“Okay, let’s do this. Are you ready?”

Ian nodded gamely and she could only respect him for that, for she knew how emotional he could be, how vulnerable to any of the emotional stressors of life. Never mind this—this was incomprehensible. And for Ian, even more so.

They heaved the corpse clear of the water with less effort than she expected.

She took a deep breath but kept her gaze away from the body.

"It's not a crime."

"What are you talking about?"

So much for taming her aggression, but she could feel the tears brushing the surface of her reality and anger was the only thing that would tamp them back.

"To cry."

"I won't."

"I know. You never do," he said softly. "Do you think it was tribal revenge?" He hesitated. "Or something else?"

"It's the twenty-first century, I'd go with something else."

But saying those words didn't make her feel any better and they didn't help the situation with Ian. His face was pinched, his lips thin. He glanced into the emerald mystery that surrounded them.

Her gaze followed his and for a moment it felt as if they weren't alone. But it was as impossible to conclude that as it was impossible to see past the first feet of dense foliage. Trees grew on trees. Vines twisted through low-growing plants and climbed upward, seeming to cling to every living thing. Hanging over it all were the massive trees whose tips grazed the sky as they formed the forest's canopy. It was all rather mysterious and today it appeared inhospitable.

"Whoever it was, they might still be around."

"Stalking us! Oh my God, Savannah." His voice went up a notch and he gasped in air looking desperate. "Or it was an accident, or an animal." There was almost relief in his voice to entertain those options. "Either way, he's still…" His voice choked. "Dead."

Savannah ached for the pain Ian was feeling. She'd seen the relationship growing between him and Malcolm, a relationship that had ended so tragically.

They had agreed to meet Malcolm farther upriver. When he hadn't arrived last night, her team of entomologists had scoured the area in safely controlled distances from their starting point. None of them were navigators, or overly familiar with the jungle, but they had two-way radios to keep in touch. They had spent the night in a deserted hut. The hut where Malcolm had said he would meet them over twenty-four hours ago.

Savannah squatted down beside the body. She had to get it together. But all she could think of was that whatever was out there—whatever had taken Malcolm—might be waiting, for them.

She sucked in a deep breath as she forced herself to look at what remained of Malcolm. She was the team lead on this expedition. It was up to her to take care of the team.

She had failed.

****

What the hell?

Matthew thought as he watched the tabloid unfold in front of him.

A man and a woman.

A dead Iban guide, headless.

It was all rather disturbing, even for him. He'd managed to inch close. Still, he was well hidden in the dense rain forest that bordered a clearing leading to the river. There was no way they'd see him. He'd passed the rest of the team earlier. Since then, he'd seen them through breaks in the foliage. He'd been as aware of their presence as they were unaware of his. That was over ten minutes ago. At the speed they were moving, they were no threat for the next five or so minutes and, besides, they were coming in from the opposite direction from where he watched, and—he had to admit, waited. He'd taken a shortcut to bring himself here, well ahead of them.

The turn of events stunned him. He couldn't believe that their guide was dead, headless. Who or what would have killed him? It was ironic how this was playing out. The dead headless guide, all of it, considering what his intent was. All this pissing around was grating.

To hold back, to wait, was taking patience that he never knew he had. Sure, he feigned patience. That was his job. He was always the afterthought, the backup. But not here, here he could be the man. The man he was meant to be. The Iban thought they knew this dense forest that tourists called a jungle. Little did they know that there was someone who knew it even better. His blood was boiling with desire, with need. It was often like that preceding a kill.

His attention diverted to the couple. Fortunately, they were oblivious to everything around them. He wasn't sure how in hell they had survived in the heart of the rain forest this long. But they had, and that was only to his advantage. Without them he'd have to deal with his cravings. But with them, so many of them… he had to fight to control his breath. For it was speeding up as he thought about the gratification that one of them would give him.

He'd been tracking them since he'd heard of their

expedition by the convoluted way that constituted communication in the rain forest. Someone told someone who told someone. This had been front page news. For, while having epidemiologists in the rain forest wasn't a one-off experience, it wasn't an everyday experience either. He'd tracked them almost from the beginning. It had been tricky for he had to skirt the long house and he had to avoid Aidan. In the end he'd had to shimmy up a tree to get the lay of the land and get a position. By the time he'd caught up with them, they'd already lost their guide and were a mess. It couldn't be more perfect.

And it was clear from the beginning that somewhere in the midst of that group was the prey. The prey who would assuage the hunger that was beginning to threaten to eat him alive. He needed relief and he needed it soon. He hadn't thought when he'd headed out on this walkabout that it would be about anything more than becoming grounded. He should have known better.

For this wasn't the first time that the urge to kill had threatened to overcome him.

He watched the tableau for a minute longer and then two. After a time, it became more maudlin than interesting and then downright disturbing. This pair were the most dysfunctional duo he'd ever laid eyes on. It was like watching a bad marriage at work.

He couldn't stand it another minute.

He'd move on, for now. They were too close to shelter and Aidan was nearby.

He stood up, glancing back at his prey. For now, he had them in his sights and that was enough.

Soon, of course, another would die. He pushed the thought back. For it caused the blood to pulse in his groin and distracted him from what was important—staying alert and not getting caught.

For now, this was foreplay. Eventually, when the heat became too much, he'd move in.

Chapter Two

Aidan glanced at the sky. Through the thick foliage that made up the forest canopy, he could see the glint of sunlight. From its angle, he knew that it was time to go back. Of course, it had been time to go back to the longhouse an hour ago. He wasn't out here for the good of the tribe. He was only out here for peace and to calm his nerves. He loved nothing better than leaving Kuching, shedding his city persona, and retreating to the home he had known as a boy. The Borneo rain forest, the place that most visitors only thought of as a jungle. Here, his thoughts were centered on the moment and on the plants and animals that breathed around him.

But his peace had been disturbed only hours before when he had stumbled on the Chinese poachers. The Chinese had shot a monkey, and there was nothing he could do. The animal was dead before he arrived, and they weren't protected. It wasn't illegal. It was only poaching in his mind. The monkeys to him were friends, and that's where he differed from the tribe who had raised him. But many things separated him from his tribe, including the fact that he was not Iban, not by blood. Despite his differences, in his heart, he was the same. And, like many of his Iban brothers, he could function in Sarawak's capital city of Kuching as well as he could here, in the wilds of the island of Borneo. Here country lines blurred.

He'd been raised by a mother who could only be called a child of the earth. A hippie some might call her. A flower child, for her naïve innocence and liberal ideas still went back to that era even though she'd been too young to live it in real time. With no stable base to call home, his mother still lived in whatever part of the world caught her fancy. She'd raised him for a time here, in Borneo, mostly in Sarawak. It was here where he'd found stability and a parent in the form of his Iban stepfather. Cliché and all, his mother was a modern-day, real-life Indiana Jane and the reason he had lived part of his time growing up as an adopted Iban.

Aidan took in a deep breath. The forest had carried on its noisy melody with no interference since the boat carrying the Chinese poachers had left. This was how he enjoyed the forest, alone. Still, he was on edge. He needed to refocus, find his center.

But there was no peace at ground level. The only way to regain peace was to go up, above the forest floor. Despite the habits of his life in the city, climbing was still instinctive. He'd done it since childhood. The rough trunk scraped his leg as he shimmied up. It was all so familiar. He grabbed a lower branch and paused, letting the texture ground him, and then swung up. He held on with one hand and squatted on the thick branch. Here he was at home, surrounded by the land he loved, the whisper of the animals, the silent promises of the plants. It was here, above the forest floor, that he finally found his zen—the peace in the heart of the forest. And it was as he found his zen that he immediately lost it.

He gripped the spear—one of the few belongings he treasured. Out here he kept his belongings to a minimum. There wasn't any room or any need for the material clutter of civilization.

There was a faint rustle of underbrush. Not the tread of the indigenous tribes, for their feet were silent on well-known paths, paths that were not seen by others. This was something else. Nothing he could see, but nonetheless a presence that was as obvious as the tree bark against his hand. The feeling was gut deep, instinctive, and there was no science to go on. He had learned early that feelings were often the net between death and safety.

He dropped lightly to the ground and stood quietly listening. Whatever it was, it was going to be a serious shit disturber, and on a scale bigger than the last group. He could feel it in his bones.

He raised his spear and loped in long strides, his feet landing soft and silent as he closed the distance between him and the newcomers. He stopped when only a few yards and dense jungle separated him from the intruders.

A mosquito landed on his bare shoulder. He twitched his skin and dislodged the insect without moving anything else on his body.

Then he stopped and sucked in his breath. For the second time that day, there was death in the air. Bitter and harsh, death knifed through the forest like an alien presence. His grip on the spear tightened.

In the clearing, Aidan could see two figures leaning over something in the grass. He moved closer and swallowed heavily—a body. That was obvious from the smell. He was sensitive to the smell of death. Scents that were powerful to him were unnoticeable, he knew, by others not raised here. And death had its own unique scent, present within minutes of dying. His ability to know that was like a woman's intuition or a psychic's vision, unexplainable.

****

"He was shot," Savannah said. She looked around as if expecting something or someone to emerge from the depths of the rain forest. But only the screeching insects, loud as monkey screams, punctured the poise of a land never silent.

"Murder?" Ian said in a choked voice.

"Maybe."

How safe were they? The team was separated and there was no longer safety in numbers.

"Do you think they shot him before they beheaded him?" Ian asked and gagged.

"Don't throw up again," she warned and knew her words were futile. Ian could only take so much.

"I can't help it," he said before he turned and fled.

Savannah stood up. The brush rustled. She clenched her fists, eyes riveted on the grass as it flattened in a wave, an S shape that signaled another of the many lizards both large and small that inhabited this land. Whatever it was, it carried on in the opposite direction, and the grass was soon still.

She blew out a breath that she hadn't realized she'd been holding. Behind her footsteps crunched, stepping through a graveyard of vegetation. She glanced around as Ian returned. His face was white as the chalk of a full moon. He wiped his mouth with the back of his hand.

The constant train of forest noise was masked by incessant and shrill calls that, at first, seemed to appear from nowhere. Now, they knifed through the clearing. Crazed laughter was her first thought, but the sound was coming from the sky. She sat back on her haunches, thinking that she'd finally lost her mind.

"Hornbills." Ian's voice was filled with awe.

She looked up to see the large birds jostle each other as they flew together. Their three-foot-long red tails would have been impressive at another time. Not now. Now even the mundane had become insanity. The calls were laugh-like, but after all that had happened, that description seemed inaccurate, for the noise they made was more like an eerie taunt.

"We're not alone," she said too softly for Ian to hear. She wasn't sure why she said it. It was a ridiculous thought, or maybe a hopeful thought. They were alone—she, Ian, the remaining team. There was no help. Still, she glanced over her shoulder as the feeling merged with one of déjà vu. The birds screeched again, and as she watched them, she shivered.

Chapter Three

Shot.

As if to echo that thought, hornbills' jagged cries sliced again through the trees and echoed through the jungle canopy. As their cries faded into the distance there was only deathly silence.

Aidan frowned as their conversation filtered back to him. He squinted and moved closer. The woman's white-blonde hair was a beacon in the shadows. The trees sifted the sunshine and the vines sucked up the remaining light that danced furtively across her features. He took in a breath, startled for a moment at her beauty.

Then she moved and he had a clear view of what lay on the ground.

He froze. It wasn't a dead animal but a human body!

An animal would have been disturbing enough. But this…

He sucked in his breath. And, for a minute he forgot to breathe. For, not only did the body have no head, it looked like a tribesman. Selfishly, he hoped that it wasn't one he knew. Was it one of the many who plied the jungle acting as guides? That would explain the fact that these two appeared to be alone, ill equipped, and without a guide. What were they doing here in the middle of the jungle without a weapon between them? It was clear that they weren't hunters, but what were they? The fact that there was a dead body, that it was headless—it didn't disturb him like it might others. Death he had faced many times, both professionally and with his Iban tribe. With the tribe, death was a natural flow of life. It was there where the skull of the last head taken still hung, well over a century later, from a rafter of the longhouse.

He was a man who danced between two worlds. So, in that instant, as he remained riveted on the scene in front of him, he flipped from his jungle mind-set into private investigator mode.

Except, he didn't have time for this. He had promised to check the rice field and refill the pots that burned every night to keep the monkeys away. He had intended to do that earlier so he could catch the plane later this evening to Kuching. There was a man he needed to see about another apartment. The way real estate was going, he wanted to pick up as much property as he could before there was no further profit to be made. It was the last plane today. And now, it was obvious that he was going to miss it.

He moved closer. He couldn't hear what she was saying, but she projected confidence. They were in a deadly situation. Did she know how dangerous the situation was? No animal would have taken only the head. Of course, that was an assumption, and part of his job was to not make assumptions. But he couldn't fathom an accident, not with the head missing.

There had been some recent run-ins with locals and loggers. But there was no logging in the immediate area. Gem smuggling was lucrative, and the men involved were ruthless. As he watched, he considered the possibilities.

"Where are they?" the man asked.

So, there were others.

To the left, the brush rustled, and heavy footsteps sounded.

He considered the Chinese. It seemed strange that he had run into evidence of both groups within such a short period of time. Did they have anything to do with this? He would have thought it a good possibility except for the beheading. That changed everything.

He moved in the direction of the sound, sliding on silent feet through the forest. Within seconds, he saw the second disturbance. A group of men were making their way along a trail, the same trail that opened onto the clearing where the woman and the man waited. They were soft, that was immediately apparent in their faces, flushed and gleaming with sweat. But that didn't mean they hadn't killed. He'd seen it before.

****

Get it together, Savannah thought, as she gingerly unhooked the watch and lifted it from Malcolm's wrist. The watch had taken a beating, but her thought was that it was an heirloom that he loved and that maybe his family would want it. She slipped it into her pocket.

"Ending the expedition and walking out now is our only option. We'll follow the river as much as we can," she said as she stood.

"Sid's not going to like it."

"Sid's not in charge of this expedition," she said angry at the suggestion. "Screw Sid."

Sid's rich baritone laugh broke into the clearing. "Ah, sweetie, I only wish you would." Sid's laughter broke as he came closer.

"What the ever-livin'—?" He bit off the expletive and his Australian accent was ripe and thick with shock. "Is that what I think it is?"

"Malcolm," Ian confirmed, his voice soft, as if he was in a church.

Burke, Drew, and Jason emerged from the brush. But it was Sid who pushed forward, hunkering down beside the corpse.

"We've got to get out of here," Savannah said, relieved to see the whole team. She took a deep breath. "Sid, gather some branches we can use as poles. We're going to make a stretcher and pull him."

"Pull him where?" Drew asked. "We haven't a clue how to get out of here without his help." He gestured toward the corpse.

The desk job Savannah had left was beginning to look better and better. What had she been thinking to come here? She pulled her shoulders back taking a calming breath as she did so. She had to get it together. Her team depended on her. This was the ultimate proof that she could handle an expedition. Then again, it could be the ultimate proof that maybe, she couldn't.

"We're doomed," Drew whispered. "What are we going to do?"

What were they going to do?

Savanah repeated in her thoughts. She couldn't leave Malcolm alone to the elements, yet she knew that bringing him was not a wise idea. Dragging a corpse through a forest studded with predators. There was no choice. She wasn't going to leave him here. Here to be ripped apart…

The thought dead-ended as she fought to stop tears that licked at her insides and twisted her stomach into a tight knot.

Savannah glanced up. Through a rare break in the canopy of trees. The sun seemed to hang mid-sky, just over her shoulder. West. It set in the west. That was the direction of civilization. If they followed the river current, they'd get to one of the smaller villages. Maybe someone there could help them get to where the rivers joined; Rumah Muleng wasn't far from that. Once they reached the village, they could arrange transport to Kuching.

With branches, vines, vest, and the jackets they would be able to fashion a stretcher.

"We're going to get moving. Anyone have a belt?" Savannah asked as she slid out of her vest without waiting for an answer.

Burke unbuckled his belt and handed it to her.

"Drew, we need your jacket," she commanded.

"No way." He shook his head. "Bloody leeches are everywhere. I'm not getting those things on me."

"Give it up." She held out her hand.

Drew peeled off the lightweight rain jacket slowly, his fingers almost caressing the zipper.

When she turned, Ian was already holding his jacket out with a resigned if stoic expression.

Drew knelt down beside her. "I've made a field stretcher before." He pulled his knife from his pocket and peeled off his vest.

"Here." Sid passed his vest to Drew.

"That should hold, at least long enough for us to get out of here," Drew said as he wrapped a vine around a branch and knotted it.

"Yeah, civilization shouldn't be that far away," Burke said, brushing sweat off his forehead.

Savannah hoped that his optimism had some basis in reality. But she was beginning to have her doubts.

She almost snorted at the utter lunacy of that

thought.

Beginning to have doubts? She'd had doubts big time since leaving the city of Kuching. She'd only admit now after tragedy was threatening to destroy them all, that much of her bluster hid those doubts. Her worst fear only hours ago, was that these men, her colleagues, would discover that her confidence was all show. What did she know about an expedition into the jungle? And now, unthinkably, they were about to find out. They'd just hit worst-case scenario.

"I still think we should wait," Burke muttered, but despite his doubts, he wasn't backing up from being her right-hand man.

"Here, use this." Sid handed a roll of string to Drew.

"Where'd you get that?" Drew frowned.

"Does it matter?" Sid snarled.

"Guys!"

The word was sharp. Authoritative was what she had been going for. Something to get them to listen and prevent what could only end in a major blow up or even an insurrection.

She pointed to the river. "That's our best course. If we keep going that way." She waved her arm downriver. "We should be at a village by nightfall."

She hesitated; it wasn't an outright lie—there was a remote possibility. If one could keep the river in sight in the dense foliage.

In the impenetrable depth of the forest insects screeched, twigs snapped. And life seemed to breathe around them. They all sucked in deep breaths. Somehow, with Malcolm's common-sense knowledge of the forest, it had not seemed so intimidating.

"We've already done this, guys. We've been

without Malcolm for almost a day and a night. We can make it without him."

She pumped confidence into the words while her soul only felt deflated, uncertain and she was one misstep away from tears. Still, she did her best to rally their confidence.

"So, let's get moving," she said.

They said nothing as they began walking, single file, one of them pulling the makeshift stretcher.

As she walked, she thought of how and why Malcolm could have ended up dead and headless. Who had he run into? Poachers? Contraband? All criminal activities, all dangerous, and they were ill-equipped to deal with any of it.

She glanced back, her gaze traveling over them. Educated scientists, brilliant in their field, none of that was going to help them. For it was next to impossible to transform textbook knowledge into real-life common sense. And the only thing that kept replaying in her mind as she calmly issued orders was fear. Fear that maybe the headhunters were back. And with Malcolm dead, they had become the hunted.

Chapter Four

"We're lost. Ian, I told you to bring the GPS," Savannah said twenty minutes later.

She scowled at Ian. And, at the same time wondered how he could be such a good friend and yet piss her off to the point of wanting to slug him. Yes, that was what she'd like to do. And yet she wouldn't. She never had, and she never would.

She swallowed and said, "I can't believe it. Can't believe you left it behind."

"I'm sorry."

Frustration coursed through her. "That doesn't help now. Why would you give it to Malcolm?"

She wanted to wring her hands or his neck, she wasn't sure what, if either, would give her any satisfaction. None of it would change the fact that they'd lost the GPS, that it was more than likely in the river.

"He was fascinated by it. He wanted to see how it worked. I couldn't deny him that. I couldn't deny him…"

"Anything," she finished. "Yeah, got it. Love wins out."

"Great job, mate," Sid sniped.

"Let's get moving," she commanded, realizing that there was no changing yet another miserable point in a crappy situation. They had to make do. They had to figure it out for themselves. They had to, somehow, not get lost in a rain forest that sprawled over more square miles than she wanted to consider and could eat people alive.

She started walking. The others followed. The trail that skirted the edges of the jungle was becoming fainter the farther they went. Within minutes it disappeared and there was only the sky to orientate them. Malcolm had judged direction by the growth of moss on the tree trunks. He had no need of a GPS, and now that they did, it was lost. The forest was forcing them farther back from the river. The overgrown vines and swampy soil had already pushed them to a point where the river was only a muted rush in the distance. They were following the river's path by fading sound. What were they going to do once that sound was gone? They were only thirty minutes in, she wouldn't think of it.

"We have to head north and west," she reminded them.

The river would lead them to the village. That was the one saving grace, the one surety. Everything else, without Malcolm, was scarily tentative, guesswork. Even the map only existed in her head. The actual map had been in Malcolm's pack. There had been a map in her pack, too, but she had left that at the last village. They had intended to return there that night when Malcolm returned, except that had never happened. All she had left was a small day pack with the absolute necessities and no navigation tools. She swallowed, willing the panic away, but it was too late. Panic brewed beneath her calm façade.

"That way." She motioned toward the looming forest that only got thicker and darker the farther they pushed in. But that was where she was sure that river met tropical forest, where they needed to be no matter how difficult.

"We've got to get back to the river while we can still hear it."

She heard mumbling and the rough scrape of the primitive stretcher as it bounced the body along the forest floor. She wanted to tune out all sounds and sensations, that and the facts. She wouldn't think of it as anything but the body. To think of it as once human, as Malcolm, would only bring unneeded emotion into the situation.

"Get it together, guys. We've got to keep moving," she snapped.

Orders and anger numbed the raw edges, staved off the weeping that once started might never stop. She pulled her knife from its sheath and unnecessarily cut through a tangled vine. She was making a point, emphasizing her decision to push forward. A night in the tropical forest of Borneo in an unknown locale was unthinkable. If they were lucky, they would be able to veer back to the river's path and make the village before dark. There was time. At a steady pace, barring getting lost, they could do it.

****

Unbelievable.

How could Aidan show up now?

Matthew couldn't believe it. This was becoming a shit show of the worst kind. Ironically, the group had yet to know of either his presence or Aidan's. He guessed that they were soon going to learn about Aidan's.

He'd had to scramble to hide his tracks for Aidan was a top-rate tracker. One screwup and he'd be found. And he had no explanation, none whatsoever, for being here. Off the top of his head, his excuses were weak. The one vying for top position was that he was taking a mini-vacation before the tourist season heated up and his services would be in demand. He knew without a lot of thought that that excuse would be met with questions, possibly even disbelief. He blew past the need for excuses for his presence, for another need eclipsed all. He was aching to kill.

All was not yet lost. There was still opportunity, a window that was sliding slowly shut with every minute that passed.

Still, a chance, he reminded himself.

He'd maintain the distance, but to do that he had to know where Aidan was at all times. Fortunately, he was far enough away, and he'd left no trail to follow. Besides, Aidan was busy being the hero, the rescuer.

Damn him!

He pushed the thoughts that always led to resentment from his mind. He had to focus. Aidan wouldn't know that he'd been here until the crew he was tracking realized that they were missing one more.

He smiled as he turned his attention to the group and saw that one of the men was moving away from the group and north, toward him. His heart raced and he clenched his right fist as if that would calm him down.

Keep coming, baby, keep coming.

He needed this. He was long overdue.

Then, his quarry disappeared, out of sight.

Damn, he thought and moved forward, carefully, slowly.

Just a little closer, he silently encouraged. He was the right direction but still too far away. Distance still stood between him and providence, and of course, Aidan. Except for those two things, this was perfect. The man's cohorts were traumatized and, from what he could determine, lost. They wouldn't, couldn't even, be able to do much of a search when their pal didn't return. The body, more than likely, would never be found. They might never know there was another kill. Anyway, he looked at it, he was good. For, no one would suspect him. Not jovial, fun-loving Matthew.

His thoughts were hot and ready. He'd thought the first kill would be enough. That had been months ago. The man was a loner, an easy mark. No one had missed him, not at first. Now, too much time had passed, and his cravings were eating at him. He needed another kill.

Just one more.

He was crouched, waiting for the man to come close enough. The deed would be done quickly and silently. The sound of death would be cushioned by the rich depth and vibrancy of the rain forest.

He smiled as he watched the man moving along, looking over his shoulder. He was oblivious, a virgin in the forest. He was whistling some mundane tune. And then, as if he'd finally become aware of something wrong—something terribly off, he turned, and the whistling stopped. But then he began his inane whistling again, as he continued deeper into the forest. The way he was moving only led to what one might call a ravine if they lived on flat lands. Here it was a dumping spot—somewhere where a hunter's quarry tumbled in with no valid way out and no way to be seen.

The man stopped. He was more than likely—yes…

He was taking a piss.

He couldn't be more vulnerable.

Matthew's heart pounded, and he had an erection. It was like he was anticipating sex on the grandest scale.

No surprise. It was always like that, the pleasure beginning as he anticipated the kill.

A whistle trilled through the forest.

"I'll be there in a minute." The man turned his head as he shouted. And seconds later he was heading back.

Damn it all to hell! Matthew thought. The heated rush of his erection deflated quickly. For a second he was numbed, as a rush of hurtful remarks from the past flooded his memory. It was a toxic cloud that held all the insults of everyone who'd rejected him in the past.

He'd never forgotten.

Chapter Five

"Hurry it up. We need to get to safety before nightfall," the woman commanded them and veered deeper into the rain forest. Aidan knew she was trying to get to the river, but her direction was completely skewed.

In another life this might have been funny, entertaining even.

In the heart of the rain forest where life and death were determined in microsecond decisions, it was frightening at most. And, at the least, unbelievable. Aidan didn't know how much longer he could trail them. They were babes in the woods, at least one was. The others were idiotic.

Again, he considered whether he should make his presence known. Yet he hesitated as he continued to shadow them through the underbrush. He moved silently on his flip-flops. He grimaced. His silence was unnecessary. The noise they made—well, he might as well be in the city in rush hour.

He was ahead of the group now. He stopped and waited. They were moving much too slowly to make it to any settlements before dark.

He allowed his thoughts to drift as he waited. The jungle had been rife with intruders today. First there were the Chinese. Hunters weren't completely uncommon, but he usually knew in advance when they were in the area, as they were rarely without local guides. But these foreigners had been alone, and he was immediately suspicious. He'd watched them for a long time trying to figure out what they were about, if they were really alone. Eventually he determined that they did have a guide, one who had headed upriver and was set to return. Still, he'd watched them. Large men—large in an overfed way, with skin taut and shimmering in the tropical heat. Their laughter had grated in a place where he anticipated human silence. And their words still ran through his mind.

The language they had spoken was Mandarin, a Chinese dialect that Aidan understood, among others. As a private investigator, languages came in handy. But they'd switched at times to English, and that combined with some of their mannerisms made him sure that they were businessmen. Men with enough money to relieve their boredom, and this had become their game board.

"We've got to get out of here unless you want to spend the rest of your life in the jungle. Pedro is overdue. He said he'd be back in an hour. He was serious. His kind know time." The man paused. "It's instinctive."

It had been clear, despite the slurs, that they were speaking of their missing Iban guide, for there was no one else. Anger still rushed through Aidan at the memory. Those men hadn't belonged here. Their presence had been an addendum to their real life.

His hand brushed against a stem of grass, grounding him. Wasn't that what he was? In a loincloth, carrying a spear, and pretending to be something he was not? When his real life was Kuching and the thrill of a new case amid the rush and hum of the city?

No, he was not the same. He could never be the same.

He forced his attention to the present. He watched as the woman strode ahead of the group. Her femininity was unmistakable. Her figure outlined beneath clothes that only clutched and clung in the turgid tropical heat and flattered every curve. They were heading straight for a tree where he could see a good-sized python dozed, deceptively still.

He considered revealing himself. To the uninitiated, a python that size could be terrifying. He doubted if she knew that right now it was more vulnerable than she. The python was well camouflaged and sated after a meal that could have been days ago. There was no danger there.

The blood-curdling scream curled through the heat and raked shrill fingers down his spine.

He held back his initial urges both to push forward, and to offer help. He stood his ground and waited. There was much to learn here and no danger, yet.

It was telling that she hadn't been the one to scream.

He watched her walk over to a man who stood quivering, staring up at the python. Her hips swung sweetly, and the seductive movement was out of place in the jungle, out of place in his thoughts. What was wrong with him?

He was going to have to show himself soon. The group was obviously lost, and there was nothing more he could learn from remaining out of sight. It was time to change tactics.

****

"Move it," Savannah hissed at Ian while her stomach quivered, and her natural instinct was to run away.

"Move, Ian!" She repeated, her voice sharp even to her own ear. "Don't look at it. Just move. One foot in front of the other—go!"

She grabbed his arm, pulling him along.

"Ouch, Savannah," Ian protested as he twisted his arm free.

"Keep moving," she snapped.

"I can't," he gasped.

She glanced at him with a worried frown, fearing that he was right. Years at a desk had made him soft, out of shape, despite the fact that he had only, like her, just turned thirty.

"He was huge," said Sid when they reached the group. "Can't stand the buggers myself."

"Are you okay?" she asked as they moved away, putting distance between them and the snake.

Ian nodded. He took a gasping breath, but his color was returning. "It startled me."

"I've heard a girl scream less," Sid said.

"Shut up, Sid," Savannah snapped. "I'm over the top with your sexist comments. Actually, with all of your comments. Quit turning on others and sweep your own back door."

"Back door…" He grinned and glanced at Ian.

"Don't you dare say it," Savannah broke in.

She clenched her fists as she reminded herself of all the reasons that she shouldn't have contracted Sid. And she'd almost followed up on those reasons except that professionally he was the best. And they'd needed the best. Besides, one of his references had vouched that he'd turned a new leaf. She knew now that she should have looked at that recommendation more closely. And, more importantly, she should have listened to her instincts.

Around them the jungle vibrated with the sounds of

millions of insects. The screeching sent a different type of shiver down her spine. Like a long-anticipated treat, it never disappointed her. The thrill was always there. Snake or not, it always came down to the insects. This was what they all lived for, what they loved. This expedition had been eagerly anticipated by all of them. She hated that she had to cut it short. And while the insects pulled her, fear drove them. Not justice for Malcolm and not grief. It was fear that they had to get out before they were hurt too. She hated that about herself—about the others.

Drew glanced behind him. "I'd be more comfortable if we put some distance between us and that…"

He pointed back to where the python had been.

Ten minutes later, with the snake well behind them, Savannah stopped and glanced back at the group. Now that there was nothing to divert Ian's attention, she could see that the panic had taken over again.

"Ian."

He wouldn't look at her. He continued to plod forward.

He was pale, his breath coming in small gasps, but at least the hysteria was gone.

"Ian, take a deep breath. Don't think about Malcolm," she said under her breath so the others wouldn't hear.

"I'll be okay, I think," he said, but his words were stilted.

She squeezed his hand and held on. He'd been there for her through much of her life, his family living next door to hers. Her love of insects had fed his, and as children they had been inseparable. They had collected and studied insect specimens together, crawling through the imagined wilderness of their neighborhood. They'd ended up going to the same university for their undergraduate study in entomology. Ian's knowledge of beetles was unsurpassed. But more important, he was a loyal friend. If it meant holding his hand through the rest of the forest, every square mile, she'd do it.

Despite everything, she marveled at where life had brought her. That she was finally here in the Borneo rain forest. Failed mission or not, she was leading the expedition. But now she was in way over her head, with a group of men who looked to her for answers. How had that happened? She knew how it happened. She knew herself better than most people, at least she liked to think so. She was focused, accepted who she was and what she wanted. And it was that and determination that had brought her here.

She had planned this trip carefully. The entire study would be completed in a series of day trips. For the last two weeks, every night had been spent in a nearby village as they followed the course of the Rajang River by boat and on foot. It was an expedition tailored to city-bred scientists. Physically it had been relatively easy, until now. She would never have brought Ian for anything more arduous. He wouldn't survive. His hysteria could get them all killed. She gritted her teeth. She wouldn't let it.

Chapter Six

"Where do we go from here?" the slight man asked the woman. "Do you think that way?" He pointed.

"Don't be utterly ridiculous," another man said as he emerged from the brush and into the small clearing. His voice was full of disdain. "We go that way." He pointed.

"I believe you're right," the woman said.

Aidan watched, surprised as the group turned and as a unit moved east, towing what was obviously a body behind them.

For the love of Mike! They were making more noise than a pipe band.

"Stop!" His command was involuntary, he hadn't meant to reveal himself yet. But he couldn't stand it. They were inordinately incompetent, and it was apparent that they needed help. From what he had seen so far, they were innocents abroad.

They hadn't heard him. But who could hear anything over the noise their heavy boots and the stretcher were making? The forest was oddly silent. He didn't like it. Some of what watched and waited knew far more than this idiotic group, and some of what watched and waited might be hungry. Smart and cunning, and waiting for an opportunity—an opportunity like this.

The woman stopped and seemed to look right at him before turning her attention to the stretcher. "We've got to get a move on. We've got to get to Rumah Muleng by dark."

The village—unbelievable, they were nowhere near there. They'd never get to the village before dark, not the way they were going. They were too far away, unless they had a boat. He took another look at the group and shook his head. He glanced at the stretcher and again wondered what had happened to their guide.

Aidan moved vines back, exposing his face. They only had to look in his direction.

He was so close he could have reached out and touched her. She was delicate, out of place here in the midst of this wilderness. Her skin, even beneath the sweat and exertion-stained flush, was fair. She wasn't built to be here, she was too slight to survive, too weak, too…

She glanced up. A frown immediately seared her face.

"Who the hell are you?" she snarled.

He bit back a smile. She should have screamed. She hadn't. All tiny limbs and fragile beauty, and yet she attacked first.

He let his gaze rove over the group, refusing to be influenced by her attack.

One of the men looked panicked, the others seriously stressed.

He shifted his spear to his other hand. He waited, taking the warrior advantage of time and observation. The silent often learned much about their enemy.

"Put that down." She gestured to his spear.

His fingers loosened for a millisecond before gripping the spear tighter. Was she out of her mind? Green, innocent, and totally forest-illiterate, but she was feisty.

Feisty? She was seething, hot, absolutely pissed—about what, he wasn't sure. Her anger didn't make much sense. Nothing about this afternoon made much sense.

"I won't be threatened. Put it down."

Her voice was rock hard, although he could hear the soft dulcet tones that would be pleasant at another time.

What was he thinking? He didn't know her. He stared silently back at her. Unfortunately, silence was not something she understood.

"Speak English?" she asked in the slow precise diction that one saves for small children and the very elderly suffering dementia.

He fought to unclench his teeth as anger ate at what remained of his zen. He wanted to shake each one of them and send them on the next Otter out of here. He bit back the comment and purposely pulled his attention to the makeshift stretcher.

"He's dead," he stated the obvious as he strode forward.

"You're swift. Can you help us?"

"Why?" he retorted.

"Why?" She drew herself up, tried to make herself taller, like the lizards that puffed to twice their body size. "Where did you come from?"

He pointed in the direction of his longhouse.

"You're from a village?" Her voice took on a hopeful tone.

"Yes." Somehow it satisfied him to give her only guttural answers, to see the annoyance on her face. And the longhouse, well, it was a village of sorts. At least it was a community and the closest available before nightfall.

"I see. Doctors?"

He raised an eyebrow.

"Not for him." She glanced at the pallet. "Him." She pointed at the slight man who swayed behind her. "He needs valium. A sedative. It's been too much for him."

The other men were as silent as the man she referred to. Apparently, these men were eunuchs of some sort. They would let anyone lead, he realized, as long as they didn't have to take responsibility for themselves.

"Is there a doctor?" she persisted.

He nodded. Her aggression only made resistance and one-word answers that much more pleasurable. Oh, he wouldn't leave them in the tropical forest. They were a threat to themselves and the inhabitants of the forest, crashing around the way they were. But he sure wasn't going to make their rescue easy. What would her reaction be when she met the doctor?

"Let's go." She waved a hand as she directed the men around her. "Show us the way." She turned to Aidan. "I need to get them to safety. Whoever did this to him"—she gestured to the corpse—"might still be out there."

Aidan glanced at them. The men stood behind her waiting. One actually glared at him, but not one of them said anything.

That confirmed it. These weren't men. They were useless. The only one with a set of balls in this group was a woman. Interesting. Not that lady balls weren't a reality. He'd met more courageous women than he could count. He just hadn't met them as strangers in the middle of the Borneo rain forest.

"What happened?" he asked.

"He washed up on the riverbank, mate," the Aussie sniped.

"Dead," the one with the high, thready voice choked.

"Shot," a third replied.

He nodded and turned away. This was a criminal investigation. He considered the possibilities before ditching the idea of getting more involved than he already was. Mark could handle it.

"Are you going to help us or what?" She frowned, hands on hips. "Can you help us get out of here and to a village? We can make Rumah Muleng if we can get a boat or plane."

"Not today."

"Why not?"

He'd had enough. Here in the jungle conversation was not an art, only a means of communication, brief, efficient, with long periods of silence. He would not be talked to death. He started to walk. He knew they'd follow. What other choice did they have?

"Wait." There was an edge of panic in her voice.

He kept walking.

Behind him they crashed and thumped. He imagined the stretcher bouncing over the rough terrain, as they struggled to follow.

"Sid, can't you see the stretcher's coming undone?"

He didn't turn around. Instead, he listened as her busy footsteps moved away from him. He'd sensed her presence just to his left and, just behind him. Now, she was moving back to her group. He didn't glance back, but from the scurrying and lack of male voices she'd obviously decided to go back and fix the makeshift stretcher herself.

"Okay, let's get going before we lose him."

The command carried loud and clear, and he held

back an unwanted shiver of pleasure at the silk in that voice. He walked faster.

There were many things he wished to demand of them. Why the body was headless, for one. Why they were in his forest. He would ask them none of those things, not yet.

"Hey."

She was beside him, brushing up against him. "Talk to me."

He ignored her and only walked faster. Gorgeous or not, she was out of place. This was his home. And she was affecting him in ways he couldn't control and didn't like.

She followed him.

He kept walking.

He led.

She followed.

She grabbed his arm.

He shook her off and motioned with his spear. The gesture should have been enough to set her on her heels. It had stayed the deadliest of jungle inhabitants. It did not stay her.

She swung in front of him. He had to stop or push her aside.

"Follow me or stay here."

She had forced the words from him.

"Why should I follow you? You haven't told me where you're going. Can we get out of here once we're at your village?" She glared at him. "What's the name of this village?"

He didn't meet her look.

"It's not a village, is it?"

"No," he admitted.

"We're tired. Ian's hysterical. Malcolm, well, what's left of him..."

She put her hand to her mouth, her eyes awash with tears that shimmered on eyelashes that swept long and dark against her fair skin. Skin that he wanted to reach out and touch. He clenched his free hand. She blinked heavily and looked beyond him.

"Look, you. I don't know who you are or where you're going. Why should we follow you?" She was so close he could touch her.

"Why?" She pushed her forefinger at his chest.

He captured it and met her gaze, and he was caught. He was drowning in hot blue eyes, dreaming of sun-washed summer days, and longing to claim her lips and never let them go.

"Let me go."

He grunted. This time his response wasn't a ploy. He truly couldn't say anything.

"Let me go." This time, she enunciated the words slowly and yanked her finger free.

He surfaced, confused as if he'd been caught in some delirium that had taken his free will away. This never happened, not here, not anywhere. His life was planned, organized, and his love life... He swallowed. His love life lately had been sadly abysmal. Maybe that was his problem—he was woman-starved and now he had literally stumbled over one.

"Sorry," he muttered and immediately knew he had lost his edge.

"Where are you going?"

"To my longhouse. There's food, shelter from the night."

"Your longhouse?"

"Muleng is too far."

He glanced at the sun.

"We wouldn't make it before dark," she finished.

He let silence be his answer.

She frowned, considering her options and obviously realizing she had none. She met his gaze and he wished she hadn't. He looked away.

"Okay, great," she amended. "Thanks."

He didn't acknowledge her. She was trying to be gracious, but really what choice did she have? The alternative was finding her own way out of the jungle. She knew that. She led this group with an ease no one questioned and a femininity that remained unshaken despite her authority—like the women of his tribe. Mentally he shook himself and moved his thoughts forward to home, comfort, and safety. A peace and comfort that he was about to destroy, at least for himself. For the rest of the tribe this would only be excitement in an otherwise mundane day.

****

Matthew knew that he was playing with the fates by continuing to hunt them. The problem was Aidan. Since he had joined their group, it had become a game of pitting his skills up against one of the best.

Didn't matter, Aidan was still an outsider. For, despite mostly growing up here, Aidan wasn't born Iban. He would always have that against him. Not that he wasn't an outsider too, but at least he didn't play at being one of them.

He wondered how they could have bloody well found Malcolm already. He grimaced at the thought of the man or at least what was left of him. He was a puzzle that he hadn't quite figured out yet. He had no idea who had killed him or what had happened. For he hadn't had any part in the killing. He had no idea who had, but he'd seen the body at the same time as the boys. That had been many miles downriver. With that thought, he turned south, dropping back from the group. Now, he was far enough behind that there was nothing for Aidan to pick up on.

He would have to keep tracking, keep his distance and wait.

Kill and run.

And then return to life as normal. That was still days away. For now, he must wait.

His hand slipped to the hunting knife at his side. He'd sharpened it only two nights ago.

He was ready.

Chapter Seven

"What's your name?" she demanded.

Aidan ignored her. It was rude, but it was only a tactic like any other. Make them uncomfortable, make them squirm and involuntary information might be forthcoming.

"Hey!"

She hurried to match his stride. The makeshift stretcher rustled and scraped through the underbrush. To his jungle-sensitive ears, the noise was an intrusion, an aberration. "My name is irrelevant."

"Irrelevant," she repeated.

A faint aroma of something flowered and sweet drifted around him as she shouldered her way through the foliage to walk beside him. Yet everything about her was delicate, despite her efforts to the contrary. He knew she forced her edge, knew the effort it required. It was evident in the tenseness that surrounded her as strongly as the scent of flowers. She was feminine to her core and warrior to her soul. She was trouble.

"So, you're not going to tell me?"

He kept walking."

"Well, I'm sorry. I wanted your name in exchange for my own. The civilized thing to do."

"Hmmph," he shot through gritted teeth.

"Well, that was profound, Mr. Irrelevant."

He pushed past her, the back-and-forth play-lead-follow becoming a game between them. He was power walking, stretching his own ability to break distance. He could hear her behind him and knew it was futile to push ahead of her. She was determined to talk to him, and she'd do whatever it took to keep up. Apparently, his name, his identity, had just become of utmost importance to her. He wouldn't give it. Exchanging names was dangerous. It implied a relationship.

There would be no relationship with these people. He would drop them at the longhouse and that was it. Mark would see them to Muleng as soon as possible, deal with the body, and then get them to Kuching and that would be it. Mark would love the challenge. He had been complaining that there was no crime in the forest, that he'd like to practice his criminal investigation skills. Aidan sighed.

His time in the rain forest was exactly the opposite. He was here to escape crime and interrogations, to relax, to find peace. He pushed a hissing breath through his teeth. There would be no peace until he got rid of this group. But it was apparent they couldn't keep his quick pace. They were weak, the men especially, obviously city bred with no fortitude.

"Could you slow down, please?"

She touched his arm, a willow wisp of touch, but again her scent was overwhelming and seductive.

"There's not much time before dark," he replied.

"C'mon, guys, pick it up," she bellowed.

Her full red lips issued the order with the confidence of any mud-ugly drill sergeant. She was a dichotomy—that was for sure. A dichotomy he wanted no part of. He'd get them to the longhouse. Get Mark on the reporting, investigation, and burial and slide back out to the jungle. His time here was limited. Besides the brief flight he had planned tonight, the one he'd have to cancel, he didn't have much time left here. He wasn't going to waste any more time than necessary on this group.

"Hey," she shouted again, and the underbrush crackled, her footsteps quick and sure as she raced to catch up.

"Now what?"

He didn't slow down. Instead, he remained intent on the trail ahead.

"Could you step it back a bit? Ian's having a hard time, and I don't think our stretcher is going to hold together."

Her perfume was making him pay attention to things he had no right to notice. How she curved in all the right places, softly, subtly, nothing overblown, nothing too much or too little. How she'd fit perfectly beneath his arm, how…

"How much longer?" she murmured.

Her voice seemed for him alone, and that was almost more seduction than he could bear, especially with that damn perfume. Tantalizing, soft, sexy wafts with every breath. Why the hell was she wearing perfume?

"You're wearing perfume," he gritted. *Idiot, why had he said that?*

"Perfume? Don't be utterly ridiculous!"

Damn, could this get any worse? That alluring scent was natural and all her. He ached to pick up the pace and peel away from her.

"What are you doing here?" he asked, desperate and curious.

"We're collecting insects for research."

"Entomologists."

"Yes." She glanced at him with surprise and then asked. "What time is it?"

"Four," he bit out.

"Oh. That late." She bit her lip. "We're really not going to make Muleng or the plane."

He didn't say anything.

"It's too late, isn't it?" she repeated this time asking instead of telling. It was as if she hadn't really believed it the first time that he'd told her.

He nodded.

It wasn't just a plane she wasn't going to make, but he'd wait. This was a potential crime and an investigation that would begin long before they left the jungle. But there was no point adding fire to an already volatile situation. He breathed lightly. That didn't help. The perfume, her scent, was more intimate than any caress. She was too close. He was too ready. For the second time in his life, he almost dropped his spear.

That couldn't happen for the spear was valuable to him. His father had given it to him, the man who had raised him. Long after his mother had left her tribal lover, the man had still been a father to Aidan. Akan was the only father he had ever known. His biological father had been only that, a brief forgotten interlude in his mother's life.

He walked faster, again trying to put a distance between himself and the woman. It was pointless. She trotted to keep up.

"How much longer?" she asked, obviously oblivious to his torment.

"Over an hour even if we pick up the pace."

"Okay." She nodded and hurried back to her team.

He sighed and tried to settle his wayward thoughts. If he breathed lightly, maybe her scent wouldn't be so intoxicating. And maybe he'd wake up and find himself in his newly decorated city apartment too.

Chapter Eight

"Malcolm should never have left us," Sid said. "He knew it was dangerous. We could have been killed."

"He didn't leave us," Ian snarled. "He was killed."

"Too bad for you." Sid bent down to tie one of the vines that had come loose on the pallet.

"Shut up!" Ian shouted.

"Cool it, girl," Sid shot back.

"Don't call me that," Ian said, and his voice raised an octave.

"We know you had the hots for him. No, according to you, he couldn't do any wrong. Even though he left us all to die." Sid glared at Ian. "He left you, too, girl."

"Sid!" Savannah barked as she went to grab Ian, whose fists balled up as he looked ready to launch himself at Sid.

Ian shook her off. "Leave me," he whispered, glaring at Sid before stalking back to take his turn at the stretcher.

"Enough, Sid. He's been through a lot," Burke said.

"We all have," she agreed.

She turned, as she struggled to keep her anger leashed. "Sid, keep your ignorant comments to yourself."

She turned away. She didn't trust herself to make eye contact. And she cursed her stupidity in thinking that his expertise would somehow override his abrasive personality.

Minutes later when she did a quick scan of her team, making sure they were still all together everyone had calmed down. Still, tension ran through the group. Ian was uncharacteristically silent, and Sid's mouth was clamped in a hard line. She doubted that either man had the energy for further baiting, or even arguing. That's how it went with those two. Ian was someone for Sid to take his frustration out on. He'd taken the breakup of his marriage hard. She suspected that now it was more a matter of bruised pride. Either way, the aftermath was this game between Sid and Ian where they sparred and ducked and then retired to their respective corners.

She glanced ahead trying to clear her thoughts from the distraction of the continual head butting and baiting among her team. Ahead, their rescuer was marching along, leading the way. She ran to catch up. He continued to walk, ignoring her.

"I'm sorry we interrupted your hunting," she said as she matched his pace and kept just behind him, allowing him for the moment to break trail.

Nothing.

He continued to walk, silently, without rustling a leaf or a vine.

How did he do that? she thought as she assessed him. His blonde hair curled softly down to his shoulders and only softened the tanned planes of his face. His bare back glistened as if he had added suntan lotion. She wondered if that was some jungle remedy to prevent sunburn. She discounted that idea. His skin was burnished a deep, sun-glazed brown. Why was he tramping around the jungle in almost nothing? He was wearing a loincloth, flip-flops and nothing else. Bare chest, bare legs, bare everything. He was dressed from another century. He was dressed as if he'd walked off a stage or as if he just didn't want to let go.

She supposed that it didn't matter whether he was clothed or unclothed. She choked back a sob. None of it changed Malcolm's tragic end or their current situation. She took a breath concentrating on not losing control. Then, she glanced back and saw immediately that Ian was struggling to keep the pace. "Burke, spell Ian off, please."

Burke nodded, and they changed places. Still, Ian's complexion was flushed. She was hoping to get a plane to take them out first thing in the morning. One night and they would be seeing the authorities, turning this problem over to them.

"Excuse me," she said to the blonde-haired giant.

He ignored her. She should be getting used to it. But they'd fought through miles of jungle to get here. She wouldn't be ignored now. She swallowed back temper. No matter what she felt, they were at his mercy. There was no other rescuer in the vicinity. He held their lives in his hands. Mitts, she amended. His hands were huge. She peeled her eyes from his hands, pissed for noticing anything about the primitive beast. He was a means to get out of here—that was it.

She pushed her thoughts away and saw that he'd gotten way ahead of her again. His legs covered twice the ground of hers.

"Excuse me!" This time she shouted.

Around her, screeching erupted from nearby branches.

"Holy shit," Jason muttered.

"Damn it, Savannah, keep it down," Sid snapped.

"Your voice startled god knows what."

She threw Sid a scathing look and broke into a jog to catch up with their rescuer.

"Ease up, Sid," Jason said.

Behind her she could hear the remaining crew hurrying to catch up.

"Excuse me." This time she tapped him on the shoulder.

"What?" He swung around.

"I…"

She choked in the face of his unconcealed aggression. She hadn't expected that.

She smiled. Aggression she could manage.

****

"Fuck, they're pathetic," Matthew muttered as he anticipated what they might do next and when there'd be an opportunity. The wait gave him time to think about things that he hadn't considered in a very long time. Like when and how he'd first felt the need to kill. He wasn't sure when the desire had begun. Now, he guessed it had always been there. For there were memories from his childhood that others had called abhorrent, and that he'd found pleasurable. But the real moment was the car accident when he was twenty. That had changed everything. He'd watched a stranger die and he'd known then that he'd been hunting the wrong thing all along. He'd needed to start at the top of the food chain, not at the bottom.

This situation had presented him with what might have been a very rare treat—an easy kill. And Aidan, the fucking bastard, had stepped into his playing field.

Aidan.

Because of Aidan he was forced to wait. And

because of that, as the seconds turned to minutes, the need became a raging fire deep within him.

Chapter Nine

"Are we close?" Savannah asked.

Only the sound of footsteps crushing the underbrush was her answer.

She hadn't realized how much noise they made until now. Maybe that was a good thing and kept the predators away. She looked at him and waited.

Nothing.

He kept walking as if she weren't there.

Jerk, she thought as she glanced back at her group. They were struggling to get the primitive stretcher back in order and get the—she almost choked—the body strapped back into place.

She looked away, back at him.

"I'll get you there. I promise."

"Thanks."

She felt sorry for thinking anything derogatory for, she realized now what the extra words may have cost him. The man of silence might not be an act.

"And then we'll go to the village tomorrow." That wasn't so bad, she thought. One night in the forest on a wooden verandah, she could live with that.

He shook his head. "Too far."

"Too far? We, my team and I, were just there, and we have to get back there by tomorrow. We have a plane to catch." She held back the sour taste of anger. She was just too exhausted to deal with any of this.

"Undoable," he said. "How long has he been dead?" he asked in a voice that would have been average except for the slight rasp that sent pleasurable chills along her spine.

The fact that he could attract her at all only added to the anger that flared through her at the fact that he'd just dismissed everything she'd said. Despair laced through the anger as she realized the truth of his words. There was no way they were flying out of here. Malcolm was dead. Murdered. There'd be an investigation. Who knew when they'd ever got out of the rain forest.

"A day, no more. He was our guide."

"Your guide is bait now."

Chills ran through her followed by the unrelenting anger. Damn it, she thought. Blunt was one thing, but that was unfeeling. She looked furtively behind her before addressing his comment. "Are you always so blunt?"

The others caught up and pushed in behind her before he could answer.

"We could get to civilization quicker if we followed the bloody river," Sid said.

"Forget the river," their rescuer said in clipped, measured words and turned around and began moving uphill and away from the river.

Savannah swallowed. She had two options—leave the shelter of the river and trust this man, a stranger, or carry on without him.

"Come." He waved his spear in the air, pointing in the direction he expected to go and began to walk.

Just like the Neanderthal he is, Savannah thought, frustrated. She should be forever grateful to the man for getting them to safety, but all she could muster was anger.

"We can't spend another night here. Look at him." Sid waved his hand toward Ian, who was now trailing some yards behind the group. "And we're relying on that savage. Shit, the man can't even string together a coherent sentence."

"Look, Sid, it's the best we can do. We've trusted him so far."

"She's right," Jason muttered looking utterly frustrated.

"We're done," Sid muttered. He shook his head as if he didn't agree. He turned to her, his mouth taut and his eyes half wild, as if the end were in sight. "Savannah, you're nuts if you think we should follow him."

"Sid, we've got no choice. He's our best option."

"Is he?" Drew asked.

"We can't follow the river; the bush will push us back. He'll take us to shelter."

****

What was going on back there?

Aidan had listened long enough to the rebellious Sid, the effeminate Ian, the obtuse Drew, the other two. He couldn't remember either of their names, only that unlike the others, they had no habits that engrained in your mind like nails on a chalkboard. He paused, wondering where that old cliché had arisen. It wasn't like he had spent any time near a chalkboard. Not in his early years. By the time he had come in contact with a classroom, he was long past childish pranks. The other participants in the classroom were by then adults, or at least young adults. It had been university.

Where did she collect this team of misfits?

The thought of her had him glancing behind. She

was ten feet back but pushing forward. Her rich mouth was pinched, reminding him of the stress she was under. She was in a difficult situation, and for a moment, compassion lurched somewhere deep in his gut and wrestled with lust. He tore his gaze from her breasts that softly filled the whisper-thin T-shirt, a gentle size, like the rest of her, enough to make a statement. I am feminine, but not too much. Enough to pleasure a man. He glanced at his oversized hands; they weren't a handful, not for him, but they'd be enough.

Enough for what, Aidan?

What was he thinking? She was affecting him in ways that clouded his usually clear mind.

They'd stopped for a rest break where a majority of the group had disappeared into the nearby bushes. In the meantime, he forced his thoughts to the practical, to the body that they were hauling. The cause of death might be obvious, and it might not. They'd have to determine that right away. That and whether any of them had been involved. He doubted the possibility, but still…

A plan began to form. But that plan all hinged on his friend Mark's cooperation.

"I was hoping to get him to Kuching," she said.

"How?" he asked.

He realized that despite her intentions, she wasn't quite in touch with the reality of living this far from a town or city. Despite that, he knew by her insistence on getting the body to Kuching that she wanted justice. She'd mentioned that desire a number of times. He canceled her off the list of suspects, but that left the others.

Behind them the makeshift stretcher scraped along the jungle floor as the rest of the team caught up.

"This thing is falling apart again, Savannah," Ian said.

"Let's see," Aidan said and knelt beside the stretcher. The body was tied with the same vines that grew deep in the forest, wrapping around trees digging in with their sinewy strength. It was a strength that could replicate rope. He opened the amateur knots and knotted the vines in a way that he'd been taught as a boy.

"That should hold it until we get there."

She squatted down beside him. The thin, pallid young man, the one he'd heard called Ian, squatted down beside her.

"Once Jason returns, we'll get going. There's at least another hour before we're at the longhouse," she said.

"Jeez, Savannah, use your head," the angry man snarled. "Are you just going to blindly follow ape man?"

His words choked in a gurgle as Aidan had him by the throat.

"Silence!" Aidan laced the command with deadly calm. "Who's in charge?" He relaxed his hold as the man, he knew was Sid, gurgled and choked.

"Loosen up, man, she is." Sid's voice was raspy.

And then, the unthinkable happened. He wasn't sure how, for his senses were in hyperdrive in the jungle. Nothing and nobody got beside him without him knowing, sensing. And yet, she was beside him and he hadn't felt her approach.

Damn it, he thought. She was putting him off his game at a time when he needed to be more alert than normal. And yet it wasn't happening. She was here and she wasn't leaving and…

The thought trailed.

"Stop it! You're choking him."

He glanced behind, meeting her furious expression, her furrowed brow and the plump lips that were so damn kissable.

"You didn't need to choke him."

He grunted and let go of Sid's neck.

"I'm Savannah," she said, surprising him, as she held out her hand. "I would have introduced myself before, but you keep getting away on me." There was sarcasm and a trace of humor in her voice.

"Vann," he said while thinking that it was an odd time for delayed introductions. But the introduction was as effective as she'd meant it to be, a distraction that defused tempers all around. Tentatively he took her hand, and he was surprised that her palm was calloused.

"No, Savannah," she said with a frown.

"Vann," he said with a slight smile.

"Whatever," she said. "Ian, Sid, Drew." She pointed to each man as she reported their names. "We're still waiting for Burke and Jason."

"Hmmph." Aidan refused to be drawn out of his jungle persona or admit that he'd been paying any degree of attention to them and already knew the majority of their names.

"Tarzan," Ian muttered.

"I'm sorry," she said. "We're all bitchy, tired. But we really appreciate you helping us like this when we've interrupted whatever you were doing."

The look on her face said that she couldn't imagine what he had been doing.

"Speaking of delayed intros…You are?"

"Irrelevant," he muttered.

"Irrelevant," she repeated with an annoyed

expression and when he didn't reply, she turned to her group.

"C'mon, guys, let's get ready to get moving." She waved them forward. "Jason and Burke should be here any minute, and then we're heading out, no delays."

A man emerged from the edge of the rain forest. A minute later, another stepped out a few feet to his left.

He glanced at them, one was fair and sunburned, the other tan and soft. Both were out of place in this environment.

"Burke, Jason," Savannah said with a wave of her arm, not making it quite clear which was which. "Let's get going."

"Thanks," she whispered as she bent down, checking the bindings and then stood up with almost queenly grace.

"Mr. Irrelevant," she threw over her shoulder with a soft laugh as she walked past him.

It wasn't her voice or her presence or the fact that she trailed that exquisite scent behind her, or her lithe body with its subtle rhythm that was heady and overpowering. It was all of it, the full package. She was too tantalizing for any man to endure especially one who had been without for…He didn't want to think how long. What he did think was that he wanted to carry her into the rain forest and wrap himself around her and…

He shook his head. She was panicked, upset, and he was doing nothing to make things easier. Even though there was a murder and for now, he considered it his job to gather what evidence he could, at least until he could dump this mess on Mark. But his eyes kept going to her, which, considering the situation, was not normal. But death was part of life out here. With the reminder of how finite life could be only a few feet from him, he wanted to validate life, haul her into the jungle, and have his way with her—and she with him.

Chapter Ten

One hour later

The longhouse blended softly into the tropical lushness. The verandah wrapped the length of the stilted structure that was perched high above the jungle. It was in a place where rising water levels and forest life could not reach. Along the eastern wall of the longhouse, glass winked quietly as sunlight grazed the building. On the dock, a boy stared at them, his mouth slightly open and a hand wedged in the pocket of his too-big shorts.

Savannah was exhausted. They'd walked miles through the interior, finally meeting up with a branch of the same river she'd lost track of earlier. From there, it had been a mile walk to the longhouse along the tributary that led even farther from the main river.

She nodded at the boy, who dodged her eyes and fixated on Drew, who was pulling the stretcher with what was left of Malcolm.

"No," she murmured. She turned toward the stretcher, thinking to block the child's view.

"Leave it," their rescuer ordered in his rough and sexy voice.

"The child," she began.

"Will be fine."

"Savannah," she said and pointed to herself, speaking slowly.

"Hi." The boy smiled. "You're American, U.S.

Aren't you? What state?"

Savannah didn't answer. She couldn't. She was too busy trying to hide her shock. She should have spent less time studying the field guide and more the local culture. Times had changed, and from the looks of things, years ago.

Mr. Irrelevant smirked. "He speaks English almost as well as you."

Damn him, she thought. "That's obvious."

"I go to school in Kuching." The boy smiled proudly skipping over the dissention that rippled between the adults. "I'm on vacation."

So much for isolation, she thought with relief.

"What happened?" the boy asked with awe in his voice.

"I don't know," she replied honestly. "We found him in the river. I don't know who did this to him."

Their rescuer turned his attention to the boy as he spoke in a language that was vaguely familiar but still incomprehensible to her. The two turned their backs to them as they walked away

"Are we spending the night here?" Worry threaded through Ian's voice and then relief. "He's coming back."

But as Ian said that their rescuer turned his back on her and began heading up the steep weather-worn steps. He didn't even look back.

What were they to do? She fumed and briefly considered waiting for him to return. Instead, she followed him.

****

Aidan knew she followed him. Her anger wafted up behind him, an almost tangible heat. He stopped and turned around. She was all delicate limbs and temper, balancing on the edge of the wooden stairs that led up a sheer embankment from the river to the longhouse.

"Stay there."

One dead body was more than enough. Two, if he counted the monkey.

"And keep them off the stairs."

He gestured to her men, if you could call them that. They were weak—distracted and completely useless. The jungle called for strong men, not this motley group. Only Vann had any strength. Just no jungle smarts.

At the top, Aidan glanced down. She stood on the bottom step, blocking the stairway to the others. He turned back and faced the gnarled and woody face of an elderly Iban.

"I see you have a story."

The old man's voice crackled and diverted his attention. His face was withered from many years in the sun. Akan said that he had survived eighty rainy seasons. Aidan believed that it might have been more. He'd known Akan most of his life. His mother had brought him here as a small boy. She'd always lived life on the fringes, and just because she was born in New Jersey didn't preclude her falling in love with a faraway man. And so, she had dragged Aidan with her.

"Memories?" Akan asked.

"Always."

Akan took a drag from his pipe and blew smoke into the air. Through the cloud of smoke, his features were masked, making him look mysterious.

"She is like no other female you have ever known," Akan said.

"That's true."

"She will not leave."

"There, you're wrong," Aidan said, as if putting the words out into the universe would change the destiny Akan predicted.

"Maybe, boy. Maybe not."

"I'm not a boy."

"Everyone to me is a boy. And you, especially, are my boy."

The discussion was part of their ritual. And, despite his contradiction, Aidan knew that Akan expected it.

"Whatever you want, old man."

"You want her."

"Don't be ridiculous."

"She belongs here, with you."

"Now, this conversation is over," Aidan said, but there was no denying the small thrill of pleasure that settled in his gut at the thought.

"You can't face the truth, boy." Akan's smile threatened to break the deep leathered lines that crisscrossed his face.

"She's nothing more than a stranger with a crisis. Once we get a plane and get her the hell out of here, we'll never see her again."

"My gut says otherwise."

"You're wrong."

"Never." Akan took a long pull of his pipe.

"So, take it as a first."

"We'll see," Akan replied, and from somewhere deep in the forest a monkey screeched a warning and then for a few seconds there was silence.

A ripple of warning ran through him. There was no danger. Not yet. His mind jumped back to the body. He had recognized the tattoo, so common among the Iban. Yet he was sure the guide was not one known to him.

That wasn't unusual. The tribes ranged throughout the forest, some migrating to Kuching and some flitting there and back again. The corpse was a stranger, a stranger who was dead without known cause. None of that boded well for either his continued vacation or a return to the city.

He considered whether it was a murder. They'd eliminate Savannah's group of misfits first. Mark, their local authority, could do that. With any luck, despite his earlier thoughts, the whole thing was accidental. He sighed. The man had been shot and his head removed. What were the odds that it was an accident? What were the odds Mark could handle the initial investigation or that Kuching would send investigators here? He sighed as he foresaw his vacation evaporating.

Odds had never been in his favor. He doubted if they were now.

Chapter Eleven

Savannah blew a strand of hair from her forehead and held back the urge to wipe sweat from her face. With her luck, their rescuer would probably look back and take that as a sign of weakness. She wouldn't give him the opportunity to think any such thing.

"Stay here," she said to the group of men who still looked to her for direction.

"Where are you going?" Ian asked, worry lacing his voice.

"I won't be long." She knew that she wasn't answering the question as she glanced up and saw that their rescuer was gone. There was no time. She needed to see what the hell he had planned. Although, he seemed to expect that she would remain here, exactly as he had commanded. She would do no such thing.

As she climbed the treacherous wooden steps, she occasionally clutched the railing especially where the stairs disappeared to time-worn nubs. At the top, rice-covered mats dried in the sun. Ahead, the roof of the open-fronted hallway was all that separated it from the verandah. Beyond that there were rows of doorways and an occasional wooden chair outside a door. It was oddly reminiscent of a Western motel. Women sat on mats in groups, weaving and talking. A few stopped to stare.

Just ahead a group of villagers were gathered around her still unnamed rescuer. And just before that, a skull hung from the rafters. An animal skull, she assumed. She walked quietly over to it. She pushed it gently with her finger and it swung around, the whitened, aged bones leering eerily at her. She bit back the fright that threatened to burst out and make her the center of attention. It was a human skull. With the scream still lodged in her throat, she backed up and was stopped by something solid. She turned around and faced a sun-bronzed chest. She backed up farther.

Only moments before he had been in the center of the tribe and now, he was here. Mr. Irrelevant. His ability to glide silently almost through time and space was eerie.

"It's the last head hunted."

Savannah gasped and backed up.

"No worries, it's old. Well over one hundred years. But it's good luck, so they have kept it." He smiled. "Even though it is no longer politically correct."

"Politically correct!" Her voice raised an octave. It was all too much. And now a human skull hung from a rafter and…

She fought tears at the very thought that brought her back to Malcolm and what he had gone through.

"Malcolm is headless! What kind of barbarian would have done that?" Her gaze went back to the skull.

"What are you suggesting?"

She should have heeded the warning in his voice. But she'd never been good at heeding warnings, especially now, when her nerves were one jangled mess. Hell, they were in the middle of nowhere in a longhouse with a time-worn skull and Malcolm's head rotting somewhere down the river. It was too much for anyone to comprehend. She only wanted to undo this entire trip. Then Malcolm would still be alive.

"Why would the Iban kill him?"

"They wouldn't," he snapped. "Don't suggest otherwise. Don't insult them."

He threw the last words at her as he walked away without looking back. Leaving her here in the midst of an Iban longhouse with a dead man waiting at the river and a skull, seeming to leer behind her. She hurried after him.

On the verandah he said something in a guttural language to another man. Both of them glanced at her, and they parted before she could reach them. He was halfway down the stairs before she reached the top.

"Wait."

She glanced behind her and saw faces of children watching her. A little girl giggled, and for a moment she might have been anywhere in the world instead of in an Iban longhouse.

She followed him back down the stairs, past Drew, Sid, Ian, Burke, and Jason.

He turned around. "Trust me, you don't want to follow."

"The lad doesn't want you to watch while he takes a whiz," Sid said and chuckled.

"Shut up," Savannah muttered as heat crawled across her face.

"Do you have any games?" The boy they had met on their arrival appeared from where he had been hidden in the long grass by the river.

"Games," Sid repeated. "What does the kid think we are?"

"Sid," she warned.

"No." She smiled at the boy. "I'm sorry, I wasn't expecting to come here."

"Why not? There's no one else to visit around here except the poachers, and you wouldn't want to meet them." He glanced at Malcolm. "Or you already have. Do you think he was making a deal with them?"

His brown eyes were alight as he yanked up his oversized shorts, which were beginning to hang slightly below hip level. "If he got in their way, they would shoot him, but they wouldn't take his head. That's strange," the boy added. "No one does that anymore."

Ian gagged.

Sid glared at Ian. "Get it together."

"It's not that bad. I read about it at school," the boy said cheerfully. "In the old days they grabbed them by the hair and…"

Ian ran for the bushes.

"He's got a weak stomach?" The boy sidled up beside Savannah.

She nodded. "He does."

Sid came over. "What's going on?"

"Let me see that." The boy interrupted, pulling Sid's magnifier from his pocket. "Mine. All right?"

"No! Not all right," Sid snarled and reached out for the boy, who dodged and disappeared behind the same bush he'd only so recently appeared from behind. "Bring that back, you little shit."

"Sid, why do you have to be such a Neanderthal?" Savannah asked. "You might have had a hope if you'd been civil with him."

"Yeah, right," Sid sniped. He glanced around. "Where's jungle boy? It doesn't take that long to take a whiz. I think he's gone and buggered off."

"Now what?" Drew leaned against the stairs. "I'm sick of waiting around. What are we supposed to do now?"

The rain forest danced rich emerald green, a lush trap for anyone wanting to venture in, for anyone who was unfamiliar with its wiles. She had no desire to begin that journey now. Wild Man hadn't returned, and he'd had ample time to take a whiz, as Sid had so indelicately put it.

"Malcolm was killed, and maybe someone here knows something. I'm going back upstairs," she replied. "Who knows when our rescuer will return."

"He'll be back."

She turned at the sound of the new voice and faced a man whose dark skin and short stature immediately identified him as Iban. He seemed to have silently emerged from the forest.

The man smiled at her. "Mark is how the English know me. My real name means fish. The name doesn't go over well in London."

"England?" she asked intrigued by him.

"One and the same. I just got back. Love it there. And of course, I have business." He looked sharply at her. "So, who do you think did this besides one of us?" He cleared his throat. "Of course, by one of us, I mean this particular tribe. We're not all one uni-tribe, and we don't all know each other." He smiled. "Just for the record."

Savannah looked sharply at him. His English was impeccable and carried a slight touch of an upper-class British accent.

"That's not what I meant."

"I know, but you did mean it was someone like us, did you not?"

"You were eavesdropping," she accused.

"Don't feel bad. You're out of your element. How would you think otherwise? The land of the head-hunters and your mate is missing his head? Who else? Look, I'm sorry and all, but I'm also pretty darn sure he wasn't attacked by head-hunters."

"I realize that. But why the hell is he missing his head?" Savannah hated the question for it was only stating the obvious, again.

"Any number of reasons. There's a lot of illicit money being made here, timber, jewels, the animals, much of it illegal or running on the cutting edge of legal. Maybe he got caught in something like that. Or, whoever it was may have been trying to pin the blame on someone else. It's not like it hasn't happened before." He stroked his chin. "Now the head, that's another matter. I'll take a close look later."

"What do you mean?"

He waved a hand backward over his shoulder. "Go back upstairs, find a corner on the verandah. You'll sleep there. I don't know when Aidan will be back. He can be unpredictable that way. I'll get you some water and some supper."

Aidan—was he talking about their reluctant guide or someone else? But he had already turned his back on her and was heading over to the stretcher and Malcolm.

She followed him. "What are we going to do about our guide?"

"I'll take care of it." Mark gave a little motion of his hand, like he was shooing children.

She wondered if what he'd told her was true or… And why was he acting like he was the authority here. Why…The questions kept coming, and there were no answers. She drew in a calming breath, for there was nothing to do now but follow Mark's suggestion.

"C'mon, guys, let's get up the stairs and find a place on the verandah."

"We're staying here tonight?" Ian's voice was unnaturally high.

"You've got to be kidding?" Drew's voice was soft.

"He's losing it again. Snap out of it, Ian," Sid demanded roughly.

"Sid," Savannah warned before she swung around, to address Mark.

"The body?" she asked quietly.

"Don't worry." Mark squatted down beside Malcolm's body. "There's a small storage shed by the river. It's tight. Even the monkeys can't get in."

"We have to get to Kuching as soon as possible. We need to report this to the authorities."

"True, but around here, I am the authorities."

"You?"

"No one else volunteered." His smile showed white teeth against full lips.

At another time, in another place, she would have considered him attractive.

"I'll report this to Kuching as soon as I can. In the meantime, let's get some food and water into your team here before you all drop dead. Looks like it's been a deadly day." He grimaced. "Sorry, bad set of puns."

"That's all right," she replied. "I'm curious, the man who got us here. Aidan? Is that him?"

He arched his brow. "He didn't tell you his name, did he?"

His laugh was more a short, harsh bark than a sound of amusement. "Aidan does like to keep his secrets."

Aidan. So, Mr. Irrelevant had a name.

"Aidan, man of the jungle. I guess in the old days he would have been considered a Wild Man—kind of Tarzan-like, you know," Mark said and laughed.

"How appropriate," she murmured. "Wild Man."

She began to climb the stairs, clinging to the railing as she glanced back at Mark, who followed. Their conversation continued as they climbed.

"Hardly. He's actually an investigator, but I suppose for some of the year Wild Man will do."

Her hand trembled on the railing and her knees began to shake. She had to keep it together. This was no time for a delayed-reaction meltdown.

Focus, she thought.

She reached the top and the verandah. Heat shimmered off the rocks below and overhead the sun shone, brutally hot on this part of the verandah where the overhang did not reach.

Mark joined her, and behind them the rest of the team plodded.

"You mean this isn't his home?"

"Of course not. Comes here to unwind, at least that's what he says. I find it hard to believe. I go to London myself to unwind. That's home for me."

Investigator.

Somehow, Wild Man seemed so much more fitting. Wild Man. Aidan. Malcolm dead and headless.

Her thoughts spun, and as she stepped onto the verandah, the stress of it all hit her full force and the world turned gray.

****

Matthew was used to sleeping outdoors. In fact, that was what inspired many of his walkabouts. But now, another craving eclipsed that and thus made the waiting…torture. At first, he'd feared that he'd lost his opportunity. But now as he'd waded through the logistics of it all in his mind, he knew that barring a miracle or a long wait, the group he had stalked wasn't flying out. Harold had one plane that he owned. While Matthew was on contract and had come to the job with a plane, he'd leased it out for the next two weeks as he tended to do when he went on walkabout. And as far as Harold's plane, last he'd heard from him, two of his reservations for sure had been long haul flights and medically related. There was no canceling or reworking those bookings. He smiled as he squatted down on the forest floor. He'd hang here for now, for he couldn't go to the longhouse; they all knew him.

If he was right, then it was only a matter of time before they began a walk out to the nearest village where they could take a boat upriver. In his mind, they had no choice, and Aidan was a logical man. There was one other plane available, but he knew that no one would risk flying on it. There were no other words for Eric's plane but piece of crap. And without another pilot or, for that matter, even a plane, his boss, Harold, was literally stuck between a rock and a hard place. It was an unusual situation working directly in his favor, he thought with a smile.

The time he'd spent circling a distance from the perimeter of the longhouse had been torture. He needed to hunt in the worst way, and there was only one thing he needed more, to kill. For that he needed to see this team of scientists set loose in the jungle. And while Aidan would lead them, that was the only fly in a pot that was slowly beginning to fill with honey. He would watch and wait. The kill was in sight, and every cell in his body was heating up with the anticipation of the moment. One kill and then he'd be good for months, maybe even a year.

Yet he knew that wasn't true. Over the last years, the urge to kill had been coming closer and closer together. It was to the point that he'd had to take numerous expeditions deep into the jungle. They'd been expeditions far from his home where it was safe to kill and not be discovered.

He was taking a chance here, so close to home.

And he knew that it didn't matter one way or another. The urge was very quickly outstripping a need for caution. Suddenly the assuaging of that ache was all that mattered.

He took a deep breath.

Soon, he promised himself again, soon.

Chapter Twelve

"Hey! Are you all right?"

The voice was distant.

"Get back, Mark. I'll take care of it."

Aidan.

Savannah's head fell back on wood so smooth that it was almost soft, and this time, the world went black.

The next voice she heard was Ian's.

"Savannah! Damn, wake up. Shit, fainting isn't about you. That's me. I'm the fainter. I've got hysteria all wrapped up. There's no room for another participant. Wake up, damn it." His voice sounded rather panicked, but surprisingly it was minus the recent hysteria.

Something wet and cold trickled down her forehead.

"Enough. You don't want to drown her."

Aidan's voice, and then a hand, warm but unfamiliar, traced her forehead. Guttural words in a woman's voice wrapped around her, comforting in an odd way.

She opened her eyes, and she was alone. Something shifted in her vision, and then there was an old woman who gazed deep into her eyes and…her eyes fluttered shut. And for a while she slept.

Then a voice came from nowhere on a cloud of rancid breath.

"You should have left the body." A man's voice registered somewhere in her consciousness. "You don't belong here. Leave before others die."

For a minute there was only silence and then a hand traced a gentle trail along her forehead. "Anne."

Who was Anne? she thought, but there was no energy to contemplate further, to open her eyes. She only wanted sleep. She shuddered as the disembodied voice growled deep and chilling before she fell back into unconsciousness.

The next time she awoke, the smell of a wood fire stung her nostrils. She didn't know how much time had passed. The smell was unfamiliar, thick and strangely sweet. She opened her eyes and the face that hovered over hers had kind brown eyes that were intense despite the deep wrinkles that enfolded them. The face blurred, and a voice grunted in a gravelly, throaty way.

The old woman sat back on her haunches. An aged cackle echoed in the stark room. She lifted a wooden cup. "Drink."

Savannah hesitated before taking a sip.

"Stay." The old woman commanded and pushed firmly against her shoulders when Savannah tried to sit up.

"All right, for now." Her words were slurring—

A man's voice played somewhere in the fog of her memory, but she couldn't remember the words, only the chill that had followed at their meaning. She shuddered and fell back on the pallet. Outside, someone was speaking, but the murmured words were indistinct. Still, she had the oddest feeling that they were talking about her. She needed to get out there. But there must have been something in the drink she was given a few minutes ago, that was the only explanation for the room beginning to spin.

"Drugged…" The words trailed into an incoherent mist.

She sensed she was alone, and then she blacked out.

****

"What's going on, Akan?" Aidan asked the man who had once been his mother's lover and who would always be like a father to him. "If another tribe has started taking heads, what does it mean? Can we rule out tribe warfare? Or is it something else masquerading as that?"

"I don't know. And I don't like the look of this." His father's attention was focused on the rain forest that surrounded them. "So much for your vacation," he said as he pushed off the railing and turned around.

Outside the sky was darkening and the moths flitted, batting their oversized wings as they hung along the verandah. Their wren-sized bodies were attracted by the torches burning intermittently across the wooden expanse.

"Should get the verandah wired," Akan muttered.

"Big job," Aidan observed, considering the fact that the deck stretched across the entire longhouse.

"Yeah, that's why I haven't done it yet."

"It wasn't one of the tribes, was it?" Aidan asked.

Akan shook his head. "I went down and took a look at the body. Whoever severed that head had no idea what they were doing. Mark's already determined that the head was removed after death, quite a bit after death. Mark is sure a knife took off that head—so that eliminates an animal."

"Really?" Aidan sucked in a surprised breath. Mark hadn't told him that. But then he hadn't had much time to speak to Mark. He'd only just gotten Vann's team settled. They were a demanding group. "How's he sure?"

"Not enough blood."

"He was in the river," Aidan added.

"True, but he still would have bled out. He didn't. There's still quite a bit of congealed blood in his body."

"He cut him?"

"Don't sound so horrified. Considering what that body's endured, Mark's makeshift autopsy was no biggie."

"Are you nuts?"

"No, just practical. Which is what you're going to have to be if you're going to get the woman and her team out of here."

"What are you saying?"

"C'mon, Aidan. I haven't seen you so flustered since you were a little boy and your mother arrived with you in tow. Now that was flustered. I thought you were going to kick up a tantrum right there on the boat dock." He smiled, his teeth yellow and cracked with age, but his skin, although leathered, still showing hints of the beauty of the younger man.

"I never had a tantrum."

"True, and you never would, but I didn't know that then. I just saw a spoiled little white boy." Akan lit a cigarette and blew a cloud of gray-blue smoke and watched as it wafted around him. "I didn't know many white boys."

"Still don't."

Akan shrugged. "The woman, she's not like any of the women around here. She fights her power."

Akan stubbed out the cigarette. "Don't much like the taste of the bought kind. Actually, I prefer my pipe." He ground his heel into the dirt and then picked up the half butt. "She's having a time of it with those men of hers, but she'll handle them. They'll learn to respect her. Any other woman would have given up, although probably not one of ours. Of course, they would never have gotten themselves into that situation."

"Aren't you being rather racist?"

Akan swept his arms across the verandah. "Look at it, this land is all ours. There's no one else here. Racist—I can afford to be. I don't have any neighbors that I need to be sensitive about." He faced Aidan, his expression serious. "That girl is trouble. Trouble for you." He smiled. "Or didn't I say that?"

"You did. You figure you say it enough times and I might believe you?"

"Something like that." Akan pulled another cigarette from his pocket and lit it.

"The hunting tourism is coming too close for comfort," Aidan said, changing the subject. He didn't want to talk about Vann with Akan. The old man sensed too much already.

"Found a monkey, shot. A group of Chinese hunters were probably the culprits. But I didn't get a chance to see who was guiding them. I followed them to the river, but the guide was just out of sight. And just after that is when my distressed scientists decided to make an appearance."

"Sounds like an LA freeway rather than a tropical rain forest. Makes you miss the old days." Akan took a long drag and blew a smoke ring. "Okay, maybe not. I'd be lost without my laptop." He looked at Aidan. "And you, you're still in the last century. Loincloth." He laughed lightly and shook his head.

They exchanged a smile. The loincloth wasn't

unheard of, but it was a throwback to yesteryear. Aidan didn't care. He could get away with it here, and it only added to the feeling of freedom a vacation here gave him. But as for the rest of it—life had changed. It was obvious that technology and the rain forest had met years ago, beginning with the introduction of satellite. The longhouse now had television and telephone. Men like Akan had embraced the technology as an opportunity in an isolated environment to feed their curiosity and remain in touch. Unfortunately, Internet access was still nonexistent. Akan claimed that the laptop allowed him to keep his records in order, and on his trips to the city he could get immediate access to the world. Since the laptop, Akan's excursions into the city had increased to once a month. Aidan suspected he was succumbing to the lure of the Internet.

"To get any answers you might have to delay them," Akan said interrupting his thoughts.

Aidan nodded. "Put them under pressure to prove innocence or possibly culpability. The easiest way to put them under pressure is take them on another trek."

At the other end of the verandah, raised voices ended their conversation. Aidan could see one of the men, the thickly set man, Sid, waving his arms around. His face was red, and although the words weren't clear, it was apparent he didn't like what he had been told.

"I better handle that." Aidan clapped his hand briefly on Akan's shoulder.

"I sure don't envy you."

Akan's words followed him as he headed toward the mismatched group of highly excitable scientists. How this particular group ever entered the forest on their own and how they had survived with or without a guide was difficult to comprehend. He wouldn't give them odds of survival past a few hours, they were all that incompetent. Except for Vann.

Vann.

She acted different from many women he knew. She led a group of men with aplomb which was interesting in itself.

Chauvinist.

It was the distinct voice of his mother, and he grimaced. Her dictates still returned to him, even now as an adult. He supposed it was true with most people. He had no personal experience, having no children himself, although there had been one child—the child who had adored him. The child he would never forget. And the child he refused to remember.

Chapter Thirteen

Her team had calmed down before Aidan was even within speaking distance. Despite that, he veered, going to check on Vann. He squatted beside her, watching as her slight frame rose and fell with the rhythm of her breathing. Sedated, she would sleep and, as the shaman promised, gain strength. Emotional strength was what she needed and what he knew on first meeting her that she had in spades. This was just a recharge of her batteries. Aidan had no doubt that tomorrow she would face what was ahead better than any of her team. He brushed a finger across her brow, lifting her hair and settling it off her face.

"Sleep," he murmured before heading outside and down to the river, where he could see Mark bent over one of the fishing nets.

"They've been keeping you busy?"

Aidan nodded. "It's been a crazy day. Look, I want to hold her team up, delay a return to Kuching."

"Put the heat on?"

"Yes. When is Harold's Otter scheduled back?"

"He's booked through the week barring a miracle. And he's the only pilot on duty right now. The other is on vacation. If we're lucky, Monday at the earliest."

Mark pulled a white, dirt-streaked cloth from his pocket and wiped the palms of his hands. "I wish they had another pilot."

"Maybe it's for the best. I need time with them alone." Aidan ran splayed fingers through his hair considering a change of plans. "We'll get Eric to take the body out."

"So Eric takes the body out. And they won't notice a slightly decrepit Otter roaring in here?" He laughed in that good-natured way of his. "I'm assuming you have a solution for that too."

He frowned. "You may be right. It will be easier if I don't have to give explanations. A day trip into the jungle. I'll get them deep enough, so they won't hear a thing."

"You're saying you're counting on Harold being available on Monday."

"That's the one," Aidan said.

"What's the scoop?" Blue asked as he came up on the two of them. His wire-rimmed glasses gleamed in the sunlight. He smiled broadly at Aidan and thumped him on the back. "Hey, bro. Hear you've caused some excitement." He hitched up his belt before leaning into a hip-thrusting slouch.

"That's one way of putting it."

"Hell of a way to go," Blue continued. "Some animal got him?"

"Not likely," Aidan said. "He was shot."

"Shot!" Blue pushed his glasses higher on his nose. "Accident?"

"Maybe."

Mark shielded his eyes and looked across the distant riverbank. "Blasted monkeys are heading for the rice field again." He turned to Aidan. "Did you light the smoke pots?"

"Forgot."

"Can't see why." His tone was slightly teasing. "Never mind, you've got your hands full. I'll get one of the boys to do it."

"You'll never get the body out of here in time for a timely autopsy," Blue stated.

"No matter," Mark replied with an edge in his voice. "I've examined what I could, what's necessary."

"Let's take it one step further. I walk them out," Aidan said. "That way if one of them was involved, they'll break soon enough. It's three days out on foot, plus a day trip waiting in hopes of a plane makes four."

Blue swung on him. "Unbelievable! You'd take them straight through the forest."

Aidan nodded.

"Missing the road?" Blue scowled.

"It's eighty-six miles by road, under twenty through the forest."

"Twenty miles of dense rain forest that's almost impassable in places," Mark said. "But you know that. You think one of them is guilty?"

"No, probably not. But if someone knows something it will be the easiest way to get it out of them. When they're least expecting it and the most stressed. One-day reprieve and then…"

"You hit them with full artillery." Blue frowned. "I'm sensing it will be futile."

"I'm sensing you may be right," Aidan agreed. "But it has to be done."

He left Mark and Blue standing there and headed up to the verandah and his temporary charges.

****

Savannah woke to the sound of Sid and Ian on the edge of an argument. She sat up. Her head ached, and her mouth was thick and dry. Beside her was a glass of something that looked like juice or could be another dose of what put her out in the first place. For she had no doubt that's what had happened. She passed on the option of wetting her mouth with whatever was in that glass.

Sid was getting wound up again. She could hear it in his voice. She dragged her hand through her hair and stood up.

"We could make a break for it, early tomorrow morning. We don't need them." Drew was sounding panicked.

"That's insane," Sid snapped. "You don't even know where you are."

"What would you suggest?" Burke asked.

The usually calm man had an edge to his voice.

Sid didn't respond.

Silence with Sid was not a good sign. She pushed open the door. Her team stood in a cluster on the verandah in front of her.

The door thumped shut behind her and got their attention as they all turned. Ian's face was flushed. And Sid looked ready to hit someone.

"We don't have any choice," Savannah said. "We're here for the night. Tomorrow we're out of here."

She hoped that was true. And she had no idea if it was or not.

"You're feeling better?" Aidan asked as he walked up to the group.

"We're leaving tomorrow?" She faced him with the question and statement both. "I'm assuming by boat, or can I optimistically assume plane?"

He slowly shook his head. "The body was examined. A rudimentary autopsy if you will, and there are some conclusions about cause of death."

"What!" Ian burst out.

Aidan held up his hand. "It had to be done."

Ian's lips tightened, and he looked away.

Jason looked pained.

Aidan's attention turned to her. "Mark," he answered her unspoken question. "He has medical knowledge and some training with the Kuching pathologist."

"Mark?" Savannah repeated, as a chill shot through her.

"It couldn't wait."

Her stomach churned, and for a moment the ground weaved beneath her.

Aidan touched her elbow, steadying her.

His touch was comforting and disturbing at the same time. She pulled away. "What did you find?"

"Nothing more than you already know," Aidan said.

She bit the edge of a nail, realized what she was doing and dropped her hand. She hadn't come this far to resort to nervous nail biting. She rubbed her fingers together, thumb across forefinger. "We can get out of here tomorrow?"

"Probably, as long as the communications are up, we're good. We can phone for an Otter."

"Communication?" she asked.

"Satellite, phone's out right now. Might be up tomorrow," Aidan replied before he turned and headed for the stairs and the river.

Savannah hurried after him.

"Hey," she called as they reached the boat dock. Vaguely she noticed that there weren't any boats, only one very worn-looking longboat. "What are the odds? I mean of us getting out of here in the next twenty-four hours."

"Not great."

"You're kidding me." Her voice wasn't much more than a croak.

"Unfortunately, I'm not. But there are two options, that is if you're determined."

"I am."

He nodded, noticing the I and not the we.

"So give it to me straight," she said.

He was silent for a second before she broke that silence.

"Please."

"Okay. Flying straight out of here to Kuching in a few days, is best case. But I'm guessing that it's not going to happen. At this point, we have one pilot and one decent plane that's way overbooked. You can take your chances, or…"

"Or?"

He cleared his throat. "Head to Rumah Muleng on foot and get the plane or a boat out of there in three days."

"Three days and that's after days of walking?" Her head ached worse than it had a few hours ago. "What about closer settlements?"

"With any luck, this isn't going to be a problem and we can get out of here by the day after tomorrow."

"You're not sugar-coating the possibilities, are you?"

He was silent as he looked out over the river.

"What about Malcolm?" She spoke to Aidan's back, his body silhouetted in the darkness.

"I think you know the answer to that."

"You're right," she whispered and knew he meant that they weren't getting Malcolm to Kuching any time soon.

When she returned to the verandah, it was silent. The longhouse appeared tucked in for the night. Only her team sat waiting for her, refusing to settle down where blankets and reed mats were laid out for them.

"Let's get some sleep, guys. It's going to be an early call tomorrow. We don't want to miss any opportunities of getting back to Kuching." She wasn't sure what that meant exactly, and she cursed herself as she played the same empty promise game that Aidan had played with her.

Chapter Fourteen

"Mark, you've got everything you need from the body?" Aidan asked later that night.

"Yeah. Eric just confirmed he's flying in day after tomorrow. I had to hold him off, he would have arrived tomorrow if we wanted. Especially, once he heard about the cargo. I swear that man has a macabre streak." Mark grimaced. "Eric shouldn't even be flying that thing. More than him and a couple of hundred pounds and I can see it crashing again. Literally. But if we don't get the corpse out of here, it's going to be too late."

"He wasn't my first choice. Harold's new hire, Matthew, is better, but I hear he's on vacation. Does these what he calls walkabouts like he apparently did at home, in Australia."

He shook his head. "Strange, as he's not aboriginal. Anyway, it appears he's on one now. Not that it matters. Either way, he's leased out his plane, and we're stuck with Eric to get the body out of here."

He straightened the collar of his polo T-shirt. "What about your scientists?"

"What are you talking about?" Blue asked as he joined the two.

"The investigation," Mark said shortly and turned his back, facing Aidan.

Aidan frowned as he looked at the two men. What was the deal? It was Blue, a man they'd known from childhood, Aidan's adopted brother. And yet every time Blue was around, Mark acted strange, almost distant.

"The headless guy?" Blue asked. "What makes you so sure one of that team isn't guilty? All of them even."

"If they were guilty, why wouldn't they have left the corpse? Buried it, dumped it back in the river or something. No, I have a good idea that they're not guilty. But it's better to ask the questions and make sure. They may have heard something, seen something." Aidan shrugged.

Blue pushed his glasses up his nose and hitched up his belt. "You'll let me know what you find?"

"Of course."

"I don't have time to stick around or I'd help. Might have another group to guide—big money if it doesn't fall through." He began to walk away, and then stopped dead and swung around. "I'm serious. Whatever the outcome, this could affect the tribe. Tell me everything before you contact the authorities."

Aidan nodded, and Blue returned the acknowledgment before disappearing into the forest.

"Why'd you agree to that?" Mark asked.

"Why not?" Aidan shrugged. "It made him happy."

"Has anything made him happy lately?" Mark asked.

Aidan shook his head as he remembered the flat look in Blue's eyes. "Blue's never gotten over Anne's death, after all this time."

"He should have married again."

"He still can."

"Maybe."

"He's changed," Aidan replied. "And I regret we lost touch. He's my brother. I shouldn't have let it happen."

"I think you're making a mistake," Mark continued. "Agreeing to tell him anything. Like you said, he's changed."

"My mistake. My choice."

Mark shrugged. "We can't let them see Eric's plane. The men, at least some of them, might try to get on. They wouldn't listen to us."

"That would bring the plane down."

They were silent, thinking of the tragedy last year when Eric had picked up a mother and her two daughters as well as a hundred-pound box of cargo. The plane had come down just across the river and one of the girls had died. It had been a sad time. Unfortunately, the plane had suffered only minor repair issues and was still in the air. Except now the only human cargo it carried was its pilot. Eric refused to be grounded. He flew cargo back and forth and nothing else.

"In the meantime, we keep the body on ice, so to speak. Until tomorrow."

"Ice," Aidan murmured.

"Kind of makes you think of something long and tall, with a twist of lime and…"

Aidan grimaced. But he guessed that the easy flip between mundane and macabre was a result of Mark's month spent assisting the Kuching coroner.

"Sorry," he said easily. "I'm torturing myself with tempting thoughts of cocktails while you can't get your mind off—" He hesitated. "The body. I hope Eric keeps his word and gets in here tomorrow. I've autopsied what I could, and we need the body out of here."

"And Vann and her team won't leave the body." Aidan scratched the back of his neck.

“Bang on. So we tell them he’s buried. Tonight.” Mark stuck his hands in the front pockets of his shorts and rocked back on his heels.

“Iban tradition.”

“Exactly.” Mark laughed. “I’ll leave the lying up to you. But I think it’s important that what we tell them, the rest of the tribe doesn’t hear.”

“What are you suggesting?” Aidan frowned slightly disturbed at the inappropriateness of the laugh.

“I don’t know. Call it a gut feeling. I’m not so sure that it wasn’t an Iban involved in this one.”

“That’s a big leap.”

“And it will need further evidence. Which I can…”

“I trust your skill, Mark.”

“But you’d like to call on the experts.”

“I’d like to consult with Andrew,” he said, referring to the Kuching coroner.

Mark nodded. “I’ll get the body on the plane and keep it as quiet as possible.”

“Thanks for that. So we get them out of here. Plane or no plane.”

Across the river, the trees presented a dark, thick outline.

“I don’t envy you. Three days trapped with them could drive any man insane. Of course, if you count tomorrow’s day trip, you’re going to be doing four, probably five. Almost a life sentence, my man.” Mark smiled.

“I thought we were leaving that to you.”

“You’re the investigator.”

“I was hoping to see about some real estate in Kuching. Besides, I want to get back out there as soon as possible, alone.” Aidan emphasized *alone*. That was what he craved in his life. A childhood raised with a mother who seemed to trail white noise like an exhaust plume behind her made him crave silence and solitude. In the rain forest, he could disappear easily. While he wasn't a loner, he loved his time alone. And that meant women too. He had no need of marriage for the sake of marriage, as so many of his cohorts had done. He grimaced. He was no better, divorced once. But at least he had decided that once was enough. Marriage to a woman like Penelope and all the women that had preceded and followed her had only confirmed for him that women loved conflict. Aidan hated conflict.

Conflict reminded him of much of his childhood and all of his marriage. His ex-wife had always been high maintenance. She had been all quick wit and lanky beauty. He'd loved her. He just hadn't loved her enough, and she hadn't loved him at all. And definitely not when she discovered he wanted to spend half his life here in the Borneo rain forest. But he had spent a year of his life in London for her. One day he had looked up over the clear glass dining table, shifted the delicate wrought-iron chair back, and met the distaste in her gaze. It was as simple as that. It was over.

"Then this is perfect. This excursion will have you out there, just not alone."

"Pardon?" He frowned as Mark's words brought him out of his thoughts.

"I said you are getting out there. This trek takes you right back to where you want to go and with a woman."

The forest was settling for the night. Wings brushed against wings, as leaves settled into the carpeted mulch on the forest floor, and a low-grade crackling filled the dusk. Amidst it all, the night creatures prepared to flee the predators that were slowly awakening.

"Damn it."

"Wow, I don't think I've ever heard you swear, man. Even if that's rather a mild word, if you're going to swear go for the gusto."

"Mark!"

"If it bothers you that much…I'd consider letting you off the hook."

"Thanks," Aidan replied.

"I said consider. Would I let you off the hook? Get real, my friend. Call this a professional obligation." Mark winked. "Women really are a bitch, aren't they? Especially when you're attracted to them."

"I'm not." He stopped, realizing how juvenile his denial sounded. "All right. There's just something about her."

Mark slapped him on the shoulder.

"But it's never going to happen. Wrong time. Wrong woman. Wrong everything."

"Whatever you say." Mark laughed.

Aidan frowned. The human condition could be strange. He'd seen it often enough, romance, attraction, even love occurring at completely inappropriate times. He thought of his reaction to Vann. The timing couldn't have been more off, the place more wrong. But it was as one psychology professor had said. The human instinct to survive is primitive and strong, especially in times where individuals are in survival mode. Problem was, he wasn't the one terrified of death—he had been the rescuer and his thoughts had been abominable.

"Sorry, old man, you've had a rough go of it today." Mark looked at him sympathetically.

Together they walked slowly along the river. Above,

on the verandah, voices carried, the raised voice of Sid or Ian, followed by a softer feminine rebuttal.

"Do you suppose I should have offered her my room?" Mark asked. "I could have slept outside. Actually, I was planning to anyway."

"No," Aidan disagreed. "She wouldn't have accepted. She'll stay with her team. They're her responsibility."

"You know her pretty well, considering you just met," Mark said and laughed. "Interesting. I never thought it would happen."

"What are you suggesting? Never mind, pretend I didn't ask that question."

An hour later, it was silent on the verandah. "Do you suppose they're all asleep?" Mark asked.

"Maybe." Aidan was doubtful. "I'm turning in."

It had been an emotionally trying day. But when he closed the door to his room, he couldn't sleep. He stared blankly at the four walls. Finally took his blanket to the opposite end of the verandah far from the motley crew he had rescued earlier in the day.

As always, he was awake at first light. He stretched and gazed silently over the forest as the sun began to rise, and the night's mist-filled shroud began to thin. Cooking fires were on, and the jungle was awakening.

He was aware the moment she awoke. Expecting answers from him, expecting action.

Chapter Fifteen

Savannah slept very little. Instead of sleep, she'd thought about Malcolm and how he might have died. Why would they behead him? Who had shot him and why? And had they taken his head for some sort of trophy or left it at the bottom of the river? Or had there been two…

That thought was more disturbing than any of the others. Had it been two different perpetrators? She'd heard Aidan and Mark talking, heard the easy rise and fall of their voices. She'd fallen asleep for a bit before waking again in time to see Aidan lie down at the opposite end of the verandah. His presence had been oddly comforting, and after that she had slept fitfully.

This morning, there were people moving around, but they were busy with their chores and paid no attention to her. She walked slowly around the longhouse, taking in the well-made verandah that stretched two hundred feet out. The verandah seemed to be the common living area; just yesterday she had seen the elderly women chatting and weaving reed mats there.

She had never been in a longhouse before. Despite the fascinating surroundings, all she could think about was the tragedy they'd endured, and Aidan. He was the first man in a long time who made her think about things she would rather not. Against all logic, she would like nothing better than to haul him into the jungle and have her way with him, stroke that sun-gilded skin until he moaned his surrender, taste the silky maleness of him… They were ridiculous thoughts, as out of place as everything else that had happened in the last twenty-four hours.

And that realization only added to the feel of a walking dream as she found herself drifting down the steps until she stood at the edge of the river.

"Sleep well?" The disembodied voice came from a stand of brush. It was as if her thoughts had conjured him.

"What are you doing here?"

"I live here." Aidan grinned. "At least some of the time."

"I don't suppose I can get a good cup of coffee?" Yeah, that was classic, Savannah, ask for coffee in the middle of nowhere. Good move.

"You supposed wrong. You can get a great cup. Hope you don't like cream, though. That we can't provide."

"Excellent." She turned toward the stairs and reality.

"Look, give me a minute, and I'll go up with you." He stepped into the clearing, pulling green netting behind him. "I was fishing. Got a few, but I want to toss the net again. Do you want to wait?"

All she could think about was keeping her eyes from another part of his anatomy covered with a worn piece of cloth. In a short time, it seemed to have become his trademark. She looked up, morning mist drifted between them as their eyes locked, his lips curved in a subtle yet definite smile, and he made no attempt to hide the fact that he had seen where her gaze had just been resting. She smiled back at him and let her gaze drop down, sweeping across his chest. Down. She couldn't do it. She looked up.

"Do I make you uncomfortable?"

"Why would you think that?" She made her tone as businesslike as possible. "If I'm uncomfortable, it's because this is a difficult situation. I have a dead man literally rotting in the jungle. Well, maybe not a jungle, but a shed on the edge of a rain forest."

A dead man, and that alone should have deterred her ridiculous thoughts, but as a scientist she knew otherwise. It was a primitive survival mode, and instead of ignoring the survival gene when it reared to the surface, she had indulged it, that had been wrong.

"He's buried."

She started. "You did it without me?"

"Tribal tradition," he said and looked away.

"I don't believe you. Tribal tradition doesn't work that fast."

"You're right. Mark and I thought it would be best to get him buried now, not to involve you as that would mean involving your team. They're rather difficult, if you haven't noticed."

"I'll give you that, but why the rush? We would have taken him with us today." She looked up at the longhouse. "We do have communications now, don't we?"

"There's no plane—not today."

"And you buried him." She shuddered. "But there was no choice," she murmured, resigned.

"No," he agreed. "There wasn't."

She wrapped her arms beneath her chest, as if warding off a chill or the sign of worse to come. "Malcolm's death kept me awake most of the night."

He stood silent as she wrestled with thoughts that roamed half finished even in the reality of daylight.

"Was it possible that someone removed his head after he died? I mean, long after he died. Someone other than the person who killed him?"

He was looking somewhere over her head into the forest beyond.

"I'm onto something, aren't I?"

"I don't think that's realistic." He still wouldn't look at her.

"Don't or won't admit that it might be? How long does blood take to congeal? What did Mark find?"

"Let's not talk about this. It's an open investigation."

"His tendons were ragged." She willed back the bile that rose in her throat but kept pushing forward. "It was a hack job. Why?"

"Don't think about it."

She was so close she could touch him. "What did you find?"

"I can't say."

"It was amateur. Akan said so."

"Akan talks too much," Aidan growled.

"I overheard," she admitted sheepishly. "You were talking right outside the shaman's room. I just caught a bit of your conversation before I fell asleep."

"Discount much of what Akan says."

"There was no blood," she persisted.

"He'd been in the river."

She began to cough, choking on the revulsion that roiled hot and tight and so very close to the surface. It was as if the horror meshed with passion, flared into anger, and acted as a front for what she didn't want, and had already done—physically break down.

He reached for her, his hand rubbing her back, his other resting on her shoulder. The coughing subsided and there was only the heat and closeness between them. She was pressed against a half-naked man in a loincloth. Somehow all of it was too much.

She pushed free.

"I'm fine," she said, taking a controlled breath. "So someone killed him, and then hours later someone removed his head?" She couldn't help it, she had to persist. She sensed the truth behind what she was saying. "You are taking your findings to Kuching?"

"Of course."

She looked at him as if analyzing each of his features would gain the truth. He looked almost guilty, like he was hiding something. "When?"

"Mark is competent at this. He's trained with the best. He has enough evidence for when he meets with the Kuching investigators and pathologist in a few weeks, hopefully less. We'll see. Maybe tomorrow even."

"A few weeks or maybe tomorrow? What are you saying? The communications are still down?"

Something wasn't right here.

She frowned for his answers no longer flowed, and his body language appeared almost stilted.

He looked at the river before redirecting his attention to her. "Hopefully Akan will get things running today. If not, we have two choices. Stay here and fly in with Mark whenever we get an Otter in. If Akan doesn't get communications fixed in the next two days, then we have a serious problem. Especially as our regular transportation is currently short-handed as well. So, we wait or…"

"What if we wait for a boat? Would that be faster than the other options?"

"You don't want to do that. The tributary is rough enough, but where it meets with the river it becomes even more deadly, especially for a small boat. But you've probably already seen that. The logs coming down from the logging, the current…Need I say more?"

"No, apparently you've said enough."

It was too much. She could feel his stare even as she ran up the stairs.

****

"The missing head is what gets me," Mark was saying to Aidan later that morning. "No one would have murdered someone and then taken their head. There was no point, especially as the body was so easily identifiable. So I asked pretty much everyone in the tribe."

"And…" Aidan prodded, his patience thin.

Mark shrugged. "Nothing. But then, I didn't think I would find anything. It's one for the history books, not real life. Well, at least it wasn't until…"

"What about the boy?" Savannah asked as she came upon the two of them.

"What boy?" Mark asked as Aidan scowled.

"The one who met us when we arrived at the longhouse. He seemed to be everywhere and know what was going on. Maybe…" Savannah hesitated when she saw the expression on Aidan's face, harsh and impenetrable.

"No," he snapped.

"Why?" she couldn't stop herself from asking, even though it was obvious that the thought was upsetting to

Aidan.

Aidan turned and walked away.

"What'd I say?" Savannah asked Mark.

Mark watched Aidan go, a sad expression on his face and seconds ticked by before he answered her question. "Aidan had a sister."

"Had?"

"She drowned when she was ten. She was much like the boy you met on your arrival at the longhouse, the eyes and ears of the village. There were developers snooping around. She followed them and no one's sure what happened, but she was found later that evening. Drowned. She was eight years younger than Aidan. I think he still blames himself. In a way he was in worse shape than Akan."

"What are you saying, she was Akan's child?" Savannah asked almost forgetting to breathe at the revelation.

"Yeah. Sunshine's mother buggered off shortly after she was born, so Aidan and his sister were close. When she died, it was a tough time for Aidan. Without Akan, I don't know if he would have made it."

"That's horrible, but what does it have to do with this boy?"

"Everything. Aidan's not going to want to get him involved. He has an overwhelming need to protect."

"But a few questions, surely that won't harm."

"Aidan will go back later. He'll get the answers we need. He has to. That's what he does." Mark leaned against a tree trunk. "He's one of the best investigators in the country."

"He never mentioned that," Savannah admitted. Of course, he hadn't even mentioned his name. He'd kept his identity well hidden.

"He wouldn't. That's the way he is. But if anyone can find out what happened to your guide, it's Aidan."

"This is a murder." Savannah paced a few steps away from him.

Mark nodded. "And if that's true, he's handled that before."

"What if the killer is still out there?" The thought, even within the safety of the longhouse, was disturbing.

"He's armed."

She swallowed. The spear was tolerable, but a gun? She thought of Ian's hobby. Handguns at a firing range were one thing, but carrying a gun and knowing you might one day use it, whether in self-defence or not…it was unthinkable.

"Colt .45—sweet little piece. I told him to get something newer. He's only fired it once. Most of the time he can get himself out of a situation with his martial arts."

"What kind of situation?"

"Man, has he got the stories. Look…" Mark slapped her lightly on the shoulder. "Another time."

"Right. Of course." Savannah was reeling and not from the gentle buddy-like slap Mark had inflicted. This was more than she anticipated. She knew Aidan was an investigator, but she hadn't thought what that might mean. Aidan, the pacifist, the one concerned for the animals, the one who rarely even seemed to swear—carried a gun. And apparently was sure that he could solve the case of Malcolm's death singlehandedly, potentially facing up to a murderer. She shivered. It was a combination of fear and desire. She wanted to ignore the latter. She was an expert at that. She'd deny her feelings until the bitter end.

Chapter Sixteen

"Any news?" Savannah asked as she approached Aidan later that day.

"No."

She looked at Aidan. "Communication is still down?"

He nodded. "Akan's working on it. He could fix it quickly if he had the part. But he may be able to work around it. In the meantime, he's sending one of the boys to the longhouse north of us to see if they have what we need."

"So what does that mean?"

"We should hang around at least through tomorrow because an Otter is the best way out of here. If it's not working by then, well, we might have to walk out. We can leave for Muleng first thing Saturday if communications aren't up and running."

"That's another two days." Her voice rose slightly.

He shrugged. "I've wanted to ask…"

"Ian?"

"Yes." He nodded, surprised. "What was Ian's relationship with Malcolm?"

"Ian's gay," she said softly. "But you know that, and he had a thing for Malcolm."

She eyed him. "Ian wouldn't hurt anyone. What happened out there almost killed him."

"Was there any time when Ian wasn't with you?"

"Obviously there's bathroom breaks and a few times he followed Malcom, but they both came back. And then, when Malcolm left to scout the river, Ian walked with him for a ways." She bit her lip. "That was the last time we saw Malcolm alive." She took a deep, shaky breath. "Ian couldn't kill anyone and definitely not someone he cared about. Never mind, no one—he's the gentlest person I know. I'm sorry, I'm repeating myself, but I won't have any of my team blamed. They all have their issues, but none of them are killers."

"What about the others?" he persisted despite her assertions.

"No. They were all with me right up until Malcolm didn't return. That's when we began searching." She glared at him as if that would stop his questions. "I've known Ian all my life. It's just not in him."

Aidan shrugged. "I never said it was. I'm just exploring the possibilities."

She shivered and rubbed her arms. Her white-blonde hair lifted in a breeze that sent wisps around her delicate features.

He glanced down to the river, where her entire team was attempting to fish with nets and the help of a couple of the Iban boys.

"He would never do it," she repeated. Her eyes were troubled. "No one on my team would." Their conversation broke as a shout came from downriver.

They turned to see Ian flopping in the river with Sid doubled over laughing. Drew had tried to wade in and pull him out, but Ian was tangled in a net.

"He can't swim. The current." Savannah broke into a run.

Within seconds he had passed her as he raced to the

bank. Aidan bit back panic. There'd been more than one drowning in this river, and one he never wanted to remember. It had been long ago, and he could never forget. He ran faster. Reaching the bank in a rush, he waded through the water past shouting men and yelling boys, all thrashing around trying to untangle the net. His knife slipped easily into his hand and ripped through the netting, freeing Ian. And with one arm he pulled Ian out, man and net together in one tangled lump. He literally tossed him to shore.

"You're okay?" Savannah asked Ian as she removed the remains of the net.

He pushed wet hair back from his forehead. "Fine. Just feel a little ridiculous. Tangled in a net. Shit. I just want to get the hell out of here. When are we leaving? I can't take this much longer."

"I'm working on it." She squeezed his hand.

She left Ian and walked over to Aidan, her eyes locking with his. "You saved his life. Thank you."

"The water wasn't that deep." Aidan sucked air and tried to sound casual. Tried not to remember the time when he hadn't been there.

"What's wrong?" She lifted her hand from Ian's. "Aidan?"

"Wrong? Near drowning, nothing else." He forced the quip as he wrestled with the dark panic that had fallen on him as he rushed to save Ian.

"You're upset."

"No." He glanced at Ian. The man was soaking wet and pale, but he was going to live. He turned away. He couldn't take any more questions, any more drama. He needed to be alone. He needed the forest. And somehow, he had to survive without solitude for at least another five days. He took a deep breath and began to walk and wished he never had to stop.

Her light footsteps sounded behind him. Her natural scent wafted a tentative seduction around him.

"We need to get out of here. I don't know how we'll make another day." She was beside him.

"Look," he said. "If Akan hasn't fixed the thing by tomorrow morning, then we'll go on a field trip. One day. Take your mind off things."

"A field trip," she said then hesitated. "You're sure you won't have the communications fixed by then, aren't you?"

"Takes ten hours just for a trek to the next longhouse. He's going to need that part if they have it. So, yeah. Probably not. But a good chance we'll have the telephone working after that." Lies didn't come easy to him, but the guilt did. He couldn't meet her eyes. Instead, he strode ahead.

"A field trip isn't a horrible idea," she said slowly, tagging beside him.

He stopped, turning to face her. And he knew immediately that had been a mistake.

"There are some easy trails around the longhouse," he said as if speaking would take away the want. "But I've got one in mind that…"

He only wanted to touch her. His fingertips flirted against her cheek. But her skin was too soft, too provocative, too tempting. His lips met hers. He would have dragged her closer, deepened the kiss, taken everything she had to offer. Would have, if reality hadn't intervened in the maniacal shrill that echoed through the jungle around him. He let her go and stepped back.

"Arrogant bastard." There was a tremor in her voice.

"Not everyone wants you."

"You're going to give in sometime," he said noting the confliction in her words and her actions.

"You and me, are going to part ways long before that happens."

"My odds are on me."

"Your odds are totally out of date, Tarzan."

"Tarzan. Interesting concept. He was rather the ladies' man of the jungle, was he not?"

"Whatever you want to think. I'm going upstairs."

"Wait. See that hornbill?" He pointed overhead, where a large black bird with a prominent yellow-orange bill sat. "That was what shrieked a few seconds ago."

"It's absolutely gorgeous."

"More beautiful than those bugs of yours?"

"Hardly." She laughed. "But close."

"He's calling for a mate. See that one there?" He pointed. "She's answering. The attraction is unavoidable."

"They're birds. They follow nature, not their heads."

"Exactly. When they mate, they mate for life."

He wasn't sure why he had said that. If it were possible to retrieve words, pull them from the biosphere, he'd pull those.

"What are you suggesting?"

The acid humor in her voice confirmed, he had handed the edge in this game over to her.

"I'm suggesting that the attraction between us is undeniable and unavoidable."

"Interesting. I thought you were suggesting marriage, Tarzan." She drawled the last part out.

"Only sex." He couldn't help himself.

"Only sex. How very romantic."

She trailed her finger down his chest, sending tremors through his entire body. He swallowed, trying to keep his overheated body in check.

"I'm sorry. That was unnecessary."

"Apology accepted. Recreational sex in the jungle really isn't my thing. Not this trip, anyway. Besides, I rather like the mate-for-life idea," she said, startling him.

He should thank her. It was those words that sent his mind from his more basic needs and into the realm of other more frightening possibilities. It was those words that allowed his loincloth to settle down, and it was those words that made him question the practicality of a loincloth. Western wear allowed for a lot more forgiveness. He'd think about that in future.

She was so close that the perfume that was all her, only made him want to take her in his arms and never let her go.

He was doomed.

He swung away from her and headed for the deep foliage that grew near the river. He needed to be alone. She did strange things to him over which he had no control.

Later he stood alone on the narrow strip of flat land that bracketed the wide, aggressive river. *Mate for life* ran through his mind, and despite the heat a chill rolled through him.

****

Stupid bitch.

Why anyone could be so hyped up about the plight of a mere woman was beyond him. There was so much more to life than a woman, money for one. Money took you to a world beyond the putrid green borders of this never-ending prison. Money brought comfort and luxury and love if you needed it.

Comfort.

This was the land of barbarians, and he couldn't escape it soon enough.

They had gotten greedy, and that was what had placed him here. Here at the mercy of his partner's impetuous stupidity, and Aidan, whose blonde hair and Nordic features were completely at odds with this place and yet, who fit like he never could. Aidan, it had always been Aidan. Everyone in the tribe had loved him from the beginning.

Prison.

He had to keep calm. The rails had slipped beneath them. He had to get them back in place. His partner's actions had placed the entire operation in jeopardy. He was so pissed he could barely look at him. It was all up to him, and if he didn't keep all the players in sight, prison would be exactly where they were headed. It was an unfortunate fact that had him fighting to keep his façade in place.

He took a deep breath.

He was sure that if he held his cards close to his chest, he could turn the game around to his advantage. In the end, he would be a rich man, more so than even now, and he'd never hear the name Fish again. He couldn't stop the smile.

In the end, he'd be the last man standing.

Chapter Seventeen

"So two nights, and the start of day two in paradise," Sid said the next day. His voice had the usual edge, and Burke took exception.

"Can you quit making it so difficult on everyone?"

"Ah. Mute boy finally speaks."

"Sid," Savannah warned as she came up to the group.

"Yeah. All right. But I can't take much more of this. I had the crap bitten out of me last night, and lying around here is beyond boring. Can we get out of here?"

Savannah tried to sound casual. "The telephone is still out. We're waiting for a part; unfortunately, it's coming from another longhouse."

"What does that mean?" Sid frowned. "Don't they have internet? Crap, what is this?"

"That we might have communications by this time tomorrow."

"So we sit around here for another day," Ian said morosely.

"No," Savannah said. "We're going on an expedition today. We head out in an hour. And tomorrow, we either fly or walk out of here. Worst-case scenario, four or five days, and this ordeal will be over. One other thing…"

They all looked at her with suspicion and resignation, especially Jason. She wasn't sure what he was thinking and had no time to ask. She supposed it didn't matter. He was the quietest of them all, watching the others, his blue eyes troubled and clearly out of place in the longhouse and feeling it. He was no help now. But in the field, he might be quiet, but he was a brilliant epidemiologist. She'd been over the moon when he'd agreed to this expedition. Now, he was one more person to worry about.

"Malcolm was buried." There, she'd said it.

Ian paled. "What do you mean?"

"She means they dug a hole and threw dirt on him," Sid snapped. "What do you think she meant?"

"Shut up!" Ian yelled.

"Guys!" Savannah bellowed to get their attention. "There was no choice. He was decomposing." She put her hand on Ian's arm. "I'm sorry. Aidan and Mark did it. I had no say."

"What about the autopsy?" Ian asked.

"Mark did one. He thinks he has enough evidence for the coroner's report in Kuching."

"And the police report?" Ian asked quietly. His face was still pale, but today, unlike yesterday, he wasn't swaying on his feet.

Only a few days and they would be back in civilization with a shower and other conveniences. She caught a whiff of body odor as Drew walked by. She wrinkled her nose and tried not to think about how she must smell.

"You smell like woman."

Aidan's breath was warm and possessive, his breath hot and provocative as it fanned her ear. She started. The man was impossibly silent, even in flip-flops.

"Let's get going," Aidan said as he faced the group.

"Get your gear." He turned away and headed to the end of the verandah, where Mark sat.

"Me Tarzan." Ian laughed. "You Jane."

She lightly air-punched Ian's arm. "Hush," she chastised.

Ten minutes later they were regrouped, ready to head out.

"Let's do what we came here to do," Savannah said. "Aidan's shown me some of the nearby area, and it's similar to where we found the first sample. I'm hoping it will be the same farther out. He seems to think so."

"What are you suggesting?" Burke frowned.

"That we make this a mini excursion and look for a beetle colony like the one we found."

"Slightly optimistic," Sid replied, but his tone held interest.

"Let's go." She waved her hand forward.

Aidan was ahead, scouting the land or whatever it was he did. She tried not to watch him. Surprisingly, she found Sid beside her as they hiked along the trail that led directly along the river.

"I'm glad you're doing this."

"Doing this?"

"This trek," he replied. "I thought you'd forgotten the purpose of this trip. What with Malcolm dying, and trying to get Miss Hysteria"—he shifted his gaze to Ian—"safely out of here and then, of course, dealing with Tarzan." He gave her a wink. "Don't think we don't notice."

"Don't think it's any of your business," she shot back.

"Point taken," he said cheerfully. "Look, I'll lay off Ian."

"That's big of you."

"No. That's grown-up of me. I know I was being childish, but I'm worried about him."

He cleared his throat, covering his mouth to muffle the sound, but the others were yards ahead.

"I was panicked."

Savannah started at the admission. "You?"

"Yeah, and I'll deny it if the topic ever comes up, so don't bother. But yeah, I'd never been in the rain forest. Had you?"

"Just on day trips."

"Lucky you."

She smiled. They were headquartered out of New York. That didn't leave much opportunity for rain-forest expeditions. She had been lucky to have the connections she did. But she knew her father would never have brought her or her coworkers over here if they hadn't proven themselves. They were all young but some of the best in their field. When it was offered, the chance to spend time in Malaysia had been an opportunity that none of them could refuse. Two months after arriving in Malaysia, her team had flown into Sibu and this expedition had begun.

"Look." She turned to face him. "I need your help getting Ian out in one piece."

"You can count on me. I'll lay off Ian." He grimaced. "Okay, I'll try."

"It was Malcolm that shook him." She touched his arm, seeing his expression become rigid. "Don't."

"I can't help it. That makes me cringe, that whole guy attraction thing. No, don't say it, I'm not a homophobe. Really, I'm not. I just don't want to see it."

"A little close to the line, don't you think?"

"Maybe my tolerance is thin, I admit." He frowned. "It wasn't just my imagination, was it? Ian had the hots for Malcolm."

"You could say that." *You could say a lot of things,* Savannah thought, but she wouldn't say them to Sid. His tough-guy approach didn't allow him to show any sensitivity to the gay lifestyle. If she were to mention the embrace she'd seen between Ian and Malcolm on the last day she saw Malcolm alive, she knew she wouldn't be getting any help from Sid. He was finding innuendos difficult enough to deal with. She assumed that the reality would be well beyond him.

"Face it, Sid, you're rather fond of him," Savannah said, going for the light buddy, friend humor that Sid understood.

"What are you insinuating?"

Apparently, buddy humor wasn't working today. Savannah frowned. "Nothing, obviously. Get real," she said.

"I'll never admit it," he said.

"Don't expect that you will."

"If I'm going to keep the twerp alive or at least prevent him from killing the rest of us, I'd better get started."

"Go, Sid," she teased.

"Shut up," he said lightly as he jogged ahead.

Savannah trailed behind the others for the first twenty minutes. She enjoyed the solitude as the river rushed on one side and on the other the long grass and brush grew in the lush river soil. Insects buzzed and sang a continual backdrop. She searched for signs of beetles similar to the one they had found earlier, before everything had gone so horribly wrong. Her breath hitched as she thought of him, Malcolm. She forced her thoughts back to the living, the present, and the purpose of this excursion. For now, it was her, nature, and the possibility of a discovery.

"What are you thinking about?" Aidan's voice emerged unexpectedly from behind her, and she jumped.

"I'm enjoying the quiet," she replied honestly as she pulled her gaze from a T-shirt that only outlined the well-defined muscles that sculpted his torso. He was luscious, clothed or unclothed. She looked away. This was utterly ridiculous. These weren't the thoughts of a Harvard-educated entomologist with a doctorate in a subject that most people knew little about. Nor were they those of a woman fighting for a foothold in a corner of the world that had been up to now a man's world.

But despite her thoughts of logic, reality, and clinical detachment, an earthy scent wafted from him. A natural, masculine scent that jangled her nerves and made her want to get closer.

"It's like that for me, too," he said, his breath warm on her ear. "Maybe it's time we did something about it."

"What are you talking about?"

"You know what I'm talking about." His finger lightly caressed her upper arm.

"Don't." She jerked away.

"Why not?"

"This isn't the place."

"Where would be the place?"

"That's not what I meant. Never. Never would be the place."

"You're a poor liar."

She took a step backward and turned away.

"You know it's going to happen."

"Your ego is frightening," she replied and walked away before he saw the quiver in her fingertips, and before he realized what she found frightening was that he was right.

And then she heard a sound somewhere to their left. No one had gone that direction.

"What's that?"

****

Damn it, Matthew thought as he froze.

He'd stepped on a dead branch. It was an amateur mistake.

He watched as Aidan stopped and looked around. Matthew didn't dare even breathe for he was too close, and he'd screwed up.

Seconds seemed like minutes as Aidan had looked around, unmoving before motioning to the woman to continue. Fortunately, the others were ahead, undisturbed by the crack of dried wood.

It was then that he backed up, away from them, moving north and then west into the denser jungle, his bare feet sure like they hadn't been only a minute ago. Then, he'd been busy thinking of what lay ahead, of the kill and the satisfaction he'd feel. He'd forgotten to watch the ground. Worse, he'd forgotten to be alert to his prey.

Thinking about the act of killing made his pulse go up, and he had to take measured breaths to ground himself. He got excited at the very thought, for it had been far too long.

He only had to be patient a little longer, and then it would be over.

One more would be dead, and he'd be on his way home where he had a job and a plane to fly.

Chapter Eighteen

The next day was as hot and humid as the day prior as Aidan prepared to begin the trek that would take the scientists out of the jungle. Today would also test Savannah and her team's limits and, hopefully, their knowledge of the crime. He had told her only an hour ago that the communications were not going to be up today and that they'd waited long enough. The lies were weighing on him. He wrestled with his conscience while reminding himself that it had to be done. This was a crime scene, and they were suspects. Nothing more. Trouble was, she was everything more, and he wasn't sure how that had happened. He didn't know her. It was too soon. But yet in the other world of the jungle, it seemed that time had its own path. He closed his eyes and rubbed the back of his hand across them, as if that would clear not just his vision but his thoughts.

"So you're really going to do it? Take them out by walking through the jungle," Blue asked from behind him.

He opened his eyes and faced his brother. "Got a better idea?"

"Let it go," Blue replied. "I doubt if there's anything that group knows. Didn't you say there were poachers in the area?" He pushed his glasses up with a knuckle. "I bet there's a good chance their guide got between them and some game. I wouldn't be apt to believe what they say, not under that kind of stress. The jungle and city folk just don't agree."

"You're probably right on both counts."

Blue nodded. "I might register for another class."

"In what?"

"Don't laugh. Tourism."

"Good direction, all things considered," Aidan said but frowned at the sudden change of direction. Yet it was the first time in a long time since Blue had made any effort at brotherly closeness. When was the last time they'd had anything longer than a five-minute conversation?

"Yeah, maybe."

Blue's tone was stiff, and Aidan hesitated over what to say next.

At another time Aidan would have asked about Blue's new interest in tourism. But there was something in Blue's demeanor, in the tense way he held himself that said now wasn't the time. It seemed the natural flow to the conversation was gone. The feel of familiarity they had once had was lost, and they were again struggling for something to say.

"I suppose this is good-bye," Blue said rather gruffly.

"For now."

"Watch yourself," Blue said darkly. "You never know what can happen. Sometimes, these things are better left alone."

"Sometimes," Aidan agreed.

"Remember Akan saying about this happening before? Years ago, a dead body turned up with no head, and he never did finish that story."

Aidan frowned. "I'd forgotten."

Blue pitched a smooth river rock into the water. It skipped once and then sank with a slight splash. Their attention both remained on the water for minutes after the rock sank before Blue spoke. "There have been more accidents in the bush than usual."

"What are you saying?" Aidan asked. There was something Blue wasn't saying, something he couldn't put his finger on. He could feel it in the energy his brother was projecting. His stance was tight, self-contained, almost defensive, and he wouldn't look at Aidan.

"I've done some guiding, just tourists to see a longhouse and a few of the more remote villages, nothing more. But I've heard some stories. Violence against interlopers." He glanced back to the longhouse.

"The loggers?"

"No, not the usual protest against logger violence. Akan suspects one of the tribes farther upriver." Blue clapped his hand on Aidan's shoulder. "Be careful."

"You know more than you're saying."

Blue dropped his hand. "Maybe." He squinted into the sun. "The weather might only hold another day or two."

"Tell me," Aidan said, frustrated, as he knew that Blue had revealed everything he would for now. "What's going on with you?"

"Will you text me when you get back?" Blue asked instead of answering the question.

Aidan grimaced. Blue had shut down. There was nothing more he would get from him today. "For sure." His attention drew upward to the verandah to where Vann watched them, a slight figure in the distance.

He turned his attention back to Blue and the

unsettling feeling that he was losing his brother. Blue hadn't been the same since his wife Anne had died two years ago. Nothing Aidan did spanned the distance that grew between them. And for once in his life, he ached to leave the rain forest, to go back to work, to the city and the known.

****

She was spinning him into her web. He couldn't have planned it better if he had deliberately thrown the two of them together. He chuckled. The attraction between the two had flared like the path of a pair of hornbills in mating season. The rest only required opportunity, and that he had provided in spades.

Aidan would discover nothing. He had been sure of that from the beginning. So far everything had gone as planned. The Iban guide was oblivious to the fact that the expedition he had led the Chinese into had a dual purpose. It was a hunting opportunity for the Chinese and a possible chance to transfer blame.

But things were a long way from okay. He was still just a wanna-be, an anomaly as a businessperson, a joke to the foreigners—to Aidan. For that's all Aidan was, a foreigner, no matter what Akan tried to make him into. Aidan would never be Iban no matter how many years he spent in the jungle, no matter how retro he dressed. Just like he was an Iban, no matter how many times he tried to escape.

He gritted his teeth. He was tired of only visiting civilization. He was so much more than this place, this prison. Soon Aidan would know all he could be. But when that happened, he would be well away from the primitive world that was once his destiny. No longer Fish—it was Europe all the way. He glanced at his watch, at the calendar that marked the days until this was over and he was on the first plane out, never to return. So far everything was going according to plan, neat and clean, a perfectly civilized ending, just as he'd planned.

Chapter Nineteen

While Savannah rejoiced at finally seeing the end of this expedition, she dreaded the journey ahead. She was anxious about leaving a potential discovery behind, even for a short time. Oddly she felt a small tug of regret at leaving the longhouse.

"Good-bye," she said to Akan and shook his hand.

"This isn't good-bye," he said gruffly.

"What do you mean?"

"You'll be back," he said and winked.

"Maybe, depending where my next expedition takes me."

"No maybe," Akan said. "Safe journey."

She walked back to the end of the verandah and leaned against the railing. On the dock, Aidan was talking to Blue. The two men were so engaged in their conversation that it made her consider what they might be discussing. Then Blue looked up and the Stetson he was wearing masked his features. She gave a slight wave, feeling foolish and reluctant to acknowledge Aidan's tribal brother. His gaze met hers, but his glasses glinted in the afternoon sunlight and hid what he might have thought. Then he waved and smiled before he reached for his belt and hitched it up.

She turned her back to the dock and returned her attention to the longhouse. Already the tribe went about their daily activities as her team headed down the stairs.

She had said her goodbyes to the women she'd had some contact with and to the shaman, who eyed her and said she would look forward to her return. It was all rather strange and unsettling as she hurried down the steep steps for what she considered to be the last time.

They weren't off to a good start. Trekking long hot days to the village before they could hope to find a plane that would get them out of here was a daunting thought. Especially considering Ian's emotional state and his continued upset over what he called Malcolm's indecent burial. And Sid sliding back into his previous unpleasantness was getting to them all before they'd even begun.

Earlier, Mark had outlined the route to her and explained some of the hazards they might face. Nights on the ground, centipedes, snakes—nothing she didn't already know and nothing she wanted to think about. Aidan, of course, had remained silent about it all.

She liked Mark. He was easy to get along with, had no edge, nothing, just easy conversation and logical suggestions. He even admitted that three days was optimistic, it could be four or more depending on her team's pace.

She knew after talking to Akan that there was no guarantee that a plane would be at the village when they arrived. They were so far off course, that Rumah Muleng was no longer the first destination. They were going to hop and skip across country and downriver.

None of it was ideal, but it was the best they were being offered. And all things considered, the alternative hadn't been so great. They could be lost in the rain forest or dead for that matter. They had much to be thankful for. But at this point it was difficult to pinpoint what those things were.

Unfortunately, a few hours into the trek, Aidan mentioned the possibility of the absent plane in full hearing of her team. Like he wanted to get a reaction, and she wasn't sure why. He grated on her like no other man did, and yet at the same time she was reluctantly drawn to him.

"What do you mean there might not be a plane when we get there?" Burke's tone registered his total disbelief. "Then how do we get out?"

"There'll be a plane," Savannah said.

"Don't be too sure about that." Aidan sounded altogether too cheerful.

"It's only a chance, a distant possibility. He's only mentioned it so you'll be prepared," Savannah said, fighting to stave off a group panic. "Worst-case scenario, we spend a night or two in the village. But there's a good chance the plane will be there on the day we arrive. That's what we're shooting for. On the upside, we can call out from there." She glanced at the team, hoping her words were having some effect. But Ian looked like he might throw up and Sid like he might punch someone.

"One other thing. It will take three, maybe four days. It's up to us how quickly we get to Rumah Muleng."

"Savannah, I can't take much more." Ian's voice indicated that he was close to the edge.

"I know, Ian. It'll be okay. We have Aidan and Mark. They know the area, it'll be fine."

"I'm trying."

"I know you are."

"This expedition has turned into an acid test," Burke said.

"You're not kidding," Sid agreed as he wiped the

back of his hand across his forehead.

"Look, guys, suck it up. This is what we've got to do to get out. You can either make it tolerable or extremely unpleasant. It's your choice," she said.

"Complete fiasco," Sid muttered and stomped ahead.

But they picked up the pace, none of them anxious to spend an extra day out here. They slept on the ground the first night. The fire that Aidan built was the only thing reassuring to any of them. Fire kept the predators away, and despite the heat they all crowded around it. There wasn't much sleep that night. By the time daylight arrived none of her team wanted to sleep another night in the open.

The next day dawned sunny but emotionally bleak, for they were at the end of their endurance, bitchy with themselves and each other.

On the banks of the river, the heat pressed in a heavy band of thick, still air. It was a frighteningly suffocating feeling. Savannah wiped sweat that dripped down her face as she knelt beside the rushing water to cool her overheated skin. She splashed water over her face, careful to keep her lips closed, to keep water droplets from entering her mouth. Parasites didn't need much of an invitation, and the last thing she needed was to get sick. She wiped her face and sat back on her haunches as she took in the never silent beauty around her.

"Get back!"

She jumped at the edge in his voice and almost lost her footing, and then Aidan was beside her. His hand was on her arm, his grip tight.

She twisted to look at him, and if she didn't know him better, she would have thought he looked like he was about to panic.

"I'm sorry, I didn't mean to startle you. Others have slipped too easily on these banks.

His hand dropped as she stood up and his gaze roved over her, and something curled soft and pleasurable in her gut.

"You look good," he said in a voice that could have seduced a well-fed python out of any tree.

"Get lost," she snapped. She was tired. And it seemed confrontation was the only defense from an attraction that had burned between them since the beginning.

"That might be difficult." Laughter threaded his voice. "Unlike you, I'd never get lost here. And I don't think you'd want to find out how that was again. The rain forest isn't exactly your thing, if you know what I mean. When I found you, you didn't even know I was there. I watched you for a while."

She looked sharply at him. "Ian heard something not that long before we met you, voices he said." She frowned. "That wasn't you."

"There were tourists, hunters, in the area. I was listening to your crashing through the bush and listening to them as well. That's probably what Ian heard."

He paused, looking at her thoughtfully. "Ian. What is he to you?"

"A good friend." She smiled. "We grew up together. Neighbors and friends."

A stick insect rested on a nearby branch. She considered her next words as she admired the simple genius of a skeleton that allowed the insect to merge so easily with his environment.

"I've loved insects since I was a little girl in

Minneapolis. Ian did too."

"Minneapolis," he said slowly. "I lived in Detroit before here."

"Me too." She smiled. "Until I was five. I don't remember it much. My parents died in a car crash. My adoptive parents were actually distant cousins, at least my father was."

"I'm sorry."

"Don't be. They've always been father and mother to me. My birth parents, I was too young to remember." She smiled sadly. "Enough of that."

He nodded. "What drew you to this?"

"I think I always loved insects. Instead of a prom dress, I begged my father to allow me to accompany him on his latest field trip." She looked out over the river as around them the jungle continued its noisy melody. "But this. The Borneo rain forest and leading an expedition here is what I've always dreamt of."

"A hard road from the sounds of it."

"You could never imagine."

"What brought you here on this expedition?"

"I wanted this for forever, to head an excursion into Borneo." She twisted to look at him. "It took me six years to finally get a yes from them."

"Malcolm's death ended what should have been a victory," he finished, finally beginning to realize the impact all of this had on her.

"There's none of us whose career didn't ride on this expedition. And there's none of us that would have considered killing him. Look, I've got to see how they're making out."

He watched her leave. Deep in his gut he believed her, but his job was to ask questions. Hard facts won every case he had ever investigated, and the only hard fact he had now was a body—a dead, headless body.

Chapter Twenty

Later in the day, Aidan managed to get time with the two quietest of the group. Burke and Drew were trailing behind the others, and he easily slid back to join them.

"Are you okay?" he asked. He offered the question with little interest. But he assumed that's what they would expect him to ask, and so he played the game.

Drew glared at him. "What do you care?"

"Fine," Burke snapped.

"I know this isn't easy," Aidan said.

"Do you?" Burke asked quietly. "We witnessed a murder. We're stuck in the jungle, lost, dependent on a stranger."

"Witnessed?" Aidan asked. This was an interesting turn.

"Not literally," Burke amended.

"You're sure it was murder?" Aidan pushed.

"What else? He was shot," Drew snapped. "I can't believe this happened."

"Not what I signed up for," Burke replied. "This is it for me. Any field trips and we're talking good old U.S. of A."

"The head was taken off with a knife and not a very good one," Aidan offered and waited for their reaction.

Burke's face drained of color. "He was a good guy. I hope you find the bastard that did this."

"Do you know what I've been thinking?" Aidan

asked.

They both stopped walking and stared at him.

"What?" Burke asked.

"That someone in your group knows what happened." His stare hit each of them.

Drew looked away first.

"He was meeting someone." Aidan provided the idea that had no basis in proof—not yet.

"How do you know?" Burke snapped.

"Do you know who he was meeting and where he was meeting them?" Aidan continued and ignored Burke.

"He didn't say," Burke said.

"I heard him say he was going to meet someone upriver. I assumed it was another guide. Who else would be that far in?" Drew added.

Yeah, who else? Aidan thought.

"I'd ask Ian," Drew added.

"I will." But that was one interview that could wait. A few more days in the jungle and he was confident that Ian would tell him everything he knew.

****

"He's a strange one. Incredibly gifted and all, but strange," Sid said an hour later as he shrugged in Ian's direction. "But they're good friends. I don't know why she puts up with him as a friend—a scientist, yeah, I get that. Don't get why she's never with a guy either, just a gay guy. She's a looker." He clapped Aidan on the shoulder. "No worries, mate. Not my type."

"Is that any way to talk about your boss?" Aidan wished he could rephrase, but he'd felt compelled to defend her.

"She's not my boss. At least she's not normally my

boss, just this trip. Otherwise, we're equals, friends of sorts. This trip she heads it. Next one—if I survive this one, maybe I'll head."

"Really?" He eyed the short yet burly man and considered why Sid was suddenly so open with him. There was obviously an agenda, he just wasn't sure what. Of all the members on the team, Sid was the one that seemed to have an agenda. Whether it was an agenda with an accessory to murder…he wouldn't rule that out.

"Yeah."

"Then I'd suggest you pull your dick back into your pants." Aidan prodded the man. "Quit acting like a rebellious teenager."

"You have your nerve, mate."

"Shut up, Sid. It isn't all about you. You're the only strong one she has on this team, but all you do is bitch."

"Bugger off, man." Sid's fist came up lightning fast but not unexpected. Aidan caught it and at the same time delivered a solid blow to the man's midsection. Sid doubled over.

Aidan waited until Sid got his wind; the others were ahead now and apparently hadn't noticed their altercation. After another minute, Aidan offered a hand to Sid, who surprisingly took it. "Grow up, Sid. You've got real potential if you'd quit hating the world," he said as he pulled him to his feet.

"Yeah, whatever. I'm just going to hang back and get my breath," Sid said as he straightened, and his gaze met Aidan's.

"Don't get too far behind."

"Right, mate," Sid replied, and there was respect in his tone.

The incident with Sid had been one of the strangest

interviews Aidan had ever had. He didn't dwell on it. With no new information in the investigation, they needed to get shelter before dark. For already the air had the humid, heavy feel of a potential storm. While he tried to set a quicker pace, the group walked slower than nursing-home candidates.

"Night's falling. We set up camp soon," he ordered.

He glanced behind and saw Sid jogging to catch up. The man's face had returned to its normal color and he looked almost happy.

"Where were you?" Burke questioned him.

"Letting someone else lead," Sid replied.

"We've got to get it together quickly," Aidan encouraged them. "Before dark."

"We?" Savannah challenged.

He smiled for he only saw desire in her eyes. Another time, another place—he looked away.

"Go for it, man," Sid said in an undertone as he came up to Aidan.

"Sid," he warned. "Drop it."

"All right, man." Sid held his hands in the air; apparently, he now considered himself Aidan's buddy.

That wasn't quite what Aidan was going for, but he had seen it before in those brash, push-the-envelope types like Sid. He wasn't going to encourage it.

"Sid," he said, ignoring the man's comment. "Watch for small dry branches that we can use to start a fire later.

"Burke…"

"Stop!" Vann cut him off. "You're not in charge of this team."

"I am now."

"You're not," she said. "No way. This is my expedition."

"Egging for another dead man, are you?" he said and almost smiled. The war of words was on, the battlefields marked, and the passion flared despite it all.

"That was unfair."

"Was it? If you want to lead this team, then lead it, but take my advice. You've got to get a shelter up soon. You can't be traipsing around the jungle at night, and dark will fall quickly." He glanced upward to the trees.

"Children, children." Mark pushed his way to the front. "If it will settle anything, I'll be in charge, for now." He glanced at both of them. "Unless, of course, you can quit your squabbling long enough to get camp in order. This is survival, guys, the real reality version. We need everyone engaged with nature, not fighting with each other. The enemy is out there, remember, and to them we could be just a light bedtime snack."

"You're right, man," Aidan said as he clapped a hand on Mark's shoulder.

"That was encouraging," Savannah muttered and glanced at Ian, who appeared not to have heard Mark's comment.

"I'm willing to try working together if you are," Aidan said. "But I think we need to get moving. I don't like the feel of the air. There's a heavy feel that could mean a storm."

She swallowed. "Okay, we'll set up camp. Here."

"No," he commanded and pointed. "We still have a way to go."

"He's right, Savannah," Mark said quietly.

"I know it," she admitted, and then as an aside to Mark she said, "But I don't have to like it."

"Go, girl," Mark said and laughed. "You're ballsy, I like that."

"Sid, Savannah!" Ian's excited voice cut through the hyperbole and had them all running.

Savannah was there first. Aidan was right behind her.

A line of coal-black beetles made their way along the forest floor. The line of insects seemed endless.

"They're smaller than our specimen, but everything about them looks the same except they're wingless," Savannah said breathlessly.

Sid squatted down beside her.

"They're carrying something out."

She peered closer. "Plant material of some sort."

"I've never seen anything like it," Sid breathed.

Aidan watched them, fascinated by the awe that registered on both their faces. To him they were beetles, nothing more. And as he thought that, Savannah pulled one out of the line with tweezers. The markings on its underside were a streak of yellow.

"Like the sample," she murmured as she dropped it into a specimen bottle.

Her gaze locked with Sid's. "Could it be possible?"

"Farming?" Sid's voice was raspy like a kid's on Christmas morning.

"There are few species on earth that are known to farm." Savannah's hands shook. This was beyond anything she could have imagined.

Aidan squatted down beside her. "You think they're farming? You aren't serious?"

"I am. Insects are actually as good or better farmers than mankind. They've been doing it longer, millions of years longer. Beetles, termites, ants, and only a few species of each. Mostly they farm fungi. To find another species of beetle…" She sat back on her haunches. "I can't believe this. Can you mark where we are? We can't lose this."

Aidan's hand rested lightly on her shoulder. "I'll mark it. Meantime, I hate to say it, but we've got to go. Darkness will be setting in soon. We need to have set up shelter before then."

She turned to him. "This is major, Aidan. Just another few minutes. I'd like to get a few more samples, study the habitat just a bit more…"

"We must go now," he cut her off. "Or risk being caught in weather that has been known to kill a man. There's no guarantee if the storm will hit us or not, but if it does…"

Her lips pinched. "You're right." But the words were laced with regret.

"It'll be fine," he whispered in her ear. "I'll bring you back here, soon."

She shivered. And he only wanted to take her in his arms. For he knew that, despite the find, things were still a long way from fine.

Chapter Twenty-One

It was the night from hell. Savannah hadn't thought it possible, but it was worse than the night before. The ground was rock hard. The night more humid than any other. The temperature didn't drop through the long hours of darkness. It felt like they were in the midst of a Swedish sauna.

"This is insane," Ian whispered. "I can't sleep in this."

"None of us can," Savannah whispered back. "Just close your eyes and try to rest. Think of the beetles. A new specimen of C*oleoptera,* imagine what the community will say. It was incredible, wasn't it?" But speaking the words only filled her with unease. She wanted to be there now, examining her find, marking the territory as hers. Instead, she was miles away with no idea how to reach her discovery.

"You're not kidding. I'm not sure if it's the heat or thinking of beetles that farm, but I'm just too wired to sleep."

"Me too," she admitted. "We'll get moving again as soon as there's a shred of light."

"That's something to look forward to," Ian said.

An hour later, there were deep snores all around her. Foliage rustled as the voiceless occupants of the forest slid quietly about their nightly business. She shivered despite the heat. It was difficult not to feel helpless when she couldn't see what was moving in the forest around her. And it was impossible to sleep when a murderer might still be out there; and the find of a lifetime was just out of reach.

The campfire's flames danced in the night sky. She could see Aidan squatting back on his heels on the other side of the campfire. With the fire between them, he was a shadowy yet comforting figure. She had tried to distance herself from him. Instead, she wrestled with the desire that escalated with every minute she spent with him. She hadn't anticipated how difficult it was to keep control in an environment where she was at odds. She wasn't giving up, but she was tired of pushing, tired of being the one that was strong. She got up, picking her way among her team sprawled at all angles around the fire.

"The forest is more alive than most nights. I don't like it," Aidan said as she came up to him. He glanced at her as he continued to stir the embers. The fire leapt as he placed another piece of wood on it. Around the fire sat rocks that had been in this spot for generations to prevent the chance that the campfire could spread.

"What are you thinking?" Savannah asked as she settled cross-legged, beside him.

"The weather's about to change. The rainy season is almost on us, but this has the feel of something more. Typhoon off the coast, heavier rain, I'm not sure."

"We should be at the village before that?" Savannah asked.

"Maybe. That's two days away; a lot could happen."

"I'm not sure Sid could handle that, Jason and Ian…" She laughed. "Never mind Burke—he's not doing too well either."

They were silent for a moment. He cleared his throat. From the far side of the clearing, her team snored and in the forest the predators roamed.

"What are you going to do when you get back?" he asked.

"What do you mean?"

"You're determined to come back. The beetle…"

"I have no choice."

"Then let me guide you…"

"You're not always here," she said.

"True. But if I can't, let me pick a qualified guide."

She hesitated. She couldn't rely on him, not for anything. After he got them out of here, it was over. She couldn't confide in him, not about her future or the reality that she would return not just once but over and over because she may have found her life's work. Revealing that meant an intimacy of more than the physical kind. That intimacy was dangerous.

"I've never met anyone as passionate about what they do as you," he said and shifted in the darkness, his arm brushing her shoulder.

"There's something about insects. They're one of the most tenacious creatures on the planet. They've survived for millions of years and will probably survive millions of years after we're gone."

He picked up a stick and snapped it. He threw it into the fire, and they watched the flames spark and whoosh, lighting the dark sky. Overhead something screeched and then chattered in what was clearly an undertone, a muttering under its breath.

"Sorry, old boy," Aidan muttered.

"A monkey?"

He nodded. "So, insects endure all. An admirable

feat but not grounds for lifelong study. What got you hooked on studying bugs?"

She laughed. "Bugs?"

"I understand an interest in botany, but it's your phylum choice that has me crawling." He grinned at his own joke.

"To think I called you Wild Man only days ago and thought of you as a monosyllabic entity."

"Monosyllabic?"

"You've got to admit you were doing your best to distance yourself from us."

"It didn't work," he murmured as his lips skimmed over hers.

The kiss was as light and gentle as the warm night air. As he began to deepen the kiss, she broke away.

"Tell me, why bugs?"

"I told you. My father is an entomologist, so I was exposed early."

His fingers laced through hers.

She pulled back but, it was all she could do not to turn into his arms. To begin another kiss where his last kiss had left off.

"Dad was passionate about his work. After Mother died, I think it was a way to get close to him."

"How old were you?"

"Eleven."

He handed her a stick.

She snapped it and threw it in the fire. "The insects caught me even before that. I spent hours studying them. I begged to go to Father's lab with him. I couldn't get enough. Insects mutate to fit their environment. They are incredible, ever-changing, and we know so little about them. How could I not be passionate?"

"Never not," he murmured, and his knuckle grazed a sensuous trail down her cheek.

"Aidan," she warned.

"What?" But he dropped his hand.

Her heart thumped, and she couldn't stand the feel of him so close and still keep her distance. She shifted away and pulled her knees to her chest.

"I can picture you as a little girl."

"Don't," she said, scared of where this was going. Her skin tingled in places she wanted him to touch. She shifted another few inches away.

"Why not? What were you like?"

"By the time I was twelve, I had my own laboratory set up in Father's garage."

"You were serious. I picture a pixie."

It was too much. The questions were building an intimacy that, despite the kiss, she had done everything to avoid.

"What happened between you and Sid earlier?"

"Why?"

His arm once again brushed her shoulder. Somehow, he had gotten closer in the last few minutes.

"He was acting differently. I know he said he'd cooperate, but it's difficult for him to cooperate when he's afraid."

"Afraid. Why would you say that?" With only the light of the fire reflecting in the night shadows, his voice was comforting.

"Why else would he have all that aggression except to mask his fear?" she asked.

"You're an amateur psychologist?"

"You could say that. On this trip it's come in handy. Anyway, behaviors don't change that quickly unless something interceded. I'm thinking it was you."

"Actually, it was my fist."

"You hit him? Aidan!" His name came out warm and breathy.

"I like when you say my name like that."

"I didn't say it any special way. I was just surprised," she objected and tried to still her hammering pulse.

"Well, then stay surprised," he said as his breath grazed her skin and his lips met hers.

"No," she protested but it was half-hearted and without physical resistance.

"The lady does protest too much."

The sound and feel of his voice against her lips was exquisite. She could smell mint, clean and sweet. How had that happened? How had they gotten so close? Had she shifted closer to him or had he moved closer to her? She didn't know. She turned and she was in his arms.

"Vann," he murmured as his lips fully claimed hers, as her body meshed with his, as the kiss combusted in the chaos of their mutual attraction.

But she claimed him with every bit of the desire that he claimed her. The desire was hotter than any anger ever could be. There was no turning back. They possessed each other, falling to the forest floor in a knot of limbs. Their bodies, both lithe and fit, wrapped around each other in an undistinguishable mass. They both sought pleasure, hard and fast, an erotic splurge of sexual sensation.

Later, Savannah lay naked and sated beside Aidan. She ran a finger along his naked hip bone.

"You're beautiful," she said.

"I don't think a man is considered that."

"You are."

"Hmmm."

She didn't expect anything else. For now, it was comforting to lie here and catch her breath.

After a while, they slept.

She awoke to his voice.

"Vann," he whispered. "Get up. Get dressed."

She sat up, instinctively covering her breasts.

He handed her, her shirt. "You might want to put that on before the others get up. Mark has eyes in the dark."

"Really?"

"No. But he'll be awake soon."

She pulled on her pants, pulling the drawstring, and then put on her shirt.

"There can be nothing between us, Vann. Not in the long term. You know that." And with that he disappeared into the jungle.

In the darkness, leaves rustled in the hollow where Aidan had disappeared. Now there was only the shadowy blackness and her thoughts. This was a brief romance, and that's why she'd dodged it. Dodging was over. She knew that as instinctively as any invertebrate that called this place home. But there would be nothing between them once they left the rain forest. When they left the rain forest, everything changed. But civilization was still two days and two nights away.

Chapter Twenty-Two

The next day the skies opened up about noon, and the rain came down in buckets. They were soaked within seconds.

"Can it get any better?" Burke muttered.

Sid, for once, said nothing.

Ian looked like he would cry, but then lately he always looked like that. If he did, Savannah thought, there would be no way to tell as water streamed down all their faces.

They trudged for hours in silence. Finally, Aidan stopped.

"What are you stopping for?" Drew asked.

"Shut up," Sid snarled, finally getting his familiar edge back.

"Ladies, ladies." Mark smiled, holding up his hand.

It happened in an instant. Savannah hadn't even heard Sid's comment, but there was no mistaking Mark's repetition of the insult.

"Little man?"

She should have known by Mark's tone. For, in that instant the world stopped, and a window of rage opened as Sid and Mark faced off.

"Yeah, that's what I called you."

Mark launched a fist at Sid, who ducked the first blow and came up swinging. His fist caught Mark under the jaw, but Mark reciprocated and Sid staggered.

"Stop it." Savannah dove in between the two as her inner voice screamed something about the craziness of it all. All she knew was that one minute she was wrestling to pull them apart and the next she was skidding across the rain-slicked forest floor. Seconds later she sat up with a bloody nose and stars flashing before her eyes.

"Savannah, are you okay?" Ian crouched beside her. "Thank God you only got the edge of Sid's fist."

Brush crashed around them and Aidan appeared. "What happened?"

"Sid hit Savannah," Ian said without thought. "No, it wasn't like that," he said as Aidan's fists balled up.

"Aidan." Savannah struggled to her feet as she tried to stop him. But it was too late. He was on Sid.

"Bastard!"

Savannah was startled to hear the word and it was only in that moment that she realized that Aidan never swore. At least she had never heard him.

"Stop!" she shouted, but neither heard as Aidan pummeled Sid.

Mark grabbed Aidan from behind and Burke and Drew wrestled with Sid.

"It was an accident," Mark repeated after the pair of fighters were separated.

"I didn't mean to hit her," Sid said through his broken and bleeding lips.

Aidan let Sid go. Sid staggered, holding his jaw before sinking into a weak squat.

Aidan squatted down beside Savannah and gently felt her nose. Finally, he was satisfied. "It's not broken. How are you feeling?"

"Like an idiot. It was a stupid thing to do."

Aidan nodded.

"It's my fault. I shouldn't have reacted." Mark shook his head. "I can't believe I did."

"You hit Sid first?" Aidan smiled. "And here I thought you were the more civilized of the two of us. You'd rather read than fight. What happened?"

"Yeah, hard to believe, but you can only take so much. I'm not a fighter. You know that."

"I'm sorry."

"Don't, Mark." She shook her head and grimaced. "It's not your fault."

Aidan looked at her. "What were you thinking?"

She shook her head. "Shut up, Aidan," she said good-naturedly.

"We'd better camp here for the night," Aidan said.

"Don't be utterly ridiculous. It's just past noon. We've got a lot of hours yet before we need to make camp." Savannah thought of how much farther they had to go.

"She has a point, Aidan," Mark said.

"She's hurt," Aidan insisted.

"I'm fine. We'll have something to eat and then we move on."

Sid glanced at Mark. "I'm sorry, man."

Mark nodded.

"C'mon, Burke," Drew said as he followed Mark.

"You're sure you're okay?" Burke asked her.

"I'll live."

"Okay," he said and turned to follow Drew.

Savannah watched her team move to the edges of the clearing. She waited until they were out of earshot before turning to Aidan.

"You know they fought because they've reached their limit of endurance. Ian could suffer a total collapse.

He's not overly strong, in case you haven't noticed. And Sid, well, he's so angry and getting angrier. Even Burke," she said with a sigh. "They're becoming a very dangerous group. The sooner we get out of the forest, the better."

"You were right. We keep moving." He skimmed a finger along her cheek. "You're okay?" His hands dropped to her shoulders.

She brushed a strand of soggy hair from her face. "I'm a little shaky, but that's all. I'll be fine in ten minutes. A drink of water and something to eat, and I'll be good to go."

"Okay, ten minutes." He handed the water bottle to her. "Have a drink," he said, his voice laced with concern.

They were back at it fifteen minutes later. It was a quiet group that trekked through the afternoon. At the front and rear, Aidan and Mark flattened the long grass ensuring that the deadly creatures of the forest were warned of their approach. The rain had finally eased to a drizzle that dripped in a dismal litany through the leaves.

They were miserable. They had all taken more than they had ever taken before. And Savannah wondered how they would possibly survive another day and night out here. But they all knew there was no choice because the only other option was unthinkable. There had been one death on this expedition, none of them planned to see another.

Chapter Twenty-Three

Aidan feared it might take a bit of luck to get them out of the wilderness before he killed one of them. His normally good temper was long gone. He'd never punched a man before, never wanted to, despite his occupation and despite the fact that he often carried a gun. But that was different. The gun had never been pulled in anger. He'd had thoughts of punching Sid for hours before he actually did.

"Aidan."

Mark's voice cut into his thoughts.

"Sid." Mark looked worried. "Something needs to be done. The man will go off again."

"You're probably right."

"Definitely right. He is absolutely unbelievable. What would make her take someone like that on her excursion?"

"Because he's not normally like that," Savannah put in as she joined them. "Truthfully, I've only worked with him in the lab, but I've seen no sign of angry outbursts. He's always had an edge, but nothing where he loses it. On the first day of the excursion, he said something about a breakup with his wife. It could be part of the problem, but I thought that he'd get back on an even keel long before this."

"Yeah, after all, it was only a wife." Mark laughed.

"Only a wife?" She whirled on him.

“I wasn’t serious.” Mark stopped laughing but with obvious effort. “I was being facetious.”

“Yeah, well, be facetious somewhere else,” Savannah said.

Her determined, *don’t mess with me, I’ll take care of myself* look only made Aidan want to kiss her. Instead he watched as she walked away. Sid joined her, and the two began to talk. He was too far away to hear and finally he turned away.

“Aidan,” Mark whispered urgently.

Aidan turned around and saw Mark motioning to him. Mark stood on the edge of the forest with his attention drawn to something farther in.

Aidan slid up beside him. The forest was trampled. Branches were broken.

“Was one of the team here?” Aidan asked.

Mark shook his head.

“Then what?” Aidan moved silently into the area, being careful not to disturb whatever had occurred here.

“What do you think?” Mark asked softly.

“No idea. I told you about the monkey?”

Mark nodded. “You think this might be tied to that poaching?”

Aidan didn’t reply but instead squatted down and brushed leaves aside.

“What do you have?”

“A knot of hair.”

“Let me see.” Mark squatted down beside him. “Human. Dark and coarse. Might not be Caucasian.”

“Or it might.” He looked at Aidan. “But on your other thought, didn’t you say your hunters were Chinese?”

“Yeah, but this tells us nothing.”

"Yeah, but a footprint does."

Aidan brushed carefully at the disturbed ground. "Whoever they were they walked heavily."

"That's not good and not Iban," Mark said. "How long ago do you think?"

"Fairly recent. The footprint would have been washed out otherwise." Aidan examined the broken branches. "They're headed to the river. Makes sense, they probably have a guide and a boat waiting."

He couldn't believe they were here again or that they were still here. He recognized the footprint. It was the same—the same size. He'd seen it how many days earlier? The Chinese hunters, the same ones he had seen the day he had found Vann and her team.

"Do you think they might be our shooter?"

Aidan frowned. "It's still wide open. Anything is possible." He hunched down and examined the footprint. It was faint, but it was obviously a hiking boot and the two others he could find matched the first.

"The others didn't come this far. There's only one set of prints," Aidan said.

Mark sat back on his haunches beside Aidan. "Are you sure he's part of the same group?"

"I'm going down to the river and taking a look." He scowled. "Maybe they think they have time to get out. The death of an Iban guide wouldn't be reported to the authorities for a while. At least I'm assuming that was their thought process."

"Exactly." Aidan stood up. "They called their guide Pedro. They were fools and racist on top of it all. Either way, they're an aberration here."

"Aidan," Mark warned as he too stood. "Don't let your emotions cloud things."

"I won't." He clenched his fists.

"What are you going to do?"

"Put the pressure on." He glanced to the forest. "If they're still here, I'll see what I can flush out."

"Are you nuts? Don't you have enough to worry about?"

"Hold them." He nodded toward Vann's group. "Keep them moving, and I'm going to see what I can find out." Aidan didn't give Mark a chance to protest before he slipped into the forest.

"Hey!" Mark's voice called. "If the storm changes direction, we could sock in fairly quickly."

"Yep," Aidan called from the shelter of trees. "You know what to do if it does."

"Mark!" Savannah called to him as her team trudged ahead. "Where's Aidan?"

"Checking trail ahead," he said evasively.

"What? Did you find something?" She touched his arm. "Tell me, Mark, please. If I know, I have a better chance at keeping the emotions in the group on an even keel. You know, no surprises."

"He found evidence of the hunters he ran into earlier."

"Hunters," Savannah breathed. "He never said. Could they have killed Malcolm?"

"Possibly. Look, don't tell him that I've told you. Please. I told you only so you would have enough background to keep them"—he gestured with a sweep of his hand—"under control."

"Got it. No more questions about that. But I'd like to know something."

"What?"

"What happens when we get to Kuching?"

"What do you mean?" Mark frowned.

"Well, there'll be police reports, an investigation into his death. Will we all have to be interrogated?"

"I'll handle it," Mark said. "They might want to speak to you. But I doubt if the others will be of much use. And really, Aidan should be able to handle most of it."

"Because he's an investigator." She frowned. "Here?"

"Some of the time," Mark said. "Look, don't worry about it. Odds are I'll be able to get the information I need, and with Aidan's help, we may have this all wrapped up."

"At least some of us have something to look forward to," Sid sneered as he came over, overhearing part of the conversation. "Bet you're hoping we never get to that village. Making out with Wild Man at least makes this tolerable for you. Not like the rest of us. Shit, what do you care? You have him."

For a moment Savannah was speechless. Sid's anger was getting out of control. And none of them could survive another twenty-four hours like the last with Sid constantly bitching. She stopped just a few feet off the path, far enough away from the others for privacy but not far enough to be out of sight.

"Look, Sid, I'm tired of fighting with you."

"Then don't."

"Sid, I'm sorry about your wife."

"Shut up," he snapped. "Just shut up. I won't talk about her."

"You have to talk about her. Apparently, that's eating you up. You're impossible. You're making everyone else miserable."

"Bugger off," he snarled.

"I don't think so, Sid."

"Don't think what?"

"I don't care how good you are. I won't take you on another expedition if you can't show me that you can be civil. Your attitude, well, frankly, it sucks. You're making everyone uncomfortable, and considering our situation, that could be dangerous." She held up her hand, warding off his next words. "Don't even say it. I know someone is already dead. That's a little hard to ignore. But it won't happen again."

"What makes you think I want to go on another expedition with you?"

"Maybe you don't," she said. "I imagine with your pleasant disposition, word will get around. You'll have offers everywhere."

"Touché."

"So, unless lab work appeals to you…"

"Look, I'm sorry."

Savannah stared at him. She hadn't expected that. She'd expected reluctant agreement, but an apology?

"I'm human, too, you know. And Ian seriously gets on my nerves. Between that and—" He swallowed and looked away. "My wife. Well, my nerves are frayed."

"And you want to take it out on someone. I get it. Although I'm a little concerned. I'd expect you to be more open-minded."

"I could give a flying mongoose that he's gay. It's the sissy hysteria that's driving me over the edge." He looked sheepishly at her. "Okay, the Malcolm crush thing was tough to take, but I can get over that. The hysteria thing, not so much."

"I'll speak to Ian. Although I don't know what good

that will do, and we only have another day out here, hopefully." She frowned. "But there will be other expeditions, I hope, and he might be there."

"That could be a no-go point unless he kills the hysteria."

"No one surpasses his knowledge of *Coleoptera*."

He bowed. "I'll do my best to be civil."

"I'd appreciate it." She squeezed his hand. "Try counting backward."

"I will," he said.

"Thanks." She gripped his hand briefly again before turning to walk away.

"In French," he shouted to her retreating back.

Chapter Twenty-Four

From thirty feet up, nestled on the edge of the forest canopy, Aidan was able to see more clearly. Beneath him the forest floor rustled, and a monitor swished his tail before disappearing into the underbrush. In the distance, the river shimmered blue and deceptively inviting. Aidan squinted as a small figure moved and a boat launched into the river. Whoever they were, they were on their way out, too far away to follow.

He headed back to the others and was surprised ten minutes later to find Ian trailing behind the group. Ian had become a constant shadow of Sid's lately, making it impossible for Aidan to get close.

"You're back," Ian said as he swung around to face Aidan. "Where'd you go?"

"For a better view."

"Why?" Ian scowled. "What aren't you telling us?"

"Who did Malcolm go to meet that day?"

"How should I know?" Ian's scowl deepened.

"I'd guess you'd know where Malcolm went. That maybe you knew everything about him."

"Hardly. What are you suggesting?" Ian looked away.

"That maybe you had a thing for him."

"Maybe," Ian murmured, and when he looked up there were tears in his eyes.

Aidan had a hard time holding his gaze. He could

handle many things, but tears in a man were hard for him to take. He snapped a nearby twig and peeled the outer bark. "Where did he go, Ian?" he repeated the question without looking at him.

"He was meeting someone he knew from a local longhouse. He said he had a chance to make good money," Ian replied. "I think he knew whoever he was meeting well. He called him something, a nickname, I think."

"What? Who?

"I don't remember." Ian hiccupped. He wiped the back of his hand across his nose.

"And you were jealous?" Aidan asked.

"A little." He glanced at Aidan. "No, never. I wouldn't do that. That's what you think, don't you? That I killed him. I loved him!" He choked. "Or at least I could have, given time."

"But you must have seen something."

"No!"

"But you followed him?"

"Yeah. I followed him for a while, but then he lost me." Ian sighed and sniffed. "That was stupid, I know. I was lucky to find my way back to the others."

"Have you ever shot a gun?" Aidan asked. He knew the answer, but pressure could be applied through many methods. This, lies and insinuations, was one of his least favorite.

"Yes. I'm a skilled marksman."

The answer surprised Aidan, and for a moment he forgot his next question.

Ian glared at him. "What are you suggesting? I shoot targets. Inanimate objects. I couldn't shoot anything living." The tears fell now, and his mouth quivered as he tried to rein them in. "Besides, I'm unarmed. Not that it matters. I would never hurt him or anyone."

"Take a deep breath," Aidan encouraged him. "So, the last you saw of Malcolm he was heading—what direction?"

"East."

"Upriver?"

Ian nodded.

"Inland?"

Again, Ian nodded.

"What did you do after that? Did you hear a shot?"

"No. I came back, and we spent the day close to camp. That's where we found the dead specimen. And then we waited for Malcolm." His chin quivered. "He never showed up. And that's when we started moving out."

"Thanks, Ian," Aidan said quietly. He turned away. Hysterics were not something he was prepared to deal with. They bordered on conflict, they bordered on everything he had always disliked. Yet here he was in a career that required just that. The irony didn't escape him.

"Wait."

He turned.

Ian's chin had stopped quivering, and his eyes had taken on a new intensity. "Be gentle with her. Savannah, I mean. She's not as tough as she likes to make out."

"I realize that," he replied, irritated that Ian had felt he needed to remind him. Her vulnerability was evident, at least to him.

"I don't think you do." Ian's chin jutted at a stubborn angle. "She's my best friend, and she's had a rough road to this point. She was anorexic, you know. Took her a year longer to graduate because she had to drop out to get treatment."

"Anorexic," Aidan repeated. There was nothing anorexic about her now. She was all delicate limbs and soft curves. Just right.

"Not anymore. She's over it all, but this is difficult for her." He waved his arm, encompassing the area. "And you. Not being in charge." He sighed. "She's better, but she still struggles with control issues."

"Why are you telling me this?"

"Because you're falling for her. What do you think, I'm blind?"

For once, Aidan was more at a loss with Ian than when he was in full hysteria.

"We've always been the odd pair, me with my emotions, her with her control issues. But I blame that, the control thing, on her father. He was always standing in her way or refusing to acknowledge her, take your pick. She hides her feelings most of the time, and that's half the problem." He scuffed the ground with his foot. "Look, I feel bad telling you all this, but I expect you'll watch out for her. I can't always be there."

"You're assuming a lot."

"Am I?" Ian asked.

"I'll take it under advisement," he said gravely as he turned away. But what Ian had told him only confirmed what he already knew. Vann and he were more alike than either one of them wanted to admit.

****

There were few days that he didn't think of her. Anne had been everything to him. He'd never thought it would be like this. Other men had lost wives and they'd recovered, but he and Anne had been different.

Blue crumpled the edge of his cowboy hat. He'd been on the losing side of things for too long. First his father's attention when Aidan had arrived as a boy, then Anne's death. All he had left was his guiding business that had accidentally ventured into poaching. And was now poised to make him wealthier than he could imagine. If they discovered who killed Malcolm—worse, if they reported it—it was over.

It was never supposed to be like this. He had liked Malcolm, what little he had known of him. What he did know was that the man didn't listen to warnings and was too naïve to suspect trouble. If his instincts were honed as they should have been, none of this would have happened.

He shoved his glasses up, as he roughly wiped his eyes. His business partner had underestimated him. The glasses dropped, and he squinted through the smudges. This time he would be the winner that Anne had always said he was.

Chapter Twenty-Five

"Would you miss this?" Savannah asked that night after they had set up camp.

They'd made slow progress today as they'd battled a jungle thick with vines and oversize leaves. She nuzzled comfortably against his naked chest. At a safe distance, the snores of the others rattled through the small clearing.

"What do you mean?"

"Us," Savannah said softly.

"Are you looking for something permanent?"

"Don't be ridiculous. I have my career."

"Of course. Your career. And that precludes everything, doesn't it?"

"Pretty much."

"So when you're not here, where are you?"

"New York. At a desk job." She sighed. "But this is where I want to be, with the insects." She waved her hand. "The jungle is home to them. Like it is to you."

"I have a loft in Kuching," he said to her, his voice held amusement and something else.

She swallowed heavily. "Kuching?"

"Half of the year. Of course, I spent time in the States too."

A soft rustle, followed by the creak of wood against wood and something else. It was a sound that Savannah couldn't identify.

"Stay here."

His hand settled briefly on her shoulder and then drifted across her cheek in a feather touch that seared her skin.

"I'll come with you."

"No," he said flatly. "Stay."

"As if," she muttered and got up.

From the right, brush rustled. Beneath the light of the moon, the great dun body of a monitor moved through the tall grass. Its head swung back and forth before it plodded toward the river.

Aidan held up his hand. Savannah nodded, instinctively freezing. She watched as a lizard nearly as big as herself, meandered across the edge of the clearing making its way to the water.

"Those things would kill you with a bite," Aidan said as he moved back to her side.

"But they don't normally attack?"

"Not humans, not unless they're threatened. That's why it's a good idea to remain still and unthreatening. Works with many things. Of course, not all."

He glanced upward into the trees.

"Pythons." She frowned.

"Them and a few other snakes. Next to the insects, they're the deadliest things in the forest."

"Lovely place." There was a smile in her voice.

"Great place for bugs," he bantered.

"Yeah, you got me there. I'd love it for that, if I could get over the hazards. I really don't know how you do it. As for me, except for research, I'm definitely not rushing back here for a vacation."

He laughed.

But something in that laugh was a little off. There

was a sadness that laced through the humor, a loneliness that made her doubt both their motives.

Later that night the rain fell again.

****

The need to kill was overpowering. That was the only excuse Matthew had for being here. His clothes were wet, and the rain was still pelting down on the only shelter he had—a plastic tarp. Frustration warred with the craving. For he'd eaten nothing in two days that didn't come out of a can and was cold.

It was insanity, all of it, and he didn't know how to create an opportunity that just wasn't presenting itself. He'd expected an opportunity well before this. He'd actually been overly optimistic and thought he'd make his kill on the first day. Instead, he'd been forced to follow the exaggerated path Aidan had set out for these city-slicking scientists. It was clearly made to break the weakest of them. And for that he could admire Aidan, if it wasn't affecting him too. So, instead, his anger built. For it had only made his goal that much more difficult to attain. And he needed that kill. He needed it now. He needed it soon.

He opened a bag of trail mix. He was getting a bloody headache. He popped an aspirin and gulped water. But that didn't cut it either. He opened the mickey of whiskey and took a slug. He closed his eyes and took another, but still the image of his hands around a neck and that last gasp of life were at the forefront of his mind. The urge was close to out of control.

His heart pounded at the thought. He couldn't lose control, for then he'd lose who he was as a man. He'd become the urge rather than the urge being part of him.

He took another drink of whiskey.

"Tomorrow," he promised himself. If the opportunity didn't arise, then he'd have to create the opportunity. Somehow—Any way he could.

He'd make it happen.

Chapter Twenty-Six

The next day the weather cleared, but the humidity hung heavy over everything and everyone. Aidan had spent the last five minutes assessing the team, preparing for blowups. But everyone seemed resigned, almost lethargic. He turned his attention to Vann. That was a mistake. Her hips swayed slightly as she walked away. Even that was too tempting, like a siren call to him.

"I can't stand this. It's hotter than hell." Ian's tone was petulant.

"Ian." Savannah was uncompromising as she looked back and said, "Can it."

"C'mon, mate. It's an adventure," Sid said and slowed his pace.

Aidan glanced back as Sid sidled up to Ian. The two had become an odd pair of mismatched friends. There were more weird and wonderful things in the Borneo rain forest than just the bugs. Thinking that, Aidan smiled and continued to mark the trail.

He glanced overhead, and through a brief break in the canopy, he could see the sun had shifted to a late afternoon position. Then the canopy closed in again and they were in the verdant green dusk that had existed long before man ever ventured here.

He slipped ahead of the group, but he was alone for only a few minutes before he heard footsteps behind him. He didn't have to turn around to know who it was.

"Aidan," her voice whispered to him, seeming separate and distant from the others.

He could hear her unease.

He slipped silently through the foliage to where she was.

He needed her. Needed her to go back to the others. "Go back."

"Why?"

She bent down, running a finger along the ground. He wished she would go back, and at the same time he fought the urge to gather her in his arms.

"I've never seen frass quite like this." She looked up and smiled. "In layman's terms, insect poop."

He smiled softly at the incongruity of their thoughts—his on passion and hers on insect poop. And despite recognizing that their thoughts were at opposite ends of the spectrum, he couldn't stop his, couldn't quite focus on a bug.

"Something makes its home here."

"Many creatures," he agreed, but it was a gruff agreement that hid the pleasure he felt at this shared affinity they had for the creatures of the forest. She was everything he wanted in a woman, and yet she didn't belong here.

"Insects, I meant. It's an unbelievably diverse ecosystem." She trailed her finger through the mulch.

And all he could look at was the view that he'd acquired while she squatted. She was braless and her thin shirt revealed what it hadn't before. Her nipples were small, and sweetly pink, and…He closed his eyes. That didn't help. He squatted down beside her.

"Look at that. You can see where the ants have made a path. See there?" She stood up and pointed, as her breast brushed his arm.

He could only take so much. She was in his arms. He was kissing her, or she was kissing him. Her shirt was open, and neither one of them remembered how. He only knew that he was caressing heaven.

She nuzzled his neck and blew hot kisses on his already overheated skin.

But it wasn't enough, he wanted more. He fondled her breast, playfully pulling a nipple before using all his will power to pull her shirt together.

"I want you," she said, and her words were hot and ready.

But he knew that much more, and he wouldn't be able to stop. Much more and the remainder of the team would be looking for them.

"No. Button your shirt." His tone softened. "I'd say you've got just under a minute."

She was just finished when Drew crashed through the foliage, followed by the others.

"When are we making camp?" Ian asked. "I'm exhausted."

"I'm going to track ahead and find a place for the night," Aidan said, relieved to find a new direction for his overheated senses.

An hour later, they reached a spot where the forest had become thinner. The sun had shifted, and darkness was only a few hours away. "We'll camp here."

Within minutes, pup tents were up and camp had been made. Supper was stew from dehydrated packs, as it had been every night.

"I don't know about the rest of you," Sid said as he got up, "but I'm turning in."

"Me too." Ian stood.

Within thirty minutes her team had all settled in to get some sleep before the morning hours.

Savannah sat cross-legged by the fire, too keyed up to sleep. She thought of the find and ached to go back. A species of *Coleoptera* that farmed was unprecedented. And only one fear marred the discovery—that when they returned, it would be gone as if it had never existed. Across the fire she could see Aidan. His back was to everyone. She wondered what he was thinking as she pushed the flames with a stick and embers fired into the air. She shifted and glanced at where Aidan had been—he'd disappeared.

She remained where she was, her arms wrapped around her knees. Soon, snorts and rumbles and deep breathing indicated that the others were all asleep.

She got up and made her way to the edge of the clearing. Beyond, the forest was dark and forbidding. The green curtain had become a black backdrop to the night sky, a rich mystery. She stepped into the black void, two tentative steps, glanced behind her and could still see the fire, yet around her the foliage was close, hot and confining.

"Aidan," she whispered, trying to keep the panic from her voice.

"Over here."

She looked to where his voice had been, and something moved.

She froze.

"It's me."

He was behind her, and before she could turn, his arms were around her. He turned her to face him. And, in his arms she forgot all the frustration and fear she had felt. Only the overwhelming heart pounding, liquid fire of their attraction remained. His lips roamed over hers, his tongue slid along the roof of her mouth. She moaned as she envisioned other places, places that she wanted that tongue to be.

"C'mon."

He took her hand.

"Do you know where we are?" The darkness was overwhelming, unsettling, and she could only see glimpses of the campfire.

He chuckled. "About thirty feet to the right of camp, give or take."

"Give or take." She licked her lips. She trusted his abilities, yet it was so dark, so foreign, so deliciously titillating because of that.

His lips met hers again, rich and warm, and all she could do was wrap her arms around his neck and demand more. They fell in a heated tangle of limbs, rolling in the thick grass in a clearing that was bracketed by impressions of foliage shadowed against the night sky. They rolled once, and then passion clouded everything. She couldn't tell who had done what to whom, only that her body sang like it never had before.

Later, as they lay together, the velvet darkness rich and unbroken, the warm humid air sifting around them like a blanket, she sighed. She loved it here.

"What was that about?" He shifted and put an arm around her shoulders. She leaned into him.

"It's beautiful, insects or not."

"Really," he drawled.

She turned to look at him. "You've always loved it here. Haven't you?"

"True. But I'm not like most people."

"You're not kidding, Aidan. So do you have a last

name?"

"I don't know," he replied.

"What do you mean, you don't know?"

"Mother was a hippie, a counterculture type, and I never had one. It's not on my birth certificate." He shrugged. "A clerical error, no doubt. My given name appears twice."

"You didn't ask to have it changed?"

"No."

"And you won't now," she guessed.

"Precisely. At this stage in my life, it's all irrelevant."

"Mr. Irrelevant," she murmured. And now, with everything they'd gone through and all she was beginning to feel for him, he was hardly that.

She could feel his heart thump, a strong, steady beat that was comforting and oddly erotic. Overhead, the sky was a dark tapestry pierced by the shadow of the forest canopy, and the stars were an upside-down configuration of the ones she was used to viewing at home. She reached behind and drew her hand down his jawline, feeling the stubble that pebbled his jaw and brushed a pleasurable edge along her palm.

"Who are you, really?"

"Whoever you want me to be." There was laughter in his voice.

She turned over, lying on her side. The grass tickled against her naked skin. "What do you mean by that?"

"Exactly what I said."

He sat up.

"Anything I want you to be? That's ridiculous." She sat up reaching for her shirt and putting it on.

"You seem to have a need to remake things. Control

your environment, so to speak," he said smoothly, shifting the topic.

"I'm a scientist. Don't we all?"

Slowly he shook his head.

"You don't like a controlled environment? That's ridiculous. You can't work without one."

"This is my laboratory." His hand waved through the air, encompassing everything around them. "Impossible to control."

"Yes, but when you return to the city…"

"There is law and order and society. Rules I must follow." He sighed.

"Do you think you'll ever find Malcolm's killer?" she asked later after they'd returned to camp.

"Possibly. But there's still a chance we may never know."

"Are you serious? That's impossible. We can't just leave his death unsolved, unavenged."

"Unavenged? Don't you think that might be overly dramatic? This is Borneo, Vann."

"No one's ever shortened my name before."

"You like it," he replied.

"Maybe," she said sinking back down beside him. She trailed a finger down his cheek. "Say it again."

"Vann," he said softly.

"Kiss me," she said, her voice throaty, and she kissed him instead.

She claimed his lips with all the latent fire she had held back. Borneo. Harsh and wild and so beautiful, it sucked you in and, barring all that had happened, made you want to return again and again. Like Aidan, she thought as their lips met and their bodies anticipated the erotic dance. So very much like Aidan.

Overhead the off-kilter shrill call of some insect jangled around them. But to Savannah it was only an aphrodisiac, a catalyst that drove her deeper into his arms. For now, there was nothing but the passion between them. For now—and that was the last coherent thought as she folded into his arms under the darkened canopy of the Borneo rain forest.

Later when they returned to camp, she retired to her own small tent. And there she fell asleep, waking hours later disturbed by something. She pulled the tent flap open to see Jason emerge from his tent. She watched as he headed to the edge of the forest. Obviously, a bathroom break. She lay there listening to the sounds of the night. She meant to wait until he returned, but somewhere between that thought and Jason's return, she fell asleep.

****

"Fuck this," Matthew muttered.

It wasn't daybreak yet, and he was tired of waiting. Plus, there was a good chance that he might have waited too long, that an opportunity would never arise. For soon they'd be in a position to head out. It was now or never. He took one breath and then two, fighting to get his thoughts under control.

But if it wasn't one thing, it was another. The most recent, the damn rain. He'd been soaked, but the heat of the forest made it a warm rain, oddly pleasurable. He'd sat down, his back to a tree, and closed his eyes. He didn't know how long he slept, only that he'd been awakened by the footsteps of someone unfamiliar with the forest.

His heart pounded. And he held his breath and his very body still, and waited. Waited with the sky still dark, and the air humid with the rain that had stopped thirty minutes ago.

He knew the players, all of them. Except for Aidan, none of them were a threat.

And then the sound began again. The flat-footed heavy walk of someone wearing rubber-soled shoes that crushed the forest floor.

His heart raced and his palms sweated.

He lifted his hand, drifting it through the glossy black hair that had enticed so many an innocent woman. He'd fallen for none of them, instead leaving a trail of broken hearts here and in the city. He was known as a heartthrob. He wondered what they would think if they knew what he should really be known for. But that thought only brought his mind back to the feelings that ached deep within him. The feelings that he'd tried so hard to control when they'd first emerged. No more.

He watched as the man turned, he was slight, and a glint of moonlight sifted through a break in the trees and hinted that he was pale, as if he spent too much time indoors. Which was odd considering where the man was and where he'd been. But the truth was, he had a soft look to him, a city look. His mousy brown hair glinted as another spark of moonlight drifted through the foliage. The man unzipped his khaki pants and turned slightly so that his back was to him.

"Perfect," he whispered. "Bloody perfect."

He slid up behind him and wrapped his arm around his neck in a stranglehold.

His victim gasped and struggled, but he'd caught him in the perfect hold, in the perfect position. It was only a twist hard and to the left. The crack told him everything that he needed to know. The blood rushed to his groin as his victim fell.

Now work would mix with pleasure. For he needed to move the victim. He was too close to camp, and he needed the victim to be found later or never.

First, he pulled out his pistol, checked the silencer, and shot him once through the heart, for good measure.

He pulled off an alumni ring on the man's right hand.

For he needed the memory, a souvenir that would ensure he never forgot.

Chapter Twenty-Seven

Savannah woke again as the sky was beginning to lighten. A sense of foreboding ran through her. She wasn't sure why or what had disturbed her, but it had her sitting up, looking around. And then she remembered Jason.

She crawled out of her tent and went over to his tent.

"Jason," she whispered.

Nothing.

She pulled open the flap.

He wasn't there.

She stood up, her heart pounding. For dawn was on them, and Jason had left while it was still dark. She'd known it was him only by the light of the fire.

She and saw Aidan coming toward her.

"Jason's gone," she said.

"When?"

"I don't know. At least an hour, maybe more. I saw him head into the forest before sunrise, assumed it was for a bathroom break, and fell asleep. I just woke up and went to check, and he's gone."

"Could he be lost?"

"No." She shook her head. "I don't think so. Jason is methodical, careful. He'd never be stupid enough to venture too far from camp, especially at night."

"You're sure?"

"Yes. I think something has happened. That he's had

an accident, or…"

The word trailed between them dusted with all the possibilities, none of them good.

"Guys!" she said loud and briskly enough to arouse them all.

The flaps of pup tents opened. Mark emerged first. "What the flip?"

"Have any of you seen Jason?"

Ian was on his feet, followed by Sid. Her light shone on them and past where the flap of one pup tent was pulled back and Jason's portable cot lay empty.

"He's probably just in the bush," Ian said.

Ian shouted Jason's name, his voice echoing in the clearing. Seconds passed, and he shouted again.

She frowned, troubled at the haunting silence. There was no movement in the trees, no chattering of monkeys nearby, nothing. It was as if something dark and dire had happened, and the entire rain forest knew. She pushed the thought back. She was being ridiculous. But if there was nothing dark or dire, where was Jason?

"I'll search…" Ian began.

She held up her hand. "No. You guys stay here. Aidan and I will search the perimeter. I don't need more people disappearing."

"What are you suggesting?" Sid growled.

"That you're a damn poor tracker," Aidan said.

Sid swore under his breath but took a step back. He might be a lot of things, but he wasn't stupid enough to think he could take on Aidan.

"He's right, Sid," she said. "You guys stay here in case he comes back."

"All right," Sid agreed.

She turned and saw that Aidan was heading into the

rain forest. It seemed that he planned to search without her.

"Hey!"

"You stay…"

"No damn way," she interrupted him, running to catch up. "If nothing else, I'll follow your lead. Be a second set of eyes."

He said nothing.

She took that as a yes.

Ten minutes later, Aidan was bending over an area where the low-growing plants and shrubs had been disturbed.

"What are you thinking?" she whispered.

"I'm not sure. I can see that Jason was walking deeper into the jungle, away from camp," Aidan said.

He stopped in a place where, even to her, it was clear that the foliage had been crushed.

"Blood," he said. He looked back. "Not necessarily human. But there was more than one person here."

A few feet from there, it got worse.

"Drag marks," Aidan said.

"Oh my God. Now what? Do you think that he's…?"

"I have no idea," Aidan replied. "But I don't like any of this."

She sucked in a breath as he pulled out a long, lethal-looking knife.

"I need you to get back to camp. It's clear that the trail is heading away, not toward camp." He turned waving at her when she didn't move.

"What! I'm going nowhere. I'm responsible for him."

"And you're responsible for the others too," he said

grimly. "Look, this looks bad, but there's nothing you can do at the moment."

"I'm staying," she said through gritted teeth.

They trekked for another ten minutes and found nothing. They'd circled the camp, fanning out wider each time. She could sense his frustration as easily as she could feel her own despair.

"What do you think? Who the hell is out here? Is he dead?" The questions ran one into another, the last almost on a note of hysteria. She took a deep breath. Hysteria was not her.

"Whoever did this is good, damn good."

"What are you saying?" she asked, knowing in her heart that everything he was not saying had confirmed her fears.

"That there's nothing we can do. The authorities will be notified," Aidan said. "Anything more we might do now might jeopardize the others."

"You're saying we should go back?"

"No, I'm saying we are going back. Mark will mobilize the necessary resources."

For the first time, his take-charge attitude didn't grate. The thought of what might have happened was overwhelming.

"I need to get the team out of here, home—safe." Her last words were almost staccato points of action. "I don't care what it takes. We've got to do it as soon as possible."

"My thoughts exactly," he said.

It was the last words they spoke until they reached camp.

Chapter Twenty-Eight

Sunlight drifted through the trees as they plodded forward the next day. The path they followed cut through the forest and ran along the nearby river, often masked by the dense foliage. Their collective mood was low, morose even, with the loss of Jason and the dark, ever-present, and unknown danger that might still lurk.

Murder.

It was bone-chilling and frightening in a way that they hadn't been frightened before. For oddly Malcolm's death had never seemed about them but about him and someone that had been out to get him. But Jason, if he was dead—it could have been any of them. It was a thought they all shared. And as a result no one spoke except when necessary, and they'd trudged for over an hour in silence when a crack like a rifle blast broke the silence as it echoed through the forest.

"Thunder," Savannah whispered. But her heart raced, and her gut told her that it was something else, something she didn't want to consider.

"Shit!" Mark stopped.

"That wasn't thunder. That was gunfire," Ian said.

Oh, fuck! She thought of Jason, of Malcolm, of it happening again, of…

She was frozen in place.

"How the hell do you know?" Sid barked. "You wouldn't know the ass-end of…"

"I sure as hell do! I belong to a shooting club. I'm on the range regularly."

Another shot rang out.

"Shut the hell up both of you, and get down," Aidan roared.

Before she could move, Aidan had hit her in a full-body tackle. They crashed to the jungle floor with him taking the brunt of the fall, twisting at the last moment so he was beneath her. But even so, her hand ended up wedged painfully beneath her. She twisted, freeing it.

"Don't move," Aidan hissed, and there was nothing soft or understanding about his tone.

He stood up. "Stay here."

"What are you doing? You're not going after them?" She sat up, being careful to stay low even while shaking her head. "No!"

He covered her hand with his. "I'll be fine. The shot sounded closer than it actually was." With that, he melted quietly into the forest.

"How do we know there isn't more than one?" Ian whispered.

Around them the forest was strangely silent, and then seconds later in the distance, something popped and snapped.

"What is that?" Sid lifted his head and looked at Ian.

"I don't know. It's too far away," Ian replied.

Aidan is out there, Savannah thought.

"Stay here," she commanded. And like they wouldn't have done so many days ago, they did.

She'd learned something these last few days. How to issue an order, for one. And for two, she might be an amateur, but she could mark a trail well enough now to at least return to her starting point.

She moved quickly taking the path Aidan had until he'd disappeared from sight. The forest seemed to breathe damp and sweltering around her. But even after five minutes in, there was no sign of Aidan.

Then a hand clamped over her mouth, and she bit back a scream.

"Quiet," Aidan hissed in her ear. He let her go and motioned over his shoulder.

Seconds later she saw them. Two men with rifles over their shoulders, heading in the direction of the river. At a guess, their destination was the longboat that she could now glimpse through the trees. They were too far away to make out faces clearly, but their voices were loud and carried easily across the distance.

"Mandarin," Aidan whispered.

Aidan took her hand, squeezing so tight she almost gasped. His face was hard, impenetrable. She glanced back through the trees, to the river and the men. Now, there was another. But it was the hat that made her look again, a cowboy hat. Even from this distance the hat was very familiar. She couldn't place it, and yet she knew that she should. She almost held her breath in the minutes that it took the hunters to load the longboat and leave down river.

Aidan released her hand as the boat disappeared.

"You saw what the one was carrying?" he asked flatly.

And she had. A hornbill, the beautiful large orange-hued bill had been impossible to miss even from the distance they'd been at.

"They're protected," she whispered.

And what did it matter, she thought. Nothing was protected here in this jungle where it seemed killers of every stripe lurked. Nothing and no one was safe. It just got worse the lower you got on the food chain. A chill ran through her.

"You're okay?" Aidan's hand brushed her shoulder, and he pulled her closer.

She stood up, taking a step away from him. She folded her arms as if protecting herself from…

From what? she thought.

"Poachers," he said grimly. "We're going back to the others. There's nothing I can do now."

"Do you think they might have anything to do with Jason's disappearance?"

She tried to breathe, tried to control her thoughts, but the possibilities, the ugly, gruesome possibilities ran through her mind. This trip was a horror show that seemed to never end.

Aidan looked at her with troubled eyes. And she thought of what she had seen and who it had reminded her of.

"Blue wears a cowboy hat," she whispered.

"There's more than one cowboy hat in the jungle."

"Not many…"

"Blue and I had many discussions about the interconnectivity of the wildlife and the Iban. If there's anything we both abhor, it's poaching. No, whoever that was, he was Iban. But it wasn't Blue."

She hurried to catch up with him. "You said Blue was your good friend."

"He's like a brother to me. His father raised me like a son."

That stopped her. "His father?"

"Akan."

"You're part Iban." She frowned. He didn't look it,

but it made sense when she thought of how familiar he'd acted at the longhouse. Almost like he'd been coming home. And now she realized that he had.

"Nope. American, but my mother fell in love with anything counter to her own culture. You don't get much more counterculture than a tribe of headhunters. So we moved in, and here I am."

"That's leaving a lot out."

He punched a stand of long grass.

She knew snakes hid in that kind of grass. She shuddered. She wasn't sure why she couldn't leave it alone. The subject was obviously touchy for him. She wasn't that kind of woman. One that delved into the personal affairs of others, sniffing around in what really wasn't her business. But she couldn't stop.

"What was it like growing up here?" she asked. At another time it might have been a valid question. Right now, it was only to get her mind to a calmer place so she could think about all that happened with logic rather than with panic.

"I learned to hunt, to navigate the forest, to use a spear and blow pipe." His eyes narrowed as he looked at her. "To wear a loincloth effectively." He winked. "Don't think I didn't see you leering at me."

"I don't leer." She laughed. "Okay, not much, but let me tell you that loincloth would cause a stampede of women in any city." She paused. "You don't wear it in Kuching, do you?"

He laughed. "Every day."

She raised an eyebrow. "I bet. But still, I can't figure you out."

"That's how most women feel."

"And I suppose you've had many women."

She fought to look disinterested.

"Maybe you need a man."

"For what?"

"Getting through the rain forest for one."

"No!" She crossed her arms over her chest. "In fact, if I spent any time here, I would know this forest every bit as well as you. Any woman would."

"But she doesn't," he said, emphasizing *she*.

Savannah grabbed his arm and pulled him around, and he let her, like she knew he would. She rose up on tiptoes and kissed him. A hot, passionate kiss, and then she let go of his hand and pushed ahead of him. It was a kiss that temporarily swept the fear and horror and tragedy behind them.

"We need to keep our eyes on where we are. This long grass can be deadly," he said as he moved to her right.

She was to follow when she saw the telltale movement.

"Don't move." Aidan's voice was a raw hiss.

She froze as he raised his spear, and then it shot through the air and hit its mark.

The snake writhed and as suddenly stopped moving.

Aidan stepped carefully around it.

"Poisonous?" she whispered.

"Very," he replied calmly.

She shivered, clutching her arms under her chest as she stared at the dead snake. It wasn't big, but it seemed none of the poisonous reptiles were. "I'll be glad to get out of here for now."

"For now? What are you implying?"

"Nothing."

"Don't give me that. You're coming back," he

accused. “Don’t. Not without me, anyway.”

Aidan’s smile was slow and languid as his arm settled over her shoulders and he pulled her against him.

He was warm and solid. For a moment she couldn’t breathe. Her brain screamed like a pilot in a death spiral—divert, divert.

No. He was the wrong man. He was a nomad, a man of the wilderness. Despite a career in the city, the jungle was where he felt at home, where he would return.

His arm curving again around her waist reminded her of his heart-stopping nearness. She wrestled within herself. End it before she got hurt.

He belonged in the jungle, yet the elegance and grace that emerged so easily came from somewhere else.

An enigma. Dangerous.

Chapter Twenty-Nine

The next day was conflicted for everyone. For Jason hadn't been found, and there was nothing they could do. Savannah assumed that the authorities would send a search party. In the meantime, it weighed on them. She could see it in the heavy mood and in the silence. And yet, there was hope ahead. Hope as they neared the end of a difficult time, and as it became obvious that the trail was changing. Signs of civilization blossomed as a path emerged, cutting into the wilderness.

"We're not far, are we?" Ian asked.

"No, mate," Sid said. "I think we're seeing the end of this particular journey."

"We'll make the village today then?" She tried to share the hopefulness of her team while hope warred with regret and worry for her missing team members. Once it had all been about the expedition, about the search and the find. Now, what once might have been her greatest regret, that they were leaving behind a discovery, was far overshadowed by the loss of Malcolm and Jason.

"Almost there," Aidan said. Far ahead on the trail, something glinted. Glass or metal, either way it was evidence of a town, of civilization.

"Civilization." Ian's smile was huge and only surpassed by Burke's, whose gold tooth glinted in the sunlight.

"Jeez, man," Sid said. "Could you not have been satisfied with metal or porcelain like the rest of the world?" He shook his head. "Gold tooth. What an idiot."

She didn't say anything, for she'd heard Sid's harsh comments too many times to even acknowledge that it had been said at all.

"Suit yourself, Sid," Burke replied. "Just because you don't like it tells me it must have some class."

A whistle floated through the layered forest sounds. Aidan held up his hand, and the group was silent.

Aidan whistled a soft, melodious sound that shadowed the first whistle and seemed one with the forest. A dark-haired, deeply tanned, compact individual dropped from the branches and landed in front of them. He rolled back on his heels and straightened, pushing his long black hair from his face.

She frowned.

The last time she had seen this man he had been at the longhouse. Aidan's brother.

She stiffened thinking of her earlier doubts about him.

"Blue!" Aidan called.

His smile reminded her that she'd never seen Blue smile, until now. She stopped, keeping back, waiting to see what would happen next.

"Aidan," Blue said and nodded. "I wasn't sure I'd net you."

"Net me? Did you mean catch?"

Blue pushed another strand of black hair back from his face. "Wrong term. You know I still fight with my English."

"What are you doing here?"

"Shopping. Someone had to get nails and wire.

Akan is determined to start wiring the verandah."

"My fault," Aidan replied. "I listened to him."

"You know that only encourages him." There was laughter in Blue's tone.

"So you're helping Akan build?"

Blue shook his head. "Nope. That's on my return. I'm off for the next few days." He pushed his glasses up his nose and squinted into the sun in Savannah's direction.

She took a step back as if there were something threatening in the look. The sun beat down making his dark hair glow as he again ran a nonchalant hand through hair that barely touched his shoulders.

"So how are our scientists doing?"

Savannah wondered how Aidan would share the news of the horror show they'd left behind. Or she thought—would he?

"Blue, I don't think you've met Savannah and her team."

Blue held out his hand and shook as introductions were made. "Not officially. I've heard lots about you though. Saw you from a distance and, of course, Akan is still grumbling about your arrival. Kidding." He held up both hands. He turned his attention to Aidan. "Can we talk?"

Aidan clapped him on the back, and the two of them turned back to the path and began to walk.

She supposed the ease that he turned his mind to other matters, to a man who was obviously close to him, was because the men involved were strangers to Aidan. Still, they were people, one missing, the other dead. It was disconcerting on all levels.

Why had he yet to mention to his brother what had

happened? Was he telling him now? She was caught up in her thoughts as she watched.

Maybe he was waiting for the authorities, or the right people to inform. And whether or not that was the case, she knew that she needed to be part of whatever his plan was. She thought of the fact that soon many miles would be placed between her dream and a nightmare beyond comprehension. Her career now hung on the edge of success and the abyss of mediocrity. It all hinged on whether they could find the place where they had left the colony. It depended on a sane resolution to a nightmare expedition. One day she would come back. Now she just wanted to get out and send searchers to find Jason.

She'd lost a team member. She'd lost Jason. Even now he could be dead, he could be…

Her thought broke off as she forced her attention on the river, on a current that seemed to boil with rage as it swept by the village. She shuddered. Life and death ran through those violent waters. She looked away to the dock, a long expanse of weathered wood, empty except for the speedboat that bumped with the current against it. Above the dock, women crouched over vegetables laid out on blankets as they gathered together for an outdoor market. Locals with colorful plastic woven bags sauntered amid the merchants, examining the produce. It was a very different existence from the one she had just left in the longhouse.

Ahead of her, her team moved along slowly on the smooth dirt path that ran through the village.

She jogged to catch up.

"I don't see a plane!" Sid's tone was caustic.

"Of course not, Sid. This isn't JFK, where there's a

plane just waiting on the tarmac. We'll have to radio or something. Maybe there's a schedule," Ian replied.

"You're in luck," Aidan said as he joined them. "There's a motorboat ready to go to the next village. From there it's an overnight, and then you catch the boat to Kuching where I'll meet you."

"What do you mean? You're not going?" Savannah frowned. *What was going on?*

"Exactly, you, your team." His index finger trailed a sensuous path down her cheek. "This is it for now, Vann. Mark and I will get a team together to do a proper search for your man. And I'll meet you in Kuching."

She looked at the dock and the boat that waited there.

"What happened to the plane?"

It was a moot question. There was no plane, they both knew it, and she wasn't sure why she felt compelled to ask.

"Not until Monday. And not from here."

"Monday? What day is it?"

"Thursday."

She calculated carefully. That was right. They had found Malcolm on Thursday, arrived at the longhouse the same day. They had been here a week since Malcolm had died. How had that happened? They'd come in with a team of five and a guide. They were leaving with four and without a guide. One man dead and another might be.

"We'll do a proper search," Aidan promised.

"Do you think he's…"

"Still alive?" He took her hands. "No."

She pulled free, taking slow breaths, forcing herself to calm.

"We'll find the perpetrator," he promised her.

"Thank you," she said softly. "I wish there was more I could do. I wish that we weren't leaving..."

"You'll be fine," he assured her as he turned at a question from one of the tribesman.

"We're going by boat," Ian said as he came up behind her a few minutes later, and his tone reflected abstract misery. "Did you see the logs coming down that river?"

She sighed, turning her attention to Ian and silently thanking providence that he was here. Watching out for him took her mind off of all that had happened. "You'll be all right, Ian. Keep your eyes closed," she assured him with a light touch on his forearm.

Sid walked by and gave them a snort of derision.

"I'll see you in Kuching," Aidan's whispered reminder was hot on her ear, his voice a sexy growl. He'd done it again, snuck up on her. "Don't come back until you hear from me."

"Is that an order?"

And the sound of his voice, the warmth of his nearness only had her wanting nothing more than to throw herself into his arms. Instead, she turned around facing him as she folded her arms across her chest.

"Promise me. It will save everyone a lot of time and trouble if we don't have to send a team in to rescue you," he said, his hand dropping to her shoulder.

"Don't be utterly ridiculous. This will never happen again. It was a fluke, a horrible, horrible fluke," she finished softly, thinking of Malcolm and Jason. A fluke seemed frivolous in the face of what had happened.

"Savannah!" Ian butted in. "Don't be difficult."

She whirled on him and then deflated like a puffer

fish. She was being ridiculous, childish even. “You’re right.”

“Excuse me?” Ian’s tone was incredulous.

“Oh, hush,” she told him lightly and turned her attention to Aidan as Ian moved toward the dock.

“I’ll be in touch,” Aidan said. “And maybe then we can plan your return.”

“We?”

“You’ll come back despite and maybe because of the tragedy you’ve left behind,” he predicted with a grave look. “Definitely, you’ll be back. You have to for your career.”

He took her hands in both of his. “In the meantime, we’ll find your mate. I promise.”

She swallowed heavily, fighting for composure. She wondered how long before Jason was even found. She pinched her eyes shut. It was all overwhelming.

“The rain forest can be deadly, and you faced some of the worst. Don’t give up. Promise me that and promise me that you’ll wait until the perpetrator has been found and is dealt with before you make good on that. Then, I’ll be your guide, and if I can’t, I’ll choose who will be. Deal?”

“Deal,” she repeated.

“I’ll see you in Kuching,” he repeated just before she boarded the waiting speedboat.

She wouldn’t say it and couldn’t stop herself. “Promise.”

“Promise.”

He kissed her long and hard and deep before letting her go.

Sadness seeped into her being and seemed to fill every pore. For no matter what their relationship was here, no matter what their promises, with civilization in sight, the romance was well and truly over.

Chapter Thirty

Despite the cold from an air conditioning system set to high, Savannah relished the last bit of time she'd have when she wouldn't be continually thinking on her feet. She had no illusions about that. No matter how good the guide was, it was still up to her to keep the team safe.

Beside her Ian shifted and jabbed her in the ribs with his elbow.

"Ian," she hissed.

"What?" he mumbled in his half awake state.

"Move over. Better yet, wake up."

He curled up, flipped to his right side, and began to snore in sync with Sid across the aisle. She considered how future trips might play out. She wouldn't have the fiasco of this one. She bit her lip. She could hardly call it a fiasco. That was a major understatement of what had really happened, one man dead and one missing. It was unthinkable.

She closed her eyes and opened them to look out and see water spraying off the metal hull as the boat roared, fighting its way upriver. Outside the forest was a blur of green, and in the water, logs rushed by as the boat pushed at a breakneck speed against the current. Another boat passed beside them. The boat was the twin of theirs. The sleek metal body with its round top, pounded across the water at a speed of fifty kilometers with the overflow passengers clinging to the top.

It was a relief when the boat's engines cut as it slid into the dock at Rumah Muleng. But even as she felt relief, she also knew that she would never again be satisfied with lab work like she had once been. She couldn't imagine being under fluorescent lights analyzing someone else's find. She needed to be in the field, breathing the excitement.

She took a deep breath. She finally understood why the rain forest drew Aidan.

When they mate, they mate for life.

Aidan had been talking about the hornbills. Yet the words had been so intimate. And she had dodged the implication despite an attraction like none she had ever felt before. She was so sure that it could never be. Now, despite everything that had happened, she wasn't so sure.

As they emerged from the boat, the smell of leaf mold was heavy in the turgid heat. The jungle rustled and screeched, and she knew that on the forest floor beneath the dead foliage were the bustling colonies of insects too numerous to count. She thought of everything that was to come and briefly the thought hit her that this might just be the illusion of calm.

****

It had been a relief to know that Aidan had found nothing. The woman and her group had provided no additional information. He could safely let them go as Aidan had planned, except for one very important detail. He sighed. There was always that one detail. Why could things never be simple?

He'd give Aidan credit—when he fell, he fell hard. And now the woman was the catalyst for Aidan to dig even deeper. Stubborn was etched in her dainty jaw just as it had been in Anne's. Anne, he wouldn't think of her, yet he couldn't stop. Everything was for Anne.

Anne.

For a moment sorrow hit him. For she was dead. And yet, she couldn't be. He wouldn't believe it. For they had so much yet to experience together. He would prove to her that he was more than just an Iban warrior. Soon she would be living in luxury.

Meantime he had to silence the other woman's questions. For those questions were persistent and would only lead to eventual answers—he couldn't take that chance.

He pressed a finger to his aching temple. To think this had all started because of one mistake. He should not have let this become more than a one-man operation. Agreeing to a partnership was when the trouble began. That was when everyone had gotten greedy. It was really the only reason Malcolm had been shot, greed. Malcolm had wanted in on the game.

And now this group only posed a problem. He had to get rid of them. That was the only thing he knew how to do. The woman and her team had to disappear, and the easiest way to do it was in the jungle.

As long as blood was not literally on his hands, it would all be okay.

Blue drew a shaking hand through his overlong black hair.

"It'll be okay, Anne," he whispered to his long-dead wife. "Soon it will all be over."

Chapter Thirty-One

Kuching, Malaysia

"Interesting case," Andrew said, his black hair standing out at odd points around his ears.

It was as if he'd forgotten that he had hair to be dealt with before he left the house that morning. The coroner pushed the metal chair across the linoleum floor with a screech of stiff wheels. His white coat was already smeared with what looked like body fluid. But Aidan guessed it was only the remains of the pathologist's breakfast.

"So you told the scientists that you'd buried the body and then got it on the first plane out. Leaving them trapped in the jungle with you for days. Brilliant."

"Stress tends to bring answers," Aidan said dryly. Although he didn't admit the fact that it took no real brilliance on his part when getting a plane in would have taken a bit of maneuvering. And by trapping them in the jungle as Andrew had so eloquently put it had caused another scientist to go missing and endangered the others. It had been stupid from the outset.

Now he sat, he and Andrew—alone. Being alone was as he'd planned. For, although Andrew was easygoing, he wasn't when it came to whom he allowed in his autopsy room. Aidan was one of the few.

"So none of them suspected that they were trekking through the wilderness for no good reason. That they could have made the trip days earlier?"

"You got it. I can safely say with ninety-nine percent surety that none of them had anything to do with the death." He stood up. "Of course, when Jason disappeared and everything went south, there was only one option—getting out."

"So that's what you did. Got them the hell out of there," he said. "I mean, what else could you do?"

"I know. But the thought that one of them is still missing when they could have been safe in Kuching days prior…that it was all my doing…"

"What are you saying?" Andrew asked. "You're not psychic. Who would have known or even guessed? Especially, as the law of averages was working in your favor."

"I know but still."

"Don't beat yourself up, man."

Aidan nodded. He and Andrew had become friends of sorts over the years.

"You're going back?" Andrew asked.

"No choice. For now, the chief of one of the tribes on the river has started a search party, and Mark's heading out to meet them."

"Isn't that dangerous?"

"They're every bit, if not better equipped for such a venture, than an outside policing agency, at least better at tracking. Besides, they're armed, and I trust they can hold their own. In fact, my guess is if the killer is still out there, he's soon going to wish he was dead." He shook his head. "He's not only an interloper, but he's making a bad name for their home. Let me say that at the least the chief wasn't impressed. At the worst, he was ready to mete out justice."

"Not a wise thing on his part," Andrew mused.

"No," Aidan said. "It wouldn't be. I mentioned that, at which point he assured me that it was nothing more than posturing, an empty threat."

"And you believed him?"

Aidan shrugged. "No choice."

"So that brings us back to the evidence at hand. Our friend here?" He nodded to the corpse. "I just pulled him out of the drawer again this morning. Already filed the preliminary police report." He paused, scalpel in hand. "By the way, they're waiting on you."

"I know," Aidan admitted. "I've been duly notified."

Andrew chuckled. "That's what I like about you, Aidan. You're consistent. Paperwork isn't your forte, and you make no bones about it. Unfortunately, that's not making big points with the chief. Anyway, like I was saying, there was something nagging at me." He waved the scalpel for evidence. "About the body, I mean." He dropped the scalpel on the tray, pulled his gown off and tossed his gloves into the disposal. He nudged the faucet on with his elbow and began to wash his hands. "I hate the ones that have spent time in the sun."

"Isn't that most of them?" Aidan asked. "This is Kuching."

"You're right. But I did my training in mainland China. Different decomposition rate, for sure. The sun is a killer." He glanced over his shoulder as the water continued to run and he lathered disinfectant soap over his hands.

"So why do you stay?" Aidan asked, although he wasn't particularly interested, he already knew the answer.

"Beijing's too cold for me and too crowded." He shook his hands over the sink and turned to look at Aidan.

"This alone." He nodded at the corpse. "Is a strange case. Never mind the rest of what you've said."

"You think?"

"Yeah, I think. Anyway, as far as this lad is concerned…" He frowned.

Aidan waited, his mind sliding right over Andrew's habit of lifting terms from other cultures. This time he'd ventured into Scotland with his term *lad.*

"And…" he prompted.

"He was shot and then beheaded. This is where it gets a little weird."

Aidan strode across the room and then stopped, glancing back at the autopsy table, where the corpse now rested under a white sheet. "We already know that from your preliminary."

"Exactly." Andrew smiled broadly. "And he was beheaded about five hours later."

"Five hours later?" Aidan hadn't expected that. "That makes no sense."

"Exactly," the coroner replied. "This is the third body we've had land in Kuching from the rain forest in the last week. The tribes aren't taking well to some of the loggers. That being said, it's the Iban who have been winding up on my slab, and it's almost impossible to pin responsibility on anyone. This is different though. The others all had their heads."

Aidan waited for Andrew to continue.

"Headhunters. If word got out, it would kill tourism. The authorities don't want that. They might very well crack down on this one."

"Headhunters? You're insinuating that some tribesman hunted this chap down, shot him, and then five hours later beheaded him? That hardly makes sense."

The coroner's smile widened. "There lies the mystery. But it gets more interesting. Cause of death was pretty obvious. It was exactly like Mark said when he called. The bullet killed him. Tested him for chemicals and he was clean. There are scrapes on his belly, so after being killed, he was dragged. By then, the blood had already drained and coagulated.

"Another thing. See the bullet?" Andrew held the bullet between his fingers. "It's from a hunting rifle that's uniquely Chinese-made. That's different from the others."

"Chinese?" Aidan took the bullet from Andrew. He rolled it on his palm. "Seems more and more likely that it was them."

"Them?"

"Before I bumped into Vann and her group, there was another expedition that day."

"A regular traffic jam in the rain forest."

"Yeah, that's what I thought then. It's becoming much more sinister the further we delve into it. I'm assuming that their guide was one of the locals, but I never saw him. He had dropped them off and then came and picked them up by boat. It wasn't anyone I knew."

"Are you sure?" The coroner took the bullet back and dropped it into a glass beaker.

"No." Aidan ran his fingers through his hair. "I'm not. I guess I don't want to believe that it might be someone I know. Frankly, I can't imagine any of them taking blood money. They killed a monkey that day and later hornbills. Then, later, of course it got worse when we lost the man from Vann's team."

Andrew nodded. "I can't begin to imagine the insanity of it." He looked down at the sheet-covered corpse and then looked up. "I did find something else rather interesting." The coroner went over to the metal counter that lined the wall. "I don't know what validity it has, but it seems to me either the deceased collected it himself. Or maybe the killer dropped it. Some weird sort of way to put your brand on a crime. Either way, it's not indigenous to Borneo. I didn't include it in the preliminary report. I wanted you to know first." He took something from a drawer. "So what's the story on our Malcolm? Was he into collecting African bird feathers?" he asked as he turned around with a brilliant blue feather in his tweezers.

For a moment, Aidan weaved where he stood.

"Hey, big fellow. Don't get that excited. It's only a feather." He laid it on the metal stand next to the corpse. "Or is it? Do you know something about this?"

"Where was it?"

"In his inside pants pocket." Andrew flipped the feather thoughtfully. "Maybe it was a good luck charm that he picked up somewhere and carried all the time."

"No." Aidan's voice was stiff even to his own ears. "It wasn't."

"What do you mean?"

"Nothing. Look, there's something I need to check out. Could you keep this quiet until then?"

"The autopsy?"

"No, the feather. I need to take it with me."

"You mean not mention it? That's unethical." He shook his head. "And the feather, no way." He set the feather down and turned away.

"Write slow," Aidan said as he quietly took the feather, knowing he was pushing their friendship to the limits.

"That," Andrew said as he turned and beamed, "I can do. The chief has the preliminary to keep him busy. If you report what you know, that should please everyone. Meantime, I sense a computer outage happening already." He slapped Aidan on the back. "I'll need it back in the evidence room before this case is closed," he said in an undertone.

Aidan went back to where the sheet covered the body. He grasped the rough sheet, considered pulling it back, hesitated, and then dropped it.

"Yeah, he's not a pretty sight. Even for me," Andrew said as he came up beside him. "I've found over the years that even the absolutely bizarre cases can sometimes have a logical explanation. So I don't mind providing a roadblock or two for the police." He chuckled. "Yeah, some slow report writing should do it. I'd hate to see a hasty investigation."

"You would?" Aidan frowned.

"All I'm saying is, if our cop force goes riding out into the wide, wild jungle looking for the perp, there might be some innocent heads rolling." He guffawed at his own joke.

Aidan didn't laugh, somehow it wasn't funny.

"It was a joke, man."

"But some of the police were raised in longhouses."

"Exactly. There are a few that would rather not remember that. I'm not sure why. One of my closest friends has the greatest memories of the longhouse he was raised in."

Aidan nodded and wasn't really listening for he was

beginning to realize the potential implications of this case. It might be that it wasn't so much the murderer that needed to be protected. It was plausible that it might be the beheader.

"In case the murderer and the beheader aren't one and the same," he murmured, "is it possible that the beheader was Iban?"

"Exactly my question, and considering the traffic in the jungle lately, we could have a sicko with no traditional ties to anything," Andrew replied, heading for the door. "C'mon, I'll buy you a beer." He opened the door and turned out the lights. The softer light in the hallway was a relief from the harsh fluorescents that flooded the aseptic, sterile autopsy room.

Aidan breathed in and almost sighed as the door shut behind them, separating him from that room of death and from the body.

"Hurry up, man. A beer will clear the fur off your tonsils."

The coroner set out at a fast walk, actually an incredible pace for a man who didn't quite crack five and a half feet. Aidan had to pick up his own pace to keep up, even though his six-and-a-half-foot lanky build could easily eat up the distance. Andrew held his own and marked the pace.

Chapter Thirty-Two

"C'mon, guys, let's get moving." Savannah literally herding her team, the last leg of their journey ahead of them. It would be made on another boat ride, this one short. It was a boat ride that would take them to Kuching. The transport gleamed under the tropical sun, its rounded metal hull riding low on the water. The hum of passengers, mostly locals, swirled around them, and she could only think of Aidan.

The lineup moved, and they shuffled forward.

"Savannah?"

Startled, she took a step back.

"I'm sorry, I didn't mean to frighten you." His voice was hesitant, his glasses glinting benignly in the sunlight.

She took another involuntary step back. "Blue?"

"I was hoping I'd catch up with you. Aidan told me about your find. That's exceptional. Something you want to get on right away."

"You know about entomology?"

"I live in the Borneo rain forest," he said, as if that explained everything. And when he smiled, only one side of his mouth turned up, giving him a slightly endearing, almost goofy expression. His hand slid to his belt and rested there. "How could I not?" He pinched the bridge of his glasses and dropped his hand.

"Where's Aidan?" she asked. "He's not with you?"

"Headed into Kuching. Got an unexpected ride just

after you left. You never know when Eric will show or not."

"Eric?"

"One of our main pilots for getting us into the city. Aidan was a little put out that he couldn't put you and your team on that flight too. But like I said, it was unscheduled, and you were already gone." He shrugged.

"Kuching? He'll be there when we get there?" She looked back to where Sid was in what looked like a serious discussion with Ian and then turned back to Blue. "I thought he was going to tie up some loose ends." She frowned. He had never clarified what those loose ends might be. "Why is he in Kuching?"

Blue shrugged. "Business of one sort or another. More than likely real estate, that would be the one thing that would make him rush back at a moment's notice. He could be a while." He eyed her, all friendly concern. "I guessed your find wouldn't have that kind of time, so I suggested I meet up with you and take your team back in."

She frowned. "Aidan agreed to this?"

Blue's nod was brief but his wide smile more than compensated. "I'm a top-notch guide. Although I have to say he was rather reluctant at first, but he knows how important that find is to you." He hitched his belt up and dropped his hand. "He drew out a map so I can easily get you back to the site."

"Wasn't there a storm front moving in?"

"What? You don't trust me?" Blue grinned boyishly. "I've been reading weather since I was a boy. This system is going to skirt us and move on."

"I don't know you."

"Look, Aidan knows I'm one of the best. I'll get you

in and out of there, and if weather looks like an issue, we'll take samples and run. With Aidan's blessing."

It was that last promise that had her agreeing, that and the desire to succeed that drove her stronger than anything in her life.

"All right." But somehow those words didn't have the bright and cheery note she tried so hard to inflect.

****

Aidan's second beer sat untouched. "A Chinese-made bullet, what does that say?"

"I don't know, I'd think pretty compelling evidence that it might have been that group you saw earlier." Mark set his beer down.

He'd arrived in town just hours ago and caught up with Aidan shortly after his arrival and met him and Andrew at a local bar.

"Maybe," Aidan replied. He couldn't mention the feather, not now, for admitting that one piece of evidence was too painful. He was choked on that fact and on the sighting of the cowboy hat that he had so adamantly denied so few days earlier.

"Don't look so dreary," Mark said as he slouched back. "It's always darkest before the dawn and everything you're worried about may never come to fruition."

"Thanks for the momism," Aidan said.

"What? Never mind," Mark said as he glanced at his watch. "It's not that late, maybe you want to file that police report. Let them know there isn't much you could add to what they already have."

Across the room, Andrew was chatting it up with a group of associates. The bar was busy despite the fact that it was close to suppertime on a weekday.

"Yeah," he agreed, distracted for this wasn't his only trouble spot. There was the disappearance of Jason. And the fact that there'd been someone else out there stalking them was almost a certainty.

"You know I would have made the same decision in your shoes," Andrew said thoughtfully as he came back, sitting down beside Mark. "It makes sense. Make them uncomfortable, rule them out as suspects. Who would have thought that you would be stalked?"

"Stalked, no," Aidan said.

"Maybe not, but I'd put money on the fact that two different people are involved."

"Two killers?" Mark asked.

"That's my best guess too," Aidan agreed. But it wasn't the worst of what he guessed.

Blue.

He couldn't believe there was a connection, and yet he held the evidence in his hand. He twirled the feather. The feather linked to Blue, and the thought of the possibilities made him feel physically ill. How was his Iban family involved? What had Blue done, and what did Akan know?

He stood up. "Look, you're right. I need to file that report. I'll talk to you later."

"Better yet, I'll come with you," Mark said.

"Yeah, I best get home," Andrew agreed. "If there's anything else you need, I'm usually awake into the wee hours."

"Thanks, Andrew," he said, before shaking the man's hand. "You've done more than enough. I'll get what you need back to you shortly."

"What was that about?" Mark asked a few minutes later.

"Nothing of any interest," Aidan said trying to cut the annoyance from the words. What was with Mark and his nosy questions? And as he thought that he realized that because of that and other things, the thought of Mark coming with him didn't sit well and there was no getting him to back off. It was a situation where he'd be forced to deal—for now.

Chapter Thirty-Three

"The tribes are talking up and downriver," Chief Lieu said thirty minutes later. "I got word just a few hours ago. Of course, that's only because I put out the word to report anything out of the ordinary. And this group is definitely that." He looked at Aidan. "What happened to the woman and the rest of her crew?"

"They're here in Kuching."

"Are you sure?" The police chief smiled good-naturedly. "I heard some fool scientist, a woman no less, is trekking through the forest. I expected that you were guiding them." His eyes narrowed. "What's going on?"

Something froze in Aidan's throat, and for a moment he was silent before spinning on his heel. "I don't know. But I intend to find out."

"It might not be her," Mark said beside him.

"You've seen a lot of women scientists in the rain forest lately?" Aidan snapped.

"Jeez, man," Mark said and put his hands up. "Keep your shirt on, I'm with you."

"Who took her back in?" Aidan asked.

The police chief shrugged. "A local guide, I imagine." He stood up. "You said one of the men disappeared?"

"Yes, I searched and there was no sign of him. A possibility that there might be foul play, but I had the others to deal with. There's a search organized by a nearby tribe underway right now."

The police chief frowned. "I'm not liking the sound of this and if I had any officers available… Look, I can dispatch a team in the next few days. Act as reinforcements if you need them or…?"

"No," Aidan replied adamantly as he moved toward the exit. "I have to do this on my own."

"Let me know what you find."

Chief Lieu's words were cut off as the door slammed behind them, and soon Aidan was striding down the sidewalk with Mark at his heels. What was Vann thinking? There was no doubt that the scientist that Lieu had mentioned was her. Was it possible she went alone, with her team and no guide? Despite the question, he knew just as surely as the feather he'd tucked in his shirt pocket, that she hadn't. He also knew that she'd keep her word unless something or someone had intervened.

There was an urgency in his walk for he had to find her. The truth was jelling in his mind, not with answers but suspicions that if true, only solidified what his gut was already telling him, that time was close to running out.

There was only one way to get back into the jungle in record time. There was only one person crazy enough to venture in with a major weather system threatening and monsoon season clipping its heels—Eric.

Two hours later they found Eric in a local bar. Fortunately, Eric had not gotten too far into his drinking for the night and was still coherent. Since the tragedy when his shaky old plane had crashed, killing one of the passengers, Eric had drunk copiously and was drunk by sundown most nights.

"What are you up to tomorrow?" Aidan asked as he settled into a chair opposite Eric. He shook his head in the negative as the waiter came over and asked for his order.

"Why?"

"I'm going to take a chance and fly on that piece of crap you call a plane. Tomorrow. I'm going home."

"The longhouse?"

"No."

He knew exactly where she was headed, and it wasn't to the longhouse. If she hadn't gone on a manhunt herself, she would find that colony. Despite the double tragedy they'd been hit with, it wouldn't stop any of them and especially her. He knew that as truly in his gut as he knew his own name. In fact, some of it, he didn't have to guess. She'd told him.

Damn, he thought.

He rubbed the back of his neck as sweat tingled on his skin.

"Aidan, what's up, man?"

"I'm going back to Rumah Muleng."

"You're serious?"

He ignored the question thinking of how he'd manage it. The plane could only take him in so far. That meant that he would walk from the landing point. From his calculations, he'd still be able to beat Vann's group to their destination. That is, if the plane got off the ground at the first sign of daybreak tomorrow.

"Can you fly me in?"

"Hey, for sure. But it's no piece of crap. Got me a brand-new plane."

"Brand-new?"

"Yeah. Blue got it for me."

How did one describe the moment when the bottom dropped out of their world? Aidan had felt that once before. When Sunrise had died. And although Blue hadn't died, in that moment it felt like he had.

He tried to push thoughts of Sunrise from his mind. She had been so young, and it had been so unfair. He knew that was some of the reason that he strove to find justice in a world where there often wasn't any. He turned his attention back to Eric.

"Tomorrow morning, daybreak work for you?"

"Deal," Eric replied. "I'll meet you at the airport."

He would have said tonight, but it was too late to fly in. The thought of waiting until daybreak seemed intolerable, the time interminable. As they strode the short distance to their hotel, his thoughts focused solely on Vann. His stomach twisted, and for a moment he felt like throwing up as he thought about his last meeting with Andrew. The blue feather was nagging at him. There had only been two like it—he had one, and he had given the other to Blue.

Chapter Thirty-Four

He longed for civilization, for the cosmopolitan taste and feel of well-heeled crowds. He longed for history and sophistication and a pace that left one breathless—London permanently. But all that cost money.

An Iban heritage was rich, not in money but in the history and the guardianship of the rain forest. He wanted none of that. If he believed in reincarnation, he would have said his birth into the tribe had been nothing but a cosmic joke. Always he had yearned for what he thought of as civilization. He could think of no other places on earth more fitting than those metropolises that sprang from the crowded centers of the world. Places where commerce moved at warp speed. Not here in Borneo, where even the little city of Kuching was too small, too provincial. None of it could satisfy him. That's why he'd agreed to the deal. It was a deal that he had come to regret. For his partner was more unstable than he had imagined. How anyone could be that upset over the death of a woman, he could not imagine. There was so much more to life. He had known Anne, and there had been nothing special about her. She was like any Iban girl, too simple for his taste. But Blue was crazed. His obsession over a dead wife was more than evidence of that. He only wished he'd known all of that before they had ever struck a deal. All he could do now was hold it all together long enough to get what was his and get out.

Soon it would be over. Despite the intrusion of the mad man, some other killer without cause, who was creating undue interest on the rain forest, he'd prevail. Soon, he would have it all and leave the primitives, those who called him family—worse, called him Fish—and the others, far behind. For in the end, only one man could win, and he had no doubt who that might be.

****

Daybreak had well passed before they began the trek back into the jungle. Overnight, Drew had a case of traveler's illness, and for a few hours in the early morning, Savannah had considered sending him back to Kuching. It was only at Drew's insistence that they waited, and by seven a.m. they had headed out.

The first few hours had been an easy trek, and she'd found Blue a pleasant companion. He was quick to point out the various plants and animals, and it took all she had not to stop to examine many of the areas dense in insect activity. She had to focus on one thing, beetles that farmed. Everything else could wait.

"You've known Aidan for a long time?" she asked Blue later in the morning, knowing part of the answer. But she wanted another perspective, a chance to better understand Aidan, the man she was growing to love. She grimaced; if she were truthful with herself, she loved him already.

"Since he was eight and he arrived sullen, scrawny, and pale-faced, and my father called him son." His grin was slightly lopsided, and his eyes twinkled behind the finger-smeared lens. "I was appalled."

"But he became your brother?"

"He did. And for a time, I loved him."

Savannah stumbled on a vine.

"Are you all right?" Blue was at her side, his tone solicitous, the smudged lens of his glasses filming his eyes.

"Fine, thank you."

He dropped her elbow and moved forward, continuing to break trail.

"Aidan was destined to be more than this."

There was something off in his voice that hinted at something else.

"You miss him?" she guessed.

He swung around to face her, as many feet away her team followed their broken trail.

"Miss him. I prayed that he would leave. It took many years for it to come to that." Blue's smile turned wistful. "I remember when he was ten, he was bit by a centipede on our first trek through this same jungle."

"He could have died," she said, fumbling with the wild turn the conversation was taking and trying to restore some sort of equilibrium.

Blue scowled. "Never. I wouldn't let him. I took care of him and carried him back to the longhouse."

"Carried? How old were you?"

"Twelve." Blue's scowl dropped. "And he was big for his age, even then. It was a bugger getting him to safety. But I'd never have left him here." He shaded his face with his hand and peered into the horizon before turning his attention back to the trail. "Not then…"

The words trailed like a hint of frost between them.

"You've never left the longhouse?" she asked, trying to gain back the easy rapport they'd shared earlier that morning. It was becoming clear that whatever was disturbing Blue was going to adversely affect this expedition if she didn't get him back on the right track.

"Did you know that the autopsy of your guide showed no bruising? It takes a lot of force to remove a head." Blue grinned, ignoring her question. "You didn't know, did you? Or that they took the body to Kuching and had a proper autopsy done there."

For a moment, it felt like her heart had stopped beating. "Are you saying that Malcolm wasn't buried at the longhouse? How did they get the body out?"

"They? Aidan. And, to answer your question, by plane." Blue smiled slightly, and the gleam from his glasses seemed to wink obscenely at her.

For a moment, Savannah couldn't make eye contact. Then her chin came up, and she met Blue's smirk head-on. "There was no plane available."

"There was Eric's. Piece of junk that shouldn't be in the air. Not like the new one that hit the air just the other day." His grin was broad. "I got him that. I'm a rich man now, or at least I will be soon."

She wasn't sure what to say. Yet Blue's attention was fixated on her like he expected an answer. "That's great," she said weakly, unable to put enthusiasm into the comment.

Blue scuffed the ground with his hiking boot. "We took a chance on getting Malcolm's corpse out."

"Why didn't Aidan say anything?" she asked more to herself than Blue.

"He's always gotten what he wanted." Blue's voice held a slight quiver. For a minute, it seemed that it might be tears that glinted in his eyes.

Now, even the possibility of the find of the century, could not combat her nerves. She was leery of going any farther with him. On the other hand, they were too far into the jungle to make it back on their own. Tentatively, she touched his arm. "Blue?"

"Leave me." He shook her hand off his arm and stormed away.

"Blue," she called, hurrying after him.

He turned and at the same time a slash of green slipped across his face and for a minute she could only see his eyes. Eyes rich and dark like the earth, and just as mysterious.

The branches dropped, and Blue was standing in front of her. "I'm sorry," he said, and something in his face softened. He brushed a knuckle gently across her cheek.

Savannah jumped and took a few steps back. "Don't, please."

"Don't? Anne, I love you."

She flinched and pushed away from him even as he reached for her.

What was going on here?

Behind her she could hear her team still struggling through the last tangle of brush that concealed this small clearing. They'd be here in minutes. That's all the time she had to get Blue back to reality. For it was obvious that his mind was somewhere else.

"Anne?"

"No, Blue, my name is Savannah." Her body tensed, and her feet itched to run, for the look in Blue's eyes was not sane.

"I… He pushed his glasses up his pug nose, and for a moment, confusion muddied his deep brown eyes. "I'm sorry. I thought Aidan said Anne, I thought…"

She took a deep breath. "Who is Anne?"

"No one. It doesn't matter."

"She matters to you," Savannah pushed. Something had him on an emotional edge. And the one thought that terrified her was the possibility that Aidan knew nothing of his brother's emotional instability. And that thought brought others and a seed of doubt that was rapidly expanding. Did Aidan know about this expedition or had Blue lied? The thought was growing into a viable and chilling reality.

Chapter Thirty-Five

"Let's get moving," Eric commanded. He was dressed in combat boots, a worn wanna-be soldier beret and a T-shirt that sported *U.S. Army* in faded letters across its olive-green background.

Some things never changed. Eric had never been in the service. But he had a collection of stories about nonexistent combat encounters during Desert Storm.

Aidan ducked his head as he climbed up the narrow ramp into the plane. He should have known how badly Vann not only wanted but needed this discovery. But why would Blue have taken her back when he knew that to stay too long in the jungle would be a danger not just to those he led, but to himself?

He shuddered at his inability to stop what was roaring into a full-scale disaster.

"You couldn't have stopped her," Mark said.

Aidan swung on him. "How do you know?"

"She would have found another plane, a boat, whatever it took."

Aidan said nothing. He couldn't. All he could see was Eric and the gleaming hull of the new twin-engine Otter. How had Blue managed to afford it? He wouldn't make enough on the occasional gigs as tourist guide. There were only a few ways to make that kind of money, and Aidan didn't want to consider any of those possibilities. When he spoke to Blue, the whole matter would be cleared up. Despite his gut churning on the possible bad outcome, his brain said there was a logical explanation. He was sure of it.

Still, as the plane banked over the Borneo rain forest, his gut tightened. He had the dull feeling that this was the beginning of an end. He stretched his legs out and closed his eyes and prayed with everything he had that he was wrong.

Who would have thought that Blue, of all people, might have accepted money from men who raped the forest, his home, for personal gain? He wouldn't think of it. He had to think of it. He was an investigator, and his personal feelings had to be put to the side. There was too much at stake. He sucked in a deep breath.

"Nothing's for sure yet," Mark reminded him.

A knot sat in his throat, and dread lodged low in his belly.

Aidan shook his head. *The blue feather pretty well clinches it,* he thought. But it wasn't just the feather that convinced him, there was something else, and it was that that he didn't want to consider. For it changed everything.

The plane bounced and settled into a landing.

"Well, troops, should you accept this mission," the jovial Eric shouted over his shoulder as the plane came to a halt. "Open the hatch, let's march."

Mark stood up. "Let's get a move on, shall we?"

Aidan resisted the urge to smack the flippancy from both their faces. But that would serve no purpose and wouldn't change the fact that Vann was alone with Blue, her team, and an unforgiving jungle. He wasn't sure which scenario terrified him more.

On the other side of the dock, the speedboat and

driver he'd booked the night before bumped gently against the dock as the current pushed against its fiberglass hull. Aidan threw his knapsack into the speedboat before going to speak with the driver.

He sucked in a deep breath of clean air mixed with the turgid scent of outboard motor fuel as he and Mark sank into seats behind the driver. The speedboat backed up from the dock before spinning ninety degrees in the powerful current. Overhead the Borneo sun spun hot and ominous as the rain forest crowded closer. He leaned back, closed his eyes and tried to breathe calmly. Their time together replayed like a litany.

Minutes into the journey, the boat began to slow. Unease churned deep and uncomfortable in his gut. It was an unease he'd learned long ago not to ignore. His gut clenched, and all he could think of was her.

"What are you going to do?" Mark asked as the boat bumped up against the dock and he followed Aidan's leap to land.

"There really isn't much choice. They left from here this morning, there's still time to catch them." Aidan passed a hand across the back of his neck. "The description that's coming from everyone we've spoken to matches Blue."

Mark looked down before meeting Aidan head-on with a glare that matched Aidan's frown.

"Bastard."

"He has his reasons," Aidan said.

"I doubt if anything justifies this," Mark replied darkly. "If it is him."

"I didn't tell you. There was a feather on Malcolm's body. The feather belongs to Blue," Aidan said as he stepped on the dock. "There were only two. I had one and Blue had the other." Aidan turned toward the village. "It's indisputable. Rare and African. I got them on safari years ago."

"I remember. You were twelve when your mother took you to Africa," Mark said. "How did Malcolm get it?"

"I don't know." Aidan twisted the straps of his pack. He couldn't contemplate where the evidence was leading.

"Strange for him to have met up with Malcolm unless it was planned. I hate to say it, but I wouldn't rule out the possibility."

Mark might be right, but Aidan had no wish to talk about it. Blue was his brother and he owed him some sort of loyalty, but not at the expense of Vann or her team. "I don't think they could have gotten too far. Blue can't keep his usual pace with them in tow." Aidan pulled on his pack. "I'm hiking in."

"The weather." Mark scanned the cloudy sky. "It's not a great time…"

"The weather could cut it short. It is the rainy season," Aidan agreed, thinking of the monsoon that was already threatening to cut a swath down the east coast of Borneo.

Mark grimaced and picked up his pack. "Let's go."

"I'll go alone."

Go back was on the tip of Aidan's tongue, to insist that he go alone. And, he wasn't sure why, except that because of Blue, he was reluctant to trust anyone. The brother of his heart might be the biggest betrayal of his life. It was a hurt linked to a foreboding that ached deep and ragged and for now felt completely irreparable.

"No, you won't." Mark hefted his knapsack and

slipped his arms through the straps. "It's too dangerous."
He chuckled dryly. "Just try to stop me."

"I won't argue with you. If you're coming, let's get going." Aidan said and headed out without looking back.

It took over three hours before they came upon fresh tracks. The tracks were less than an hour old.

"They're just ahead of us," Aidan said.

"I just hope we make it in time," Mark said grimly.

Aidan nodded and pushed ahead. He had the same reservations as Mark. He feared they would be too late.

****

"I didn't want it to come to this." Blue's brown eyes gleamed sadly behind the confines of his wire-rimmed glasses.

"I don't understand," Savannah said, a sense of foreboding beginning to crawl through her. The rest of her team had slipped away for a bathroom break, leaving her alone with Blue. Almost immediately he'd begun to act strange, muttering to himself, looking fitfully at her. But something had been odd about Blue's behavior from the beginning. They'd trekked for hours on a route that was unfamiliar. She had questioned him a number of times, but every time he had snapped at her. Finally, she had settled in and followed. After all, previous experience had shown that she was no judge of jungle trails. Blue was Aidan's brother, and despite a slightly strange and oddly cantankerous disposition she would trust him for that reason. That and she had no choice. They would never find their way out alone.

"I'm heading back," he said. The river was just behind him, masked with layers of foliage, it's angry current a constant undertone.

"Going back? We haven't reached the site yet. We

can't go back."

"You're not going to reach it either," Blue replied softly. "I'm sorry."

"I don't understand?"

His eyes were glazed over and shimmered again as if on the verge of tears. "I'm going back. Alone."

For a minute she froze, immobilized by the enormity of what he had said. "You can't."

But the look he gave her was so filled with hate that bile crawled up her throat.

"Blue? What are you saying?"

"I'm leaving you…"

"Here," she cut him off. "No. We don't know the way out. We…"

"Don't." He held up his hand cutting her off. "I'm not immune to female pleading. But it won't work this time. The only woman I cared about is dead."

Her heart was pounding. They'd never find their way out. She had to get this right.

"Who was she, Blue?" She jumped on the only soft spot she could see, her one chance to change his mind. For it was obvious that he'd been hurt. That might be what was fueling his strange behavior.

His smile was wistful, more regret than happiness. "It won't work. Don't play psychologist. It's over."

"Is it, Blue?"

He looked away and then back at her, the expression in his eyes, flat.

"Tell me." It took everything in her to modulate those two words into a softly caring gesture of encouragement while controlling the quiver in her limbs.

For a minute the expression in his eyes softened. "She was my wife."

"What happened?" she asked as her thoughts spun and her heart hammered.

"She got sick. Look, stalling won't change my mind. But no worries, I won't kill you." He smiled. "I'll let this." His hand swept wide, indicating the forest around them.

"Why?" she asked as relief flooded her. In the rain forest, they had a chance. Not much but a chance all the same. Her mind was already leaping to options for getting them out of this mess. They were too deep in the jungle for them to find their way out. The route Blue had taken had been convoluted and impossible to remember. But somehow, some way, she'd get them out. For now, her only tactic was delay.

"You planned this from the beginning," she accused.

"You saw me that day, didn't you?" he asked softly. "The day you found Malcolm."

She shook her head and realized it was futile. He wouldn't believe her. "You were there? Why?"

He pushed his glasses further up his nose. "Don't play innocent."

"I have no idea what you're talking about, Blue." But her heart pounded at the thought of what he had implied. He had been there the day Malcolm had died, and she couldn't even consider why without her suspicion showing in her expression. She took her mind from that place. The place that screamed that Blue just might be a murderer.

"No matter what you say there's no proof one way or the other," he said as if he'd read her mind. "But, unfortunately, as long as you're here, Aidan will stop at nothing to protect you and solve this crime."

"He wouldn't quit on any crime."

"No," he said with a smile. "Maybe not. But he might be quicker to draw different conclusions, if he were say—led."

Her blood felt like it had literally run cold.

"I don't believe you."

"Oh, believe, my dear, believe." He grimaced before she could interject with either a question or a plea. "Because it affects you. He loves you." This time there was an obvious glimmer in his eyes. "Because of that you're going away, like Anne."

He turned away. "I think we're far enough in. Stay and I'll…"

"Blue, no." She rushed forward, taking his arm as if that would stay him.

He spun around, throwing her to the ground, and around her the jungle came alive as brush crashed behind her and something screeched a dark warning.

"Bastard!" It was Ian.

Savannah tried to lift herself, but her head spun, and everything was only a whirl of motion. The forest seemed alive with the crash of heavy footsteps and excited male voices.

Branches crushed in angry snaps as Sid exploded into the clearing with Ian behind him.

Ian launched himself at Blue who easily defended himself with one hand and punched him with his other.

Sid glared at Blue as he helped Savannah up. "You're okay?"

"Yes." She looked back. "Be careful," she whispered. "Don't antagonize him further."

"I'll kill the bastard," he whispered in a heated vow.

"No. He's armed, you're not."

She glanced over where Ian was bent on all fours

and obviously struggling to get up.

She realized then that they were no threat to Blue. They were unarmed and physically no match. And that was when she looked up and saw the glint of aluminum as sun filtered across the river. A boat!

Could it possibly be?

"You planned this," she accused and wondered why she stated what he'd already admitted to and what, she supposed, should have been obvious.

"To leave you here," Blue finished. "I guess I did."

Sid charged Blue and was met with a punch that had him flat on his back, motionless.

Savannah's first instinct was to go to Sid.

"You don't want to do that," Blue said looking at her and then Ian.

The words were devoid of emotion.

"Blue, please reconsider. Anne…"

It was the wrong word, the wrong approach, the wrong name on the wrong lips. She knew it the moment she'd said that name. Blue had pulled the knife from the leather sheath at his waist. The look on his face was hate-filled pain, and the knife was now over his head. It was happening in fractions of seconds and even as the knife slashed down, seemingly toward her, she couldn't help herself, she screamed. And it was the scream that she later came to regret, for it was the scream that determined the course of the tragedy to come.

Chapter Thirty-Six

The scream resonated in the still heat. Aidan broke into a run. Behind him, foliage snapped as Mark tried to keep up.

For the scream was familiar, and it was Vann.

It was seconds before he realized that was the wrong approach. He stopped as quickly as he'd burst into motion, Mark slammed into his back, knocking him forward.

"Wait," he whispered after he'd regained his balance. "I'll go in first."

"I'll follow at a distance."

Aidan nodded as he began to move quickly and silently through the trees. In seconds, he was there, witnessing a scene that was disturbingly unbelievable. He barely registered the fact that Sid lay motionless on the ground. It was Blue and Vann that had all his attention, for Blue was holding a knife to her neck.

The roar in Aidan's ears was like nothing he had experienced before. Despite his earlier words, he charged the last yards in blind fury.

"Blue, no!" he shouted, anger and disbelief propelling him forward.

It was Blue who stopped him. For the look in his brother's eyes was filled with hatred and seemed directed solely at him.

"Aidan." There was no inflection, no emotion in the

sound of his name.

This wasn't his brother's voice nor was the hate in his eyes.

"Blue. What happened here?" He struggled not to acknowledge the fact that Blue had a knife to Vann's throat.

The air felt thick as he took a step forward into what might have minutes ago been a peaceful clearing that fronted the river.

"Move and she dies," Blue spat.

Behind him he could see Mark slipping slowly through the underbrush, barefoot and silent. Moving as they had all learned as children. He was slowly trapping Blue between them.

"Blue, what have you done?" Aidan asked.

Why was he threatening Vann?

"You always had everything." The words were ragged with disdain. "And now you come back for what is mine."

"Poaching? Is that what is yours? Is that what you've been doing? Is that what the ancestors would have wanted?" His gaze focused on the knife and how close it was to Vann's throat. It wouldn't happen. Blue wouldn't kill, but as he thought it and looked at Blue, he wasn't so sure.

"How would you know, poor little white boy?" Blue snarled.

He almost recoiled at the hate in his brother's voice. He had grown up with him, and now it was as if he didn't know him. Aidan's hands clenched into fists as he tried to ground himself in a world that no longer made sense.

"You always had your escape. You could always leave here. You weren't stuck."

"Neither were you."

"You were an interloper with a crazy mother that was thrust on us. And, like I knew you would, you eventually returned to where you belonged."

"That's not true." Although some of it was. His mother was crazy. The rest of it… No… "You were a brother to me. A friend." Aidan moved one foot forward, trying to be as unobtrusive, as nonthreatening as possible. He considered options for getting closer, getting the knife from Blue's hand. The conversation was out of place, and yet he desperately clung to each revelation as if that alone would buy time, restore sanity. Except nothing was sane ever since he saw that feather less than forty-eight hours ago.

"A long time ago," Blue said. "No more."

"Why?" And even as he asked the question, he feared the full scope of what Blue might have done.

"You got out of here. Went to school."

"You could have done the same." Aidan bit back impatience. He'd play this game. He'd play whatever game it took to get Vann out of here.

"How?"

"Scholarships." Aidan paused. "I would have lent you the money."

"I couldn't get a scholarship. I didn't have your marks. And I'd never ask you for money. I made my own." His gaze never left Aidan and the knife never wavered. "You weren't supposed to figure this out." He shifted, dragging Vann back tighter against him. "Bastard!"

Vann was silent steady through it all. Although he saw a slight quiver of her hand that he knew she fought to hide. *Hang in love, hang in.*

"How'd you know?" Blue asked.

"It's my job. And it wasn't just me, Akan suspected something too. In fact, that was my first clue." He hadn't figured it all out, not yet. But he wasn't telling Blue that. He moved one step forward.

"He was worried about you and the time you were spending away from the tribe. He knew something was wrong."

Play to his emotions, he reminded himself. He dodged the look of fear in Vann's eyes and kept focused on Blue.

"You were good, Blue."

"But you figured it out anyway."

Damn, Aidan thought. Blue's voice was flat, and he seemed disconnected. He kept on the same track, hoping to get a flicker of a connection, anything to get her out of Blue's hands. "You mentioned taking a tourism class. Not unusual alone, but then I saw you guiding the Chinese, condoning illegal hunting, I knew something was up. That wasn't like you—not the Blue I knew."

"Bastard. You never knew me."

"I did once, Blue. You can't deny that."

Time was his friend he thought as he fought to keep the conversation going, to find a weak spot, to move in. Keep talking, man…

"It was you that day when I tracked you to the river, days after Malcolm died. It was your cowboy hat that identified you, and I wouldn't believe it."

"You're not the only one who wants a taste of city life now and then," Blue said not denying any of it. "Now I have the business, foreign hunters are very lucrative. Five guides full-time and five or six part-time. If it's not the Chinese, it's the Europeans, and both seem to have big bucks right now, at least the ones I'm seeing."

Dread lodged in Aidan's gut. "Malcolm was one of your guides." He continued before Blue could say anything. "What happened?"

"It was necessary."

"Was it?" Dread locked cold and slick in his belly, but his gaze kept trained on Blue.

Blue shrugged. "Malcolm wanted in on the deal. And he got greedy. He was expanding his own branch of the business, including other tribesmen. I wouldn't allow that." He smiled broadly.

"Damn Chinese were gullible enough to believe it was a shot they had fired. Never mind that I used their gun."

"It was an accident. I can understand how…"

"You wish, brother," he cut Aidan off. "I killed Malcolm. And I will kill you."

"Blue, I can't believe this." Aidan fought to remain calm, and to buy time. "You killed Malcolm?"

"Everyone will think it was the Chinese tourists. They'll be gone now. They won't want to be caught in a foreign country with a dead body, accident or not. I'd say they're in Hong Kong as we speak."

"You're right. They flew out of Kuching just a few days ago," Aidan replied.

"So now that they're gone, well…" Blue shrugged. "Congratulations, you've wrapped it all up quite neatly."

"I never would have believed it except for the autopsy. Malcolm had something in his pocket that I believe was yours." Aidan held up the blue feather.

Blue squinted and the knife wavered. "Malcolm had it?" There was disbelief in his voice.

Aidan nodded. "Even then I couldn't believe it had

been more than an accident." While they spoke, he had edged closer to Blue, the distraction of his voice hiding the subtle forward movement. "I've been away too long.

"The head was removed after death. I'm assuming you had nothing to do with that." He paused for effect, his attention never veering from Blue, but all the while watching for a chance to get the knife away from him. Through it all he was aware of Vann, and he wished against everything that she wasn't here. But there was nothing he could do but trust that his reflexes were fast enough to intervene if needed.

Blue shook his head.

"You?"

"I needed the money." Blue's tone was sharp, offensive. "And I took Malcolm's head to divert attention." He smiled wistfully, but he wouldn't meet Aidan's eyes. "From me."

Another explanation came to Aidan, formed in part by some of what Blue had just said. "You're covering for someone."

"Leave it, Aidan. Please. For old times at a minimum." Blue's laugh was dry and humorless, cutting jaggedly through the jungle's constant hum. "It was and is a good gig."

"Gig? Hardly, Blue," Aidan said sadly. "It's over. You've destroyed much in your bid for wealth."

"It wasn't all me. I wasn't alone. Mark—"

"Shut up," Mark snapped behind him.

"Mark?" Aidan's hand went involuntarily to his gun, concealed beneath his shirt. How could he have missed Mark sneaking up behind him. He was cornered! Damn it to hell.

"Don't even think about it." Mark held a handgun as

he stepped out and around him. The gun waved over Aidan, who sent a subtle look toward Vann.

"You couldn't keep your mouth shut, could you?" Mark snarled at Blue.

"I wasn't taking all the heat," Blue snapped.

"I should have ditched you months ago." Mark's gaze swept the clearing. "You always were a screwup. I would have been better off alone."

"You? It was my business."

"I would have let you live. You realize that, you idiot. If you'd kept your mouth shut."

"What are you saying?"

"Mark," Aidan said. "We can work this out."

"Work this out?" Mark smiled grimly through the slowly enunciated words. "I don't think so. You're spun so tightly into her web." He shrugged a shoulder at Vann. "I wouldn't trust a word that you might say."

"Mark, no!" Vann said, fear and desperation showing on her face. "We…"

"Shut the hell up!" He moved forward so that he was between Blue and Aidan and facing off Vann.

"You are why everything has fallen apart." His gun waved across them all. "I could be in London instead of here trying to make conversation with primitives. But no, you have him panting after you like you were a dog in heat. He dug deeper, because of you," he spat.

Mark swung the gun in Aidan's direction.

"You're not as smart as you think, Aidan. You're not the only one who escaped to the big city. When this is over, I'm going to be a thousand miles away from here." He laughed, the sound rough and dry like grit that ran a ragged path across the clearing. "And Fish," he said. "He will never return. Mark will take his place, forever." He swept the gun across each of them. "I will be the last man standing. For that's the only way any of this will work in my favor. Too bad really. Some of you were beginning to grow on me."

His eyes darted from one to the other. "I even called some of you friend, once."

"Mark, I can't believe this of you," Aidan said, the reality of what was occurring almost beyond comprehension. He focused on the facts, divorcing his mind from who and what these men had once been to him.

"Attempting reasoning. Good of you, old chap." Mark's gaze swept across all of them. "Don't get me wrong, I'm not all bad. I just have my limits. Who do you think protected Blue from his own ineptitude? When a couple of tribesmen from upriver asked questions, I gave the authorities something to think about."

"Damn it, Mark, you shot them," Aidan said as he thought of Andrew's mention of two other bodies.

"You!" Blue accused, glaring at Mark. "You told me I was the only one."

"Fool," Mark replied with iced precision. "Malcolm had potential. I was grooming him to take my business far."

Blue's face was red. And his hand clutched the knife and Vann, as if both were lifelines.

"You were only playing second fiddle to me, Blue. You know that. Who else had the potential to expand? Certainly not you." He chuckled. "If the Chinese weren't blamed for Malcolm's murder, I made sure there was a backup plan. Who do you think put that feather into Malcolm's pocket? That way there would be no doubt as to who murdered Malcolm. Case closed."

"Bastard."

"You've been outplayed, Blue," Mark said calmly. "Unfortunately, now you will all have to die."

"And how do you plan to explain that to the authorities?" Aidan asked while his mind spun through options. Behind Blue, he could see Ian moving stealthily through the underbrush. He counted on that to be the distraction he needed.

"This place is very unforgiving, Aidan. I think you know that."

It was then that Ian leapt, grabbing Blue from behind. It was enough for Savannah to slip out of Blue's grasp. Blue rocked, disoriented for a moment, the smaller man clinging to his back. He shook him off and swung around as Ian dodged the knife but not his fist.

"Ian!"

Savannah wavered.

"Run!" Aidan shouted. For it was impossible to rush to her as he wanted. Mark would bring him down in an instant. With Vann out of Blue's clutches, he had to let things play out a little longer. These weren't strangers he could kill with a single bullet. They were people he cared about; and people he had cared about.

Footsteps crashed through the brush.

"Stay back!" Mark shouted.

"Stop, he's armed!" Aidan shouted as Drew and Burke simultaneously charged into the clearing. In the confusion, Aidan dove as the blast of the gun rocked the small clearing again and again. Blue went down even as Aidan hit him, tackling him to safety—too late.

Aidan rolled with his brother's body in his arms. Blood covered his hands as he looked into Blue's face and saw only the silent stare of death. Mark's bullet had taken Blue down. And it wasn't over. Another shot exploded, and a woman screamed.

"Vann!"

He was on his feet, scanning the perimeter even as he saw the blood, so much blood trailing toward the river. Three men and the raging river and then he saw her, a small figure holding a thick branch like a club. One of the men was obviously injured, while the other, Drew, was wrestling with Mark. City soft and thirty pounds lighter, he didn't stand a chance. Then Burke moved in and almost within seconds slipped on the bank. Mark got off another shot with Vann in the line of fire.

Aidan charged without thought. But the distance was too great. A punch from Mark sent Drew into the river. Another gunshot had Burke tumble down the steep embankment and into the violent current.

It was all a blur. Vann was on her knees, no longer using the branch as a weapon but as a means to save her team from the river. Her tear-choked voice was music to his ears. She was alive and unhurt. And even as he thought that, he heard the laugh and knew what was about to happen. But even in knowing, he was too late. Mark had a thick forearm around her waist, his gun in his other hand.

"Move and she follows the rest."

Mark's grip tightened, and color slipped from Vann's face as she fought for air. He twisted and looked coldly at the water behind him. "When I ditch this place, no one and nothing will follow me."

Aidan schooled his features as Mark's dilemma came to him. He would have shot them both by now if he had enough bullets. He didn't. Vann gave him a slight lift of her brow and from the corner of his eye he followed her gaze and saw a movement, Sid.

A crack of underbrush had Mark's attention, and in that split-second, Vann twisted and drove her elbow into his gut. Mark doubled over, releasing her.

"Roll and run!" Aidan shouted as he dove, hitting Mark with his full weight and throwing both of them to the edge of the raging river. They rolled once. Mark slipped free, and Aidan swung, catching the side of his face. The punch drove Mark backward, his body twisting sideways into the river.

Minutes later, it was over. They stood on the bank, the three of them.

"Burke and Drew," Savannah said. "They didn't make it."

"Son of a bitch!" Sid drove a fist into the palm of his hand.

Aidan took a deep breath. There was only one body in the clearing, Blue. The others were gone, taken by the river and eventually, more than likely, the many jungle predators. He looked at the sky and fought for calm. In his peripheral vision he could see the treetops. The branches broke the clear blue of the endless sky, unchanged, surreal in the face of this tragedy. Blue was dead and with him had gone everything he had thought they had together. The brother of his heart had been no brother at all. The friend he had once had, Mark, gone too.

A few feet away, Vann waited for him. It was unbelievable as he took her in his arms, trembling but safe. Around them there was carnage. That four men had lost their lives here was incomprehensible.

"I can't believe this happened." She raised her head. "Blue?"

"He didn't make it."

"Oh, Aidan. I'm so sorry."

"He lost his mind. I know that. He wasn't the Blue I remember," Aidan said as his hand lightly brushed her cheek. "His loss saddens me as it will Akan, but we are both stronger men than that."

It was a silent and sad walk as the group made their way to where Aidan had disembarked so few hours ago. And when they were settled in the boat that had brought him to the beginning of this heartbreaking journey, Aidan could only close his eyes as he spun the boat neatly around in the rough current. For the second time they were leaving the remains of a broken expedition behind them.

And in the heart of the jungle more lives had been lost and one killer roamed free.

…waiting, watching and wanting, to kill again.

Chapter Thirty-Seven

"You know, don't you?"

Akan shook his head and blew a ring of smoke. "I will shed no tears. I have seen much in my lifetime. Buried many." But despite his words, his eyes gleamed. "I had my suspicions, but he was my son." He stubbed out the cigarette and put it in a rusted half-gallon pail. "As are you."

Aidan stared out into the dense green of the jungle. The longhouse was silent in midday, and in the quiet, he still wrestled with anger and guilt. Blue was his brother, he should grieve.

"I'm angry too," Akan's voice was soft. "He could have been so much. He failed every dream I had for him, but most of all he failed himself. But I am glad one of my sons lives.

"That's not all," he said looking at Aidan.

"What?"

"There's already an investigation in process and a report filed."

"The missing man." He frowned. "What was his name?"

"Jason."

"Yes." Akan sighed. "He's not missing any longer. A report came in from farther down river. A villager found the body but was attacked from behind. He managed to wrestle free and restrain his attacker. He's under arrest."

"Who was it, the attacker I mean?"

"Matthew," Akan said.

"Harold's contracted pilot?"

"One and the same."

"Damn." He was silent for a moment taking it all in. "And the body?"

"Jason."

"Unbelievable. I hate to tell Vann this, although I'm sure she already guessed that Jason was gone."

"Murderers amongst us," Akan said slowly, as if contemplating the words. "One my son. That is so hard."

"I'm sorry." Aidan put his hand over his father's still sturdy hand.

Akan looked at him, sorrow and wisdom reflected in his eyes. "There is reason to rejoice, and there is reason to grieve. One balances the other." He looked down to the river. "Your woman, she waits. Take comfort in her arms."

He dropped a thick hand on Aidan's shoulder and drew him close. The hug was brief, but it imprinted the love that lay between the two men, one sun-wizened and the other bronzed and tall.

"We'll talk later," Akan said as he turned away. "In the meantime, you must take your mind from the death and move forward to your own future." He pointed to Vann. "Go."

Aidan took a deep breath. In his peripheral vision, he could see the treetops. He thought of the peace he found above the forest floor amid the trees, and there was no peace in the thought.

His gaze dropped, and he saw her looking at him.

He came to her, reaching out his hand. "Let's get out

of here."

"I'm sorry, Aidan."

"You don't need to be sorry."

"It's incomprehensible to lose both a friend and a brother."

"There were too many losses." He drew a finger along her silken cheek. "I know they have you torn up, but in a way, we were lucky. Drew lived." It had been touch and go when they had pulled him out of the river. Drew was still under the shaman's care, awaiting transport out, but he'd live.

"I don't know if I can ever forgive myself."

"You have to."

"I'll try," she said but her voice was a thread of its former self.

Aidan took her hand, and they left the longhouse without a backward glance.

A bird called from somewhere in the rich forest canopy, and ahead something swished quickly through the underbrush.

He let go of her hand as the forest opened into a clearing, a plant-bordered paradise with water streaming down a small cliff.

She stepped into the rock alcove and drew in a breath that was audible despite the rush of water churning over the rocks and into the pool in front of them.

"It's beautiful." Her words were a sigh of pleasure.

He placed his hands on her shoulders, slight, delicate shoulders with the strength to lead an army. She'd proven that to him more than once.

She turned around, her body soft against his. "I can't believe it, a waterfall. It's incredible. Aidan?"

All he could think was that she had survived. Blue could have killed her. It was incomprehensible.

He kissed her. Warm and languid, the kiss trembled in the tropical heat and threatened to steal all reason. He broke away while he still could. And while he tottered on the edge of reality, she looked unaffected.

"Is it safe to swim in it?" she asked.

"Very," he said. "I swam here many times as a child."

"But I don't have a swimsuit. Do you?"

He shook his head. The heat was killing him, and it wasn't just the crowded warmth of the rain forest, not anymore. He peeled his shirt off.

"You're going in?"

"After you." He didn't know what came over him. Maybe it was the need for some playful relief in the midst of an emotional cauldron. Maybe it was just that he wanted to get closer to her. Whatever it was, he didn't spend much time analyzing it before he acted.

"No." She shook her head.

"Yes," he said as he lifted her and tossed her into the pool that fronted the small waterfall. She went under, and he followed her. He jumped feet-first and landed beside her. The water was warm but cool in comparison to the land temperature and a delicious contrast to the tropical heat. He came up for air almost reluctantly and playfully shook water everywhere and especially on her.

"Aidan," she protested.

She was so close he could feel her warm breath on his chest. Her hair was wet and sleek, and droplets of water clung to her cheek. He dry-swallowed, his imagination seeing her body revealed in every tantalizing curve despite the fact that she was up to her neck in water.

"Bastard!" she said good-naturedly and shoved him. He staggered, played along with her game, and went under. When he surfaced, he spun around looking for her and blinked to clear his water-blurred vision. She was really up to her neck now. And he was out for revenge.

But she stole his edge when she pulled off her T-shirt and tossed it to shore. The rest of her clothes soon followed. He was mired in desire as she trod water and laughed.

He didn't know when he consciously reached for her, but suddenly, she was in his arms. Wet skin glided in a silken haze over wet skin. She smelled like fresh air. She smelled like woman.

He wanted to kiss the life out of her, make love to her like none of the horror had happened. Hot, heavy, no-holding-back sex.

She was beautiful, and he wanted her. It was inevitable. He folded her into his arms. His head dropped to meet her lips. She was so tiny. She fit so perfectly against him. She was lost in his arms.

Lost.

What was he thinking? She was soft and strong against his side, an erotic dichotomy. His body quivered as their lips collided, as she sucked the life force from him, as her taste flooded his mouth. He didn't know what she held to all he knew was that he clung to her.

He thought he heard her throaty chuckle. It was hard to tell through the roaring buzz that blocked all coherent thought.

Her hands clutched his shoulders, and her slight frame imprinted against him. He groaned and pulled her closer. He'd never felt anything like it. And when it was over, he was more lost than when it had begun.

Chapter Thirty-Eight

It was like the playful interlude in the water had given them the strength to face what was to come. Together they climbed the longhouse's narrow worn steps. On the verandah, rice lay spread out in thin layers to dry. At one end a dog dozed, and a fly buzzed lazily around it.

"This way." Aidan took her hand.

A cowboy hat lay on a chair outside a door near the end of the longhouse. And for a moment they both stopped. Aidan ran a finger over the hat that had once belonged to his brother. He squeezed her hand. "Would you wait outside if I asked?"

"No. We're in this together." She turned the unlocked doorknob and swung open a door to a room that had housed many generations before, in a tribe that had lived communally for as long as anyone could remember. A breeze skirted along the verandah and ruffled her shirt. From the corner of her eye, she could see the skull rocking gently in the rafters. The last human skull, hunted and killed, beheaded and hung from these rafters as a prize of war, or maybe an offering for one man's bride. She shivered and hesitated in the doorway. It was Aidan who led the way into the empty room that echoed with memories and yet contained only a mat and a bamboo woven chair.

"Do you smell that?" she whispered.

"Stay here," Aidan replied grimly. "Please."

She waited as he went upstairs, where the smell emanated from. It smelled like flesh decomposing, like…

When he returned, he was pallid despite his golden tan.

"I should have gone with you."

"No," he said firmly as he closed the door behind them.

"What now?" She took his hand.

"For you, nothing. For me, I see Akan. There's something I believe my father has not told me."

"Aidan."

"Don't say it."

"All right, I'll wait."

But five minutes later found her roaming aimlessly below the verandah. She glanced down to the river and saw the boy who had met them that first day. With new determination, she headed in his direction.

"You've come to hear what I know." He smiled a rather grim smile for such a young boy.

"What do you know?"

"Not here."

He stepped into a longboat. "Hurry."

"No!"

"Do you want to hear what I know or not?"

She hesitated before gingerly sloshing through knee-high water and into the wooden boat.

The boy stood at the back of the boat with a pole in hand and easily maneuvered the boat into the current. "We don't want others to hear."

"What's your name?" she asked.

The boat rocked, and she clung to the edges.

"Don't go too far," she said already regretting her decision.

"I won't."

He smiled and dropped one hand from the pole, holding it out.

She took it and shook. "Savannah."

"Malang. Call me Mick."

"Mick?"

"Yeah, you know, like this—" And he burst into an off-key rendition of "I Can't Get No Satisfaction."

"The Rolling Stones," Savannah said and despite everything, had to smile.

"Movement up top. Get down," he hissed as he dropped to all fours.

She bent over while thinking that she might look a fool and only be caught up in a boy's vivid imagination.

"Okay, we're out of sight," he said a minute later as the rough-hewn boat rocked.

Savannah sat up.

"Blue took the head. But it had already been lopped off," the boy said as he guided the worn wooden boat along the outside edge of the river and away from the rapid and deadly current in the middle.

Lopped off. She forgot to breathe at that. This was no game.

"Who did it?"

"I can't tell you."

Water spit over the sides of the boat, slicking her arm and wetting her shirt. "Why not?"

The boy's lips pinched. "You won't tell?"

"I can't promise that."

Mick chewed on his lower lip. "They took his head, but he was already dead."

She frowned and a thought came to her, outrageous but considering it all, plausible. “You?”

He shook his head. “No.”

“Someone you know?”

“Yes.”

The slapping of the waves and the aliveness of the jungle were, for a few minutes, the only sound. Finally, Mick shook his head. “I will tell you who, so that you can help them. Otherwise, the guilt will ruin my friends.”

It was an unbelievable story and threw Savannah into the midst of a situation that she had no real understanding of. It was a relief to see Aidan standing on the dock when they returned.

“Aidan.” She jumped from boat to dock and reached over to get the rope to help Mick tie it up.

“Remember your promise,” Mick repeated.

“I will swear him to secrecy.”

“Thanks, Savannah.”

“What were you thinking, going out with him?” Aidan’s words were hard-edged and full of carefully controlled anger. “He’s just a child.”

“I’m thirteen,” Mick shot back as he stomped up the dock and faced Aidan. “I know what I’m doing.”

Aidan looked over the boy’s head. “He could have drowned both of you in that rickety longboat.”

“Hey, I’m not invisible,” Mick persisted. “And I’m not your sister,” he shot as he headed up the stairs, shaking his head as he went.

“He has a point, Aidan. He’s good at what he does, child or not.”

Aidan rocked back on his heels. “I know. And he had a point. That’s how I lost my sister. To the river.”

“It wasn’t your fault. You have to let it go.”

"It haunts me, but you're right. It's irrelevant now."

"Always relevant," Savannah replied. "Feelings always are."

She moved to his side, putting her arm around his waist. "Tell me about your sister."

He shrugged her arm off as he looked into the distance.

"The first time I realized I didn't understand the forest like I thought was when it took Sunrise. She was the only child that Akan and my mother had together. She was only ten and too young to die."

He was silent for a minute.

"That was so many years ago. I was eighteen when it happened. After that, college allowed me to escape and forget."

"And prevented you from healing. You avoided."

"It was easier," he said simply. "It's ridiculous, I know, but I felt betrayed." He looked downriver. "She was much like Mick. Independent, wise for her years. But there was nothing I could have done to save her. What keeps me sane is knowing that she was happy. I know that now. Right to the end." He sighed. "Sixteen years. That statement was a long time coming." He stared off into the distance before turning his attention to her. "So why were you on the river with Mick?"

"He had something he didn't want the others to hear." She smiled softly and rested her hand on his knee. "Something that you might be very interested in."

"I'm waiting."

"I tied up a loose end for you. Malcolm's head."

He crossed his arms, his expression grim. "So, what does Mick know that I don't?"

If she hadn't known him, she would almost have

been intimidated. Instead she faced him off, crossed her arms across her chest and told him everything she had learned from Mick.

"Why would Blue hide the head?"

"To protect them. They're just boys," she said.

"He thought what they had done would ruin them."

She put a hand gently on his shoulder. "Where do we go from here?"

"Again, to Akan," he said as he kissed her, a lazy languid kiss that had her melting into his arms, where he wanted to keep her safe—his, for now.

Chapter Thirty-Nine

After listening to Aidan and viewing the evidence, Akan retired with him to the verandah.

Akan lit a cigarette and stared off into the distance.

"Couple of young ones wanting to try the old tradition."

Aidan shook his head. "I pray that's all it was."

"It was."

"You knew!" Aidan accused.

"They're good boys. My grandnephew is going to university in three years. His friend, he just lost his mother. Maybe that had something to do with it."

"You don't believe that?"

"No, I don't. It was poor judgment on both their parts. But who am I to talk? I can't very well judge them, all things considered. Not when my own son has been defying tradition."

"So Blue found the head and tried to cover for them?"

"That's about it. He didn't tell me until just before he left to get verandah wire. It was as if he knew that he wouldn't return."

Savannah came up to them. "Where are the boys?"

"We have them contained for now," Akan replied.

"How could this happen?" She shook her head, disbelief apparent in her look.

"I asked myself the same. Then I realized it was the

way of it." Akan blew another smoke ring and the smoke wafted into the evening air.

"Tradition," Aidan and Akan both said.

"They would never consider killing anyone. The body was coming downriver, an unknown, already dead. They knew odds were that the body would never be claimed," Akan continued. "They'd heard the tale of another boy."

"This has happened before?" Aidan looked stunned.

"Once, a long time ago. In seventy-two, an expedition of scientists."

Savannah jerked, taking a step back as if she'd been slapped.

"Father," she whispered, remembering her father's story of losing a man from their expedition in that particular year.

"It was a long time ago, and they were boys," Akan said. "They're both gone now. Died too young, both of them. They were my cousins, and it was an opportunity they couldn't pass up."

He lit another cigarette. "For the boys, it's over. They're traumatized by what they did. I think, in fact, it might haunt them for life. There aren't a lot of dead bodies floating down the river. That might be the last in their lifetime."

"They're not killers," Akan said with steel in his voice.

Aidan looked at Vann's pale face and realized that her mind was elsewhere. On her team and those she had lost. He circled an arm around her waist.

"I'm sorry," Akan addressed her, his voice raspy but still strong despite his age. "It is a rarity for bodies to survive for any length of time in the river. Your friend has met a jungle burial, as has Mark." He shrugged. "For the Iban, that is an honorable end."

"Thank you for that." Savannah smiled weakly.

"You're welcome." Akan roughly patted her shoulder and turned his attention to Aidan. "The boys will be taken care of."

"How?" Aidan asked.

"You're not the only one with an in with law enforcement. I was planning to fly out with Eric tomorrow."

Akan took another drag.

"Because I pushed you into it?" Aidan asked.

"No," Akan replied. "Despite what you might think, I was on this—the boys anyway. I didn't expect outside interference."

"I'm not outside."

The silence hung over them, more condemning than a verbal yes could ever be, and her heart ached for Aidan.

"It's been over six months since you were last here," Akan said finally, and his tone had the accusatory note of any parent. "But you're still my son." A cloud of smoke wafted softly into the air and the hand that held the cigarette dropped to his side. "My only one." The words hung melancholic between them.

Then Akan glanced at his watch. "Look, I've got to get going fairly soon. We can talk more about this later. But there's a couple of tourists who want the typical longhouse tour. I'm on duty."

"You?" Aidan frowned.

"Filling in. The lads that were supposed to show them through didn't get back from the city on time."

"What are you saying?" Savannah asked as anger raced through her. "You have tourists showing up? You have continuous communication?"

"Satellite access." Akan held up his hand. "We really were having trouble with it that day when you arrived."

"Fixable trouble, I'm assuming?" she asked. "Meaning it was up and running and we could have gotten a plane out of here?"

He shrugged. "Not exactly."

"You could have gotten out, but the only plane, well, that was Eric,"Aidan said. "We wouldn't take a chance with anything that wasn't already dead." He paused. "Sorry, that sounded bad. But Malcolm had to be airlifted out, the rest of you didn't."

"There were communications before we left for that last field trip, wasn't there?" She folded her arms. "Why would you do that—drag us through the jungle for no reason? Why?"

Aidan had no excuse, no glib answer as Akan looked at him and shrugged. As he turned his attention to her all he saw was betrayal reflected in her eyes.

Akan motioned them to follow as he headed down the verandah, carrying on his monologue as if the tension between them didn't exist, as if the questions had never been asked.

"Confinement seems to have quieted the boys. I'll bring them out, and you can see for yourselves that they're relatively harmless. I think it would be in the best interests all round if the tribe handles this. I'm sure Chief Lieu will agree." Akan stopped, turned and motioned to another man, who unlocked the last longhouse room.

The boys who emerged couldn't have been more than fourteen or fifteen, both slight, neither having filled into a man's frame.

"Them? You're kidding," she blurted.

"May I?" Aidan asked, and Akan nodded.

Aidan faced the boys, towering over both of them. "I'd be interested in your reasons for mutilating a dead body," he began with his hands behind his back.

Tears glittered in the one boy's eyes. "We shouldn't have done it. I told you so." He looked at the other boy, who stared at a spot somewhere between his feet.

"He was dead," the second boy muttered.

"So you thought that made it right to decapitate him?" Aidan moved closer to the boys.

"Respect for the dead." The other boy glanced at his accomplice, who nodded.

"Headhunting is honorable."

"Was," Akan injected. "Some ancient traditions do not fit in modern-day society. That is one of them."

The skull swung from a rafter only thirty feet away. The last human head hunted by this particular tribe—until now.

"He was Iban. We thought he'd understand." The words were desperate and quick.

"When we started, we both wanted to stop," one boy said and glanced at the other, who nodded. "But we couldn't because that would have been worse."

The boys shifted from foot to foot, and she realized that Aidan's lack of response was working better than talking ever would.

"Will we be arrested?" Tears glimmered on the smaller boy's lashes.

Savannah felt a pang of sympathy for them.

"This is serious."

They both nodded at Aidan's words.

"You could be arrested."

"No, please." They both sobbed.

"It's not up to me," Aidan said. "You should have thought of these things before you did something so outrageous. Thought that the man had a family. One that would be devastated by his death and by the fact that he was decapitated."

"Did you think of those things?" she asked, feeling for the boys. Surely a parent should be here, encouraging them, supporting them, guiding them to the right decision.

Where were their parents?

Both boys shook their heads.

"They are alone," Akan said in his quiet yet authoritative voice as he stood beside her.

She looked up surprised. "How?

"Did I know what you were thinking? You have an expressive face." He held up his hand, a familiar gesture that indicated silence. "They are wards of the tribe. I think you would call it in your Western lingo. I don't think that's an excuse. They've been well loved and cared for. No one in a longhouse is ever without love or family. We take care of our own." He faced the boys. "Isn't that right?"

They both looked down and muttered something that sounded like agreement. Akan came up beside Aidan. "So have we decided when they'll be arrested?"

The boys gasped.

"You said that wouldn't happen." One boy glared at Akan.

"I didn't say anything," Akan replied. "In the meantime, I think the pair of you should be kept under house arrest until we decide what to do."

"No, please," the smaller boy sobbed.

The other stood beside him, stoically quiet except for the scuffing of his bare foot back and forth.

"I agree." Aidan folded his arms across his chest.

"It will give you time to think about what you've done. And time for Akan and the others to think what your punishment might be," Aidan said.

"You mean we won't go to jail?"

"There's no guarantee in life. This is serious," Aidan warned. "But no, I doubt you will. Not that there won't be punishment. Serious consequences. You won't get off easy, you know that?"

"No, we expect that."

"Most of the punishment has been waiting to be discovered," the one boy said.

"I imagine it has. That will be taken into account. In the meantime, I think we'll maintain your confinement and let Akan deal with this."

"Locked in." A tear ran down the smaller boy's cheek.

"Yes. Locked in. And I'd say you're getting off easy." Aidan paused. "Go. And think about what you can do for the mutilated man's family."

"Locked in?" she said. "Isn't that harsh?"

"They'll bunk with me for now," Aidan said. "They'll only be locked in alone for the next hour. Then I'll deal with them, get them settled where I can keep an eye on them."

With the boys gone, the verandah was oddly silent except for the eerie creak of the skull as it twisted in the quiet breeze.

Chapter Forty

"You won't have the boys arrested?" Savannah asked as night fell and she sat cross-legged on the dock with her heart breaking. They were going back to the city tomorrow, and then she would say good-bye to Aidan. It was almost over. She stood up, turning to face him. She knew what he had said but she needed, wanted him to say it again.

"I trust Akan. He is one of the Turah Burong," he said, referring to the group of tribal administrators whose job it was to resolve conflicts. "I think we can avoid a legal mess. But the rest is his decision."

"What now?"

"Now they go to Kuching. That is one thing even Akan cannot avoid."

"No." She hadn't expected that. "You can't do that. The city would kill them."

"Hardly. Kuching will give them a taste of reality. They're old enough. It's time they learned how to be men."

"They're boys."

"Exactly," he replied as his lips met hers and she matched him kiss for kiss. Her hands tangled in his blonde curls. Her mouth parted, wanting more, needing more. But his deception sat heavy in her heart.

"No," she murmured against his lips.

"You're right. Now isn't the time," he said as he let

her go and she followed his gaze.

She gasped. Standing in the shadows was Mick. Their eyes met briefly in the darkness before the boy scurried away.

For a minute, her breath caught in her throat. She met Aidan's eyes as the boy melted into the forest and they were finally truly alone.

His thumb skimmed her lower lip.

"Vann."

She shook her head. She would never be Vann again.

"You won't forgive me, will you?" His voice held only resigned sadness.

"You lied. You unnecessarily dragged us through the rain forest for days. We could have gotten out by plane or boat. You could have phoned."

"It was an investigation."

"I think you might have enjoyed it." But even as she said it, she knew that there was no truth in the words. They were only pebbles of hurt, of reacting to what she still couldn't accept.

"Hardly. I didn't know what you were about, and there was a possible murder."

"You mean you thought it was one of us? Make us uncomfortable enough and someone would cave."

His silence was more damning than anything he could have said.

"You couldn't have returned us to Kuching and asked the same questions there?"

"I could have," he agreed.

"But if you hadn't, Matthew would have continued to kill."

"I'm sorry. I wish I could tell you that I would have

done it differently. But despite a regretful investigation tactic, I care about you." He looked away. "Very much."

The last words were so low that she was unsure if she had imagined them or not.

"Desire isn't the basis of a relationship, Aidan."

"I think we both agree that there's more."

"No. There can never be more. It was a holiday romance, nothing more." The words were like ice chips in her mouth, hard, cold and foreign.

"I can't convince you otherwise?"

"No," she replied, and it felt like something had broken deep within her. There was nothing to do but cry or change the subject. She took a deep breath and went for the latter. "I can't believe Malcolm was beheaded by boys. It's unbelievable. Who would have thought?"

"Teenage boys and tribe tradition." He shook his head, his eyes heavy with sadness.

"I'm not justifying what the boys did. But headhunting, by Iban culture, is explainable historically. They were boys exploring their culture, their history. Malcolm was already dead. There's a lot of different ways to look at this."

"Or just one," she said. "A man died."

"We both know that it's not that simple, don't we Vann?"

"Vann."

She nodded. "You're the only one who calls me that," she said choking back tears. "And I don't think I can be that to you anymore."

"Meaning?"

"There's no point taking this any further. It would just be too painful." Her gaze locked with his and saw something that might have been pain flit in his brown eyes. It was hard to tell; her own eyes were swimming and she had to leave before what little control she had left failed her.

"For both of us." She walked away without looking back.

****

"He's a good man," Akan said that night at the longhouse as he leaned against the verandah railing. His weathered face was stern.

"I know that," Savannah replied.

"You are a foolish woman." He blew a slow smoke ring and seemed fixated on something in the distance. "He will speak to Chief Lieu, make it right so those boys can go on with their lives."

Akan held up his hand, warding off any interruption. "I raised him from a thin, annoying little boy to who he is today. If he lied to you, he lied for a reason. He lied to protect his people and to find justice for a victim, for Malcolm. That is hardly a lie. That is a sign of good character. He is a good man." He glanced away. "Better obviously than my natural son, Blue." He frowned. "I am sorry. That is no longer a good comparison." He blew another smoke ring as a bat flitted close by and then disappeared into the velvet night. "Aidan believes in justice and truth. I would trust him with my life."

"You're right," she said and felt small.

"He is also very adaptable." He smiled. "As, I think, are you." He paused, staring into the night. "You have good instincts. You will make the right decision."

"I can't promise anything. To be honest I wouldn't trust my instincts on anything." She leaned heavily against the railing. "I can't believe Malcolm, Burke, and Jason are dead."

"These things happen. Borneo is unforgiving, but I think that like Aidan, it too might be your destiny."

"Maybe." She folded her arms across her chest and shivered. "This trip was my proving ground and I failed."

"Something else." He cleared his throat. "Back in seventy-two it was me who led that scientific expedition. Your father was there too."

"You're kidding," she said as he confirmed what she had only suspected.

"I'm not. I learned much that trip. We were all young, inexperienced, and a man died. The circumstances were different, mind you, but the same in ways." He stubbed out the cigarette. "We never found the body. What I'm saying is that this could have happened to anyone. You must not let it stop you."

"I don't know."

"I do. You are stronger than that. I think maybe I will see more of you."

Savannah squeezed her eyes closed for a moment, thinking of Burke. "I don't know. Forgiving Aidan is one thing, forgiving myself quite another."

She slipped quietly off the verandah, unable to deal anymore with Akan's words of wisdom, for despite their truth they clashed with the raw emotion that she had no idea how to come to terms with.

Chapter Forty-One

It was a silent flight the next morning. Aidan stretched his legs and looked out the window. Drew had been flown out hours earlier accompanied by Sid and Ian. With Drew's stretcher, there hadn't been room for an extra person, and Vann had stayed behind. Now she sat ahead of him, and she might as well have been in New York. His betrayal stretched like a canyon between them.

Across the aisle, the boys sat beside Akan. Each of them sat almost primly, dressed in long pants and shirts, attire appropriate for the city. And both of them looked completely uncomfortable and scared. He felt for them, but he agreed with Akan. More importantly, the council members had also agreed with Akan. It was time that the boys met the city that might one day hold their destiny. They needed to learn to live in harmony with the outside rules and its mores.

The flight was short, and when they landed Akan smiled gravely and shook Aidan's hand. "I'll take a cab from here." Akan glanced over his shoulder at the two boys. "I imagine a few days here will be more than enough. Thanks for understanding."

"You knew I would."

"That I did, my boy. Come back sooner than last time. I missed you." Akan swung away and loaded his charges into the nearest cab.

One problem solved. If only they could all be solved

so easily, he thought. But it wasn't until they were in Kuching, in the hotel lobby, that he was able to say what was on his mind.

"Vann," he began. "I want to fix this between us. I love you." He couldn't believe he'd said the words. He couldn't believe he hadn't said them sooner. Despite where they were, in a corner of a hotel lobby with a potted plant to his immediate right, it seemed right. He took her hand, folding her smaller one between both of his.

Summer sky blue eyes met him head-on, and he resisted the urge to draw her into his arms. He would undo it all if he could, if he could have just one more chance with her. He took a deep breath. He'd never felt this attached to anything, to anyone in a long time. And this was so very different. But it made him think of the only pure love he'd known, Sunrise. That stopped him. It had been days since he had given her a thought, and the rush of guilt was gone.

"Aidan."

Her voice brought him back. Back to the woman he loved and the relationship he had destroyed before it had even begun. He didn't know what to do.

She pulled her hand free and took another step back from him. "I can't, Aidan. Not now. It's all too fresh. I don't know how our relationship will survive part-time, and now I'm too drained to even consider it."

The silence was thick between them.

"I'm sorry. It's over," she said, and her voice shook. But there was no hesitation in her departure. She strode away from him with her shoulders back and her head high.

He watched her leave, and a knot grazed

uncomfortably in his throat.

His zen was gone, and there was no refuge.

****

Savannah contacted her father in New York to relay the news of her failed expedition. And it was with trepidation that she awaited his reaction.

"You're all right?" His voice shook.

"I will be."

"I'm sorry, Savannah. But you're not the first one this has happened to. That's the risk and why I didn't want you to go. I felt the same way after the expedition of seventy-two. Struggled for years with the guilt, and in fact I didn't go on another expedition for ten years." His sentence trailed. Then, he cleared his throat and went on to explain in detail how he had felt and, how it had affected him. His guilt was so very similar to that which racked her. For the first time, she basked in the emotional support her father offered.

"You can't let guilt stop you. You're human. The insects are your legacy, what you will offer the world and eventually your children," he finished his lengthy and one-sided conversation.

Legacy. That one word carried so much, love, pride, acceptance.

"As far as the beheading, it's hard to understand what they did from a Western perspective, but you learn to see their side the longer you stay there. You'll realize that after you've been there for a while."

"What are you saying?" Savannah held her breath.

"How would you like to transfer to Kuching?"

"Permanently?"

"There's a lot more research to be done on this find of yours and it can't be done from New York. Are you up to it?"

"I will be."

"Your beetle might be pivotal in getting the new Kuching research center off the ground."

They spoke at length of what the transfer would entail. And when the call ended, for once in her life she couldn't stop the tears.

Chapter Forty-Two

Early that evening.

"Meet me for supper, Riverfront."

The connection ended before he could say a word.

Aidan smiled, but it was more a grim attempt than any sign of real humor. That was so like Akan. His aversion to the telephone was contrary to his easy acceptance of the computer. In fact, the latter was a shock to many, but not to Aidan. Akan had missed the convenience of one technology, but in his later years the need for ease and convenience had drawn him much more easily from the old ways.

He glanced at his watch. That was another dichotomy with Akan, he loved to be pampered, and when in the city he went all out. He'd have to dress, for the restaurant was high-end. Thirty minutes later, he met Akan at the entrance of the restaurant. When they were seated with drinks and their menus, Akan leaned forward, pushing his menu to the side.

"I'll get right to the point."

Aidan sat back and folded his arms.

"You're a fool if you let Savannah go. She is perfect for you. Strong. Independent. With her own career and a love of insects that will bring her back here again and again. You have a shared reverence for nature. What else do you want?"

His eyes clashed with Aidan's. "Do you know

another woman crazy enough to love Borneo's rain forest like you do?"

Aidan fingered the frosted beer glass and considered something stronger.

"You know she's going on another expedition?"

"What?" Aidan clenched his hand, twisting the napkin, his attention locked on Akan.

Akan's eyes sparkled, the laughter lurking just beneath the surface. "I can see you did not know about this."

"What's this expedition?"

"It wasn't you, was it? You didn't break it off." Aidan chuckled dryly. "I think it's time you took your emotions off the back burner, boy. Show her who you are and what you feel. You can't hide in the jungle forever. I should know. Your mother taught me that at least."

"Can't I?" he asked not denying the truth in Akan's words. There was no point. His father hadn't gotten it wrong.

"She's hurt and blaming herself. That was a hell of an experience, especially for a woman fresh out of the city." Akan picked up his menu but didn't open it. "She was responsible for five others. Not including her guide, two of them didn't make it. Do you not think that eats at her? Still, she forges forward despite what would have broken a weaker person. But you have let her guilt stand between you."

Guilt, Aidan thought. What guilt? Instead, he said, "It wasn't her fault."

"True. And guilt aside, maybe she blames you a little for putting her in such a position, justified or not. Would they have lived otherwise?" He shook his head at the waiter's silent question and waited as the man slipped quietly away. "I tend to doubt it. Her team threatened a very lucrative operation." He skimmed a thumb over his plate. "Too bad about the meal."

"Excuse me?"

"The meal. It won't happen. Not tonight. I'm guessing that you have some fences to mend. Fence mending with a woman who I would be proud to have as an adopted daughter." He smiled broadly. "That is, if she suits you."

"She suits. That's why I can't chance it."

"That's why you must chance it." Akan pulled a cigarette from his pocket and looked at it for a long regretful moment. "No smoking indoors, imagine that." He looked up. "She lives because of you."

"Others died."

"And may have died anyway."

"Maybe. I couldn't stand it if something happened to her. I can't live through that again."

"You're not the only one who beats himself up over Sunrise's death. Do you think I didn't feel guilt? I was her father." He turned the unlit cigarette over in his hand. "Life is risky, you know that. You can't protect everyone you love."

It wasn't your fault. You have to let it go. Vann's words sifted through his mind, a gentle reminder.

"If you love, you must expect to hurt. You know that."

"You're right." Aidan stood up. He dropped a bill on the table. "I think we'll have to put off dinner for another time."

Akan's laugh barked loud and clear through the restaurant. "It's about time, boy. Way beyond about time."

****

She had barely knocked, and the hotel door was flung open.

"You're back." Ian broke into a smile.

"How's Drew?"

"Admitted and settled into a private room just as you ordered. Looks like he's going to be fine. A few days of bed rest, good to go."

She hovered in the doorway. "Thanks, Ian. I don't know what I'd do without you. I'll go up and check on him later."

"No point, he was sleeping when we left him. Leave it until tomorrow."

She walked into the room and sat on the edge of his bed and pushed her hair out of her eyes. "I can't believe Burke and Jason didn't make it." Her hand trembled. "And Malcolm."

Ian covered her hand. "We were lucky to escape. And now Malcolm at least will get a proper burial."

"You're right. I just wish I could do the same for the others."

But nothing could change the fact that Burke and even Mark had been swept into the river's powerful current, and there was little hope that much would be left after they were dashed by rocks and discovered by predators.

"I contacted the families as soon as I got into the room. Burke's family will have a memorial at a later date, Jason's didn't state their preference, and Malcolm's are here in Kuching."

"Good. Let me know when or where the services will be."

"Malcolm's is private." Ian's voice cracked. "That's what his mother wants. Just family."

"We'll have a memorial for him later, just us," Savannah said firmly.

"Thanks." Ian stretched his legs out as he slouched in one of two chairs in the room. "So what did your father say?"

"He actually praised me," she admitted.

"You're kidding, spill."

It was time, she thought and sat down as she began to tell Ian what her father had said.

"So we have a chance to stay here?" Ian said after she told him that bit of news. "I'm looking forward to it."

"You?" she asked.

"Yeah, me. I like it here. The people are great. The weather is fantastic." He smiled at her. "And my best friend will be here. What else is there?"

But her inner voice screamed that there was so much more. "Nothing."

"Aidan," he accused. "You won't find any better, and he loves you." He looked at her suspiciously. "I'm guessing you know that."

She strode to the window, where outside traffic moved in orderly streams beneath the same sun that had caressed the jungle floor just a few days earlier. Aidan. She bit her lip. She couldn't think of him.

"There's no excuse now."

"Enough, Ian."

"Don't fall back on past patterns, Savannah. You've grown way beyond that. I'm proud, baby." For the second time in a matter of hours, she found herself wiping tears.

"See, and you cry. Big improvement," Ian said

triumphantly.

Ian was right, she thought as she left.

She had come a long way. But now that the tears had started, they seemed a long way from finished. If she could see past the sorrow, maybe there was still a chance, although whole lives could be ruined on maybes.

Chapter Forty-Three

Aidan found Vann in the hotel lounge with an untouched drink in front of her and a faraway look in her eyes. Her pixie face was sad, and he resisted the urge to rush over and gather her in his arms and somehow take the sadness away.

She looked up, and her eyes shimmered.

He sat down beside her.

She'd been sitting for a while, that was apparent, as the ice in her glass had melted.

"I was such a fool. I'm sorry," she murmured. "I let my guilt over Burke and Jason stand between us."

"What are you talking about?"

"You had to investigate us. You were right. You didn't know us. It was part of your job, and you saved our lives. I can never thank you enough for that. Without you, none of us would have survived."

Her words were running together. She wasn't acting at all like the Vann he knew. Her edge seemed to have disappeared, and he wasn't sure he liked that.

"I'm sorry. I know I'm making no sense." She turned to face him, and this time the tears were gone. She spun the straw in her glass. "Thanks. Really, I don't think I ever told you that. Or that I love you."

The last words Aidan had to strain to hear.

"Did you just say what I thought you did?"

"Don't make me repeat it."

Her hands trembled.

He smiled.

She was more like him than she would admit. She didn't handle emotion well.

And while he wanted to shout down the halls of the hotel that she loved him. He knew what it had taken for her to say those words. And so, he tried to give her what she had always given him—zen.

"What are you thinking?" she asked.

He shook his head, and instead of words he leaned over and kissed her. It was a hot kiss despite its brevity.

"Aidan?"

"There's more but not here," he said and took her hand, smiling at her slightly bemused look.

They walked outside into the warm, refreshing tropical night.

"You were serious?" he asked. "You love me?" He felt like a fool repeating it.

"I love you." This time her words were firm and clear. "But we still have issues."

"Such as?"

"Would you lie to me again?" she asked with a hint of fear in her eyes.

"Yes," he replied without hesitation. "To protect you."

"An obvious flaw," she said.

He smiled at the flirtation in her voice.

She looked up at him. "We're still very different."

"Maybe not so different as we thought. The jungle for me isn't home. Not anymore. It's peace and a place to visit. A vacation home, if you will," he said, surprised at the truth in the words. He tipped her face up to his and dropped a light kiss on her lips. It was a kiss more of reassurance than of passion. "The tribe is still family, but they're changing. And I've changed. It isn't the place of my childhood."

"That might be a problem," she replied.

"What are you saying?"

"I'm being reassigned to Kuching and ultimately a lot of time spent in the jungle."

He began to laugh. "Only you, Vann."

"You don't want to spend…"

"I said that to make you happy. Being here will make both you and Akan happy. A double win."

"You're sure?"

"I can't complain. That is where I grew up. Where, as much as I complain about it, my roots are."

He bent down and kissed her as she wrapped her arms around his neck and kissed him back with a heat that could easily match a sweltering jungle day. There was silence for a moment when the kiss ended, broken only by the scratchy chirp of an insect.

"Besides, the jungle is unforgiving. You need me."

"I won't disagree," she said softly.

"You're my zen, Vann. I meant that. I love you." He kissed her again.

"Aidan," she murmured against his lips before pulling away.

His thumb traced her lower lip and he couldn't stop himself. His thumb dropped and he followed the pattern of his thumb with his lips.

She shivered.

"Vann," he said softly.

"Just kiss me."

And he did. This time when the kiss ended, he took her hand and they walked.

"Where do we go from here?"

"What are you suggesting?" she asked, and her voice was both hopeful and serious in the darkness.

"An alliance?" His heart skipped a beat as he anticipated her answer.

"An alliance," she repeated. "What does that mean?"

"Marry me."

"I don't know what to say."

"Say yes."

"I…"

"If you think this is a joined-at-the-hip proposition, you're wrong. I love you. I want to marry you, but I don't want to hobble you."

"Marriage?" Her voice trembled in the darkness. She shivered against him, and he wrapped his arms around her.

"Everything worth doing is frightening," he said practically. "Say yes so I can help you plan the next expedition."

"What expedition?"

He hugged her close. "Your expedition. The one that's going to get that pretty little butt back into the forest and find your bug."

"Bug?" She laughed openly. "I can't believe you said that."

"Well?"

"Yes!"

"That's encouraging." He smiled. "And romantic."

"As romantic as your proposal," she said with a laugh.

He smiled and looked somewhat chagrined. "Not the Iban way."

"Or not Aidan's way.".

"I might not be romantic, but I love you and I always will."

"I love you," she said as she threw her arms around his neck. "And I'll marry you."

He spun her around, and she threw her head back and laughed. And when he set her down, she only asked, "When?"

"The wedding or the expedition?"

"The wedding."

"What do you say we make them one and the same? A wedding in the rain forest," he said softly. "Maybe this weekend. Depends when Ian's available. And, of course, Sid."

"Ian?"

"I know, to me, he's a pain, but he has your back and that's worth everything. Besides, you need a maid of honor."

"You can't stand him."

"I never said that."

"You didn't have to."

"He's important to you, and because of that he's important to me. Let's say that I'm learning to stand him. Besides, it wasn't him that was bothersome, like Sid said, just his histrionics. That aside, he's a good enough guy. He's loyal to you, and for that I'll do anything for him."

"Wow, that was quite a speech, jungle man. So, what are we going to do for a last name?" Her laugh was like the gentle flutter of moth wings in the gathering night.

"Last name?"

"Will you take mine?"

"Don't be utterly ridiculous. I'm a liberated man. No

last name has worked well through the last three decades. I'll think I'll carry on the status quo."

"And children?"

"Ah, sweetheart, you think too much. All in good time," he whispered as his lips came down and met hers, and he drew her gently into his arms as the world faded around them. They'd both found their zen where it would always be, in each other's arms.

A word about the author...

The winner of the City of Regina's writing award, Ryshia Kennie's novels have taken her characters from the depression era prairies in her first book "From the Dust" to a across the globe and back again. There's never a lack of places to set a story as the too long prairie winters occasionally find her with travel journal in hand seeking adventure on foreign shores. When not collecting odd memories from around the world, she's writing mainly romantic suspense and women's fiction. For more, visit her website at http://www.ryshiakennie.com. http://ryshiakennie.com

Thank you for purchasing
this publication of The Wild Rose Press, Inc.

For questions or more information
contact us at
info@thewildrosepress.com.

The Wild Rose Press, Inc.
www.thewildrosepress.com

CPSIA information can be obtained
at www.ICGtesting.com
Printed in the USA
LVHW021558060222
710389LV00015B/1893